GRACE

BOOK ONE OF THE REVELATIONS SERIES

LEANNE RATHBONE

*This book is dedicated to the memory of my Nan and
Grandad – Yvonne and Gordon.
Their gift of my first typewriter, together with the
unconditional love and values that they taught me,
enabled this book to come to fruition.*

Prologue

September 1st 1997 18:52
Kings College Hospital. London.

The smell…it was always the smell that did it. It stung his eyes and made his skin crawl. If his stomach wasn't already bunched up in anxious knots of anticipation and dread, it would be rolling with waves of nausea from the cold, clinical scents that clung to the inside of his nose.

He'd always hated hospitals. Avoided them at all costs. His lip curled in disgust as he asked himself, for what felt like the millionth time, what he was doing there.

He winced in pain, snapped from his self-pity as she dug her nails deep into the skin of his hand. That's what he was doing there; it was for her. He would do anything for her. She was his entire world.

He watched her face contort as she screamed in agony. It was an intense and raw sound, that sent shockwaves of panic through his whole body. He felt like someone had reached into his chest and squeezed his heart to bursting point. He hated to see her like that, her face red and her brow covered in sweat; all brought on from the sheer effort it was taking her. Twenty-two hours in and it was slowly coming to an end. Soon, it would be all over, and they would know for sure.

He had been pacing outside the room uncontrollably, not really knowing what to do with himself, when she had called for him. She needed him for support, and though he wasn't sure that he was fit for the job, he had gone to her, refusing to ever let her down. His mind still spun whenever he thought of all the things he had learned, all the things she had told him.

It felt like an age had passed since she had sat him down and told him – everything. He had laughed, gotten angry and stormed out. He'd spent such a long time in denial, convinced it was some sort of twisted, cruel joke; that it was her sick way of trying to break up with him – but it wasn't. He regretted all that now, all those wasted hours spent sinking pints, drowning his sorrows in the bottom of a whisky glass. It was precious time he should have been spending with her, helping her prepare for this.

A lot had happened since then. She'd had to make so many decisions alone, and there had been so many more that they'd made together. He had just been starting to wrap his head around it all when she had made the call – to them.

She'd dealt with them solely on her own, up until the point she had given him one instruction. Once it was all over, as soon as anything was confirmed, he had to call them and let them know the outcome. His hand went unconsciously to the phone that was weighing heavy in his pocket, like an anvil dragging him down. It felt like it was burning a hole there, a slow, ticking time bomb, ready to go off at any second and wipe out everything he knew and loved. It only added to the nervous tension coursing through him.

She screamed again, shattering his thoughts, as the sound echoed around the sterile room. The woman in scrubs was a blue blur as she darted around the room, uttering words of encouragement. He couldn't bring himself to say anything, not with everything he knew. He was worried, sick to his stomach and he wasn't hiding it well. She gave one last squeeze of his hand, one more guttural scream – and then it was over.

He dabbed at her clammy brow with a damp cloth, laying a feather light kiss upon the crown of her head. Then he heard it; the first, gurgled screams of an infant clearing its lungs. The midwife whipped it away to a table and he averted his eyes. His heart had stopped, he was frozen in this moment of unknowing. He knew what he was looking for. She had told him it would be obvious, and he wouldn't be able to mistake it, but he couldn't look for fear of it, for fear of seeing the truth of her words. The midwife tapped him gently on the shoulder. He swallowed hard as he turned to her.

She handed him a small bundle, placing it awkwardly in his arms. He cradled it timidly, inexperience shaking his every breath. He was so scared of hurting this tiny being, like it was made of glass and could shatter at the slightest touch. He held his breath and for the first time, he looked down into the swollen, pink face of the baby.

The blanket slipped and time seemed to stand still. He gasped, his arms shaking as his eyes roved over the tiny head full of soft, fiery red hair. No – this couldn't be happening. His eyes filled with tears and he choked back a sob.

"Congratulations," the midwife said. "It's a girl." She gave him a reassuring smile as she watched the tears slip from his eyes. She was used to seeing emotional parents, it was one of her favourite parts of the job, but she couldn't possibly know the real reasons behind his pain.

He looked up, his eyes finding those of the woman he loved. His horror was mirrored on her face.

"I have to go – I should go and, I should – make the call," he mumbled, his heart breaking again as he handed the perfect, little bundle to her mother who was nodding absentmindedly. She was too shocked for any actual words. He tried his best to conceal the sickening panic that was forcing bile up into his throat. He needed to stay strong – for her.

Walking from the room, he felt completely numb. They had talked in ridiculous detail about every possible outcome. They had known this might happen – hell, it was what was supposed to happen! Hadn't she told him all about it? Wasn't this exactly what they had been preparing for? He shook his head bitterly; no amount of talking and planning could have prepared him for this. It didn't matter now that he had spent nearly nine months denying the truth. It had happened, as she said it would – as it was supposed to – and now he needed to get his act together. It was time to let them know.

He pushed out into the cool night, dragging the fresh air into his lungs. Without the cloying hospital smell, his mind was starting to clear. He lit a cigarette, inhaling deep as he pulled his phone from his pocket. His fingers shook and his eyes pricked with tears as he pulled up the number she had added to his contacts, just the week before.

"Yes?"

"It's over," he grunted. "It's a girl and – and her hair…"

"Thank you for informing us." He blinked as the call ended abruptly, sighing as he pushed his phone back into his pocket. His head was pounding, and his heart ached; what would the future now hold for the little girl with the red hair?

One

"God dammit!" I growled to myself, as I pushed my way through an overgrown hedge. The branches snagged at my clothes and hair, reaching out like crooked fingers. I was in so much trouble. The thought consumed me as I rushed home. It was a small mercy that my new room didn't have a lock, because I had no doubt my mother would utilise it if it did. She'd lock me away like Rapunzel, preventing me from ever leaving the house again. She was definitely going to kill me. I shook my head as I pulled my hair free of the twigs. Maybe I was being melodramatic – maybe there would just be some light maiming. Whatever happened, it was going to be no picnic.

It was freezing, and I was freezing and that made the whole thing worse somehow. The wind howled through the trees like a scene from some sort of zombie apocalypse movie. The thin trunks were almost bent double with the force of it. It made my eyes water as I forced myself forward. My cheeks were stinging, like I'd been repeatedly slapped by someone with a very large hand.

A shiver ran the entire length of my spine and I dragged my hood up, trying to tame my wild red hair as it whipped into my eyes. My fingers were like ice and I scowled. My bad mood was worsening with every delayed step I took along the gravel path.

I didn't like this place on the best of days, and today was not nearly the best of days; but it was my only choice because once again, my attempt at time keeping had failed – miserably. I was running unbelievably late, so taking the shortcut, even in the dark, to the dilapidated old farmhouse my mother was now forcing me to call home, was my only option. The house wasn't actually that bad, but after everything I'd been through in the past year, I was still finding it hard to be nice about it.

I kept my head down and took deep breaths, refusing to be creeped out by the centuries old tombstones that spread out on either side of me. In the light, when you could see the detail of the stones, when you could smell the floral arrangements that were scattered around sporadically and read some of the sad, yet beautiful, inscriptions, the cemetery was a peaceful place. But as the night drew ever closer, and a veil of darkness as black as a raven fell across the place, it transformed the stones and cast creepy shadows around that were the stuff of nightmares.

A part of me, quite a big part, hated that we had moved so close to a cemetery. Being separated by only a sparse front garden and a very narrow lane, did nothing to endear the place to me. I understood my mother's need to up and leave London after what had happened, what I couldn't understand was her choice. There must have been somewhere better, somewhere that wasn't in the back arse of beyond, somewhere that was less – creepy. In the blink of an eye, because of one tragic night, my life had been ripped out from under me; a life I had been happy with.

I let out a sigh of relief as I looked up and spied the gate in the distance. Beyond it, if I squinted against the darkness, I could make out the warm, welcoming lights of home. I hastened to the gate, desperate to be free of the cemetery. With what had happened in London, my nerves were shot. I spent most of my time on edge and walking through rows and rows of headstones just amplified my remote paranoia.

A chill swept through me, sending ice through my veins. It had nothing to do with wind, and everything to do with the faint noise that had just come from behind me. I froze, unable to quell the fear as it fingered its way up my spine, making my heart hammer in my chest. I wasn't really in the mood for facing off against any boogeymen.

Closing my eyes, I willed my legs to move forward but they had turned to jelly. Bravery had never been something I'd had endless supplies of, but since the move I'd had a hell of a lot less. Given the circumstances it wasn't surprising, but still –

I heard it again and turned sharply, clenching my fists and mentally preparing to fight if I needed to. I wasn't sure I would be much good in a fight, having never been in one in my life, but I wouldn't go down without at least an attempt at one.

The path behind me was eerily empty. There wasn't so much as a leaf blowing across it, which was odd given how the wind was still blowing. I glared out into the night, hoping that I was giving off a 'don't mess with me' vibe. I scanned the nearby pathways and stones for any signs of movement – but there was none – nothing. I strained my ears, listening intently, but with the blood rushing through them and my heart racing so fast, it was hard to hear anything over my erratic pulse.

Slowly I backed up to the gate, ready to ditch the cemetery. I was scared to turn my back on whatever it was that had caused the mysterious rustles. The hairs on my arms were raised, goosebumps had covered me from head to foot. It wasn't a new sensation, I probably should have been used to the creeped out feeling but I wasn't, and every time the hairs on my neck rose, my stomach filled with a sense of dread.

I still couldn't see anything and there was a small voice in the back of my head, questioning whether I could be imagining things. My overactive imagination did have a rotten habit of playing tricks on me and I was already sensitive due to the scary surroundings. It could all be innocent. That same voice though was the one that reminded me of what had happened to me before the move, reminding me that sometimes I was right to be on edge. It was unnerving.

My already icy hands connected with the freezing cold steel of the gate and I wrenched it open. It creaked loudly and I winced, the sound bouncing off the graves. It could have been taken straight from the sound board of a horror movie. It echoed around me for what felt like an eternity. I shushed it, before rolling my eyes. Maybe I was going crazy – walking through a graveyard alone at night wasn't my best idea and now I was shushing an inanimate object.

Shaking my head, I pulled the gate closed as quietly as I could. My eyes scanned the nearby paths and stones again, but the darkness shrouded everything. I took a deep breath and ran all the way to the farmhouse, not once stopping to look back over my shoulder.

Two

"Grace Elizabeth Ayre, where the bloody hell have you been? Have you seen the time?" I leant against the front door, trying to catch my breath and calm my racing heart. My hands were trembling, and my knees were shaking. I steadied myself, balling my hands into fists and trying to quell the tell-tale signs of my fear before seeing my mother.

She was smart, she never missed a trick and it worried me. If she saw me freaked out, if she even suspected a hint of any dodgy goings on, much less that I was being followed, she would pack us up and move us all over again. Moving away from the cemetery wouldn't be the worst thing in the world, but I was still reeling from the last sudden move and I couldn't face going through it all again.

"Sorry mum," I called, knowing that I didn't have long before she stomped her way into the hallway to check on me. "I got – carried away." I looked down at my hands, finally feeling calm enough to face her. I dropped my bag and hung up my coat. Inside, I was still trying to work through whatever had just happened, if indeed anything had happened at all, but outside I hoped I was convincingly chill.

There had been moments for as long as I could remember, when I'd felt like I was being watched. Most of them I could vividly remember; feeding the ducks when

I was six, skating on a makeshift ice rink when I was eight, Christmas shopping when I was eleven, sketching in Trafalgar Square when I was thirteen and most embarrassingly, walking back from a school disco hand in hand with some boy when I was fifteen. It was strange, but none of those times had felt – bad. This, this was different somehow. I couldn't completely shake the unease that had stolen through me; it was just sitting beneath the surface of my skin, freaking me out.

I didn't think there had been anyone else in the cemetery with me, but something had certainly freaked me out and it had left a sickly feeling in the pit of my stomach. I knew, better than anyone, that you could never be too sure of anything.

"I'll give you carried away next time you're two hours late home young lady! What do I even bother paying for your phone for if you can't be bothered to use it? Would a measly text message have hurt, or heaven forbid a phone call?" I couldn't stop the roll of my eyes as I walked into the kitchen and found my mother up to her elbows in suds. It wasn't often I had to witness my mother's drama queen side, but I knew that it would be out in full force after my mishap.

"I said I'm sorry mum. Please don't make a big deal out of nothing. You know what I'm like when I'm in the library."

"Nothing? Nothing Grace?" She glared at me. "You know as well as I do, that I am not making a big deal out of nothing! You have got to be more careful these days Grace!" Her voice was rising, and I could feel my temper going with it.

"I said I'm sorry, ok!" I snapped, grabbing a dish towel

and picking up a plate to dry. Her reaction was to be expected, so I should've kept better control over my attitude, but it bothered me that she didn't trust me to be able to stay a couple of extra hours somewhere as mundane as a library. It wasn't as if I was out on some street corner, drinking and causing trouble.

A small wave of guilt prickled at my skin as that little voice in the back of my mind spoke up again, reminding me that it wasn't about trust. Trust had nothing to do with it. It was fear – fear for my safety. I sighed heavily. I understood my mother's need for control, but it didn't make it any less annoying.

"I just would have appreciated a call, that's all," she said quietly. She sniffed and I could feel her eyes on me. My shoulders slumped and for the first time since arriving home, I turned and looked into her eyes. The fear I saw, put me instantly on edge. She frowned. "Gracie, are you feeling ok? You look like you've seen a ghost."

I shivered involuntarily. She couldn't have picked worse words to say. The trembly feeling coursed through me again. Ghosts were the last thing I wanted to think about, especially because being in the cemetery, it wasn't beyond the realm of possibility that some short of ghoul had been the source of my unease – if you believed in that sort of thing.

I swallowed hard. It would be no use trying to explain the real reasons behind my sudden lack of colouring. If anything, it would justify her argument and give her a valid reason to lock me in the house and never let me see the light of day again.

"I do feel a bit of a headache coming on actually. Maybe I'm coming down with cold." It was a reasonable excuse and seemed to have the desired effect. My mother softened, all the anger and worry disappearing from her face in an instant.

"Get yourself to bed baby girl, I'll bring you up a nice cup of tea." I bit my lip, trying to hide the smile that turned up the corners of my mouth. My mother was so typically English; she was of the firm belief that a good cup of hot, sweet tea could solve any number of problems or even stop oncoming ailments.

I obliged, dumping the dishcloth on the side and making my way up the creaky, splinter ridden staircase to my room. It had been almost two months since we had moved in, yet the majority of my things were still in boxes. The only things I had gone to the effort of unpacking, were my iPad, my speakers and my art supplies. I couldn't face dragging all my old memories out of the numerous other boxes – not yet at least. Even my clothes were still in suitcases. I dived onto my king-size bed, which was one of my favourite places to be, and tried to swallow past the lump that formed in my throat.

Everything had changed so quickly. One minute, I was finishing school, getting my exam results, planning what I was going to do next and wondering where my life would take me; just like any other, normal teenager. Then the next minute, the whole universe had seemed to tilt on its axis uncontrollably. My little, near perfect world, had been shaken up like a cheap can of cola until it had burst. The resulting mess was the life I had been left with.

It was still a hard thing to swallow. All my hopes and dreams were suddenly – gone. The ground beneath my feet had fallen away and I'd had to start afresh somewhere new, somewhere completely different to everything I had always known and loved. I was – lonely. At the time, I'd been so numb, so wrapped up in all my own misery, that I hadn't put up any sort of fight. Now, I wondered whether I should have.

"Knock, knock, one lovely cup of tea for one lovely girl." My mum pushed open the door and weaved her way through the many boxes to hand me my cup. I didn't miss the look of disdain on her face as she saw I had still not unpacked. Her lips were a thin line, but whatever she was thinking, she was keeping to herself – for now. She'd already gently suggested several times, that I should unpack and start to make myself at home, but I'd managed to get away with ignoring her so far.

"Thanks mum, you're an angel." Her cheeks flushed lightly as she handed me the warm cup, which was welcome as my fingers still hadn't thawed out.

"You still look rather pale. Drink that tea and get some sleep. It's Saturday tomorrow so you can have a lie in and get better." She pressed a kiss to my forehead, before leaving me in peace.

The weekends arrival didn't really matter all that much. Technically, I could sleep in every day if I chose to. That was the downside of moving away from the home you had always known, not long after finishing secondary school. My dream had been to take a year out of education and travel, work my way across Europe and perhaps save up for college or university when I had figured out what I wanted to do with the rest of my life. So, when I'd turned seventeen in the September after getting my results, I hadn't immediately done anything. Perhaps it was fate, because then as December rolled around, we'd had to leave.

That's how I found myself in a ridiculously small village, in the north of England, with no clue of the area, nor what jobs or opportunities it had to offer. Worse than all that though – no friends. Every day, I made the choice to get up and go to the library, because no matter where in the world you go, a library remains the same. It was a safe place where I could lose myself, draw to my heart's content and not have to think about a single thing.

Libraries do have their downsides though. They aren't the best place to meet new people, aren't exactly hip and happening; not to mention that they're quiet places, where talking too loudly earned you dirty looks and funny stares. That was why, after two months, the librarian was the only person (other than my mother) that I had spoken to. Even then, it was always book related or a request for some computer time. She seemed nice enough, but it was hardly conversation gold and there definitely wasn't much wiggle room for socialising.

I stood and carried my tea to the window seat. It was comfy and cosy; covered in scatter cushions and thick fleece blankets, courtesy of my mother. It was another small thing that she had done to try and convince me that this was now home. It had gone some small way to making the room feel more homely. The seat was my second most favourite place in the world. It meant that even when the weather was rubbish, and I didn't want to trek to the library in the pouring rain, I could snuggle up on my window seat, feel safe and secure and sketch away my worries.

My room overlooked the garden and just beyond the dimly lit street, I could see the outline of the church and some of the taller headstones. The cemetery was in complete darkness. The small glow of the lamps that sporadically lit the pathways within, were not visible from where I sat. It made for an eerie view.

Sitting and looking out from behind the rapidly fogging glass of my window, I started to feel silly. There were a million and one explanations for the rustlings I'd heard, and they all flooded my mind. It could have been the wind, a squirrel, a fox, leaves falling from the many trees – though I hadn't seen any. There was even the possibility that it had been another person, someone who was as crazy as me. The cemetery was bordered on all sides by houses, so it was daft to think I would be the only person to use it as a shortcut. I shook my head – if it had been another person, why hadn't I seen them?

Had they purposefully hidden? Why would someone do that? What reason would a person have for hiding from another in a cemetery in the dark? The strange feeling returned to my stomach as I closed my eyes. The goosebumps rose on my arm. If I allowed myself, I could think of a few reasons and not a single one of them was good. I didn't want to open myself up to all that. I needed to stop letting my mind wander to those dark and sinister situations. We had moved, I no longer needed to worry so much. Deep down, I wasn't convinced.

I drained the last dregs from my cup and got myself ready for bed. It had been a long day and I needed to switch off. Whoever, or whatever it had been, had done a thorough job of freaking me out. As I climbed into bed and wrapped myself in my duvet, I prayed that the next time I had to venture through the cemetery, it was devoid of any scary sensations.

There was still the persistent voice, even tinier now, in the back of my mind that was screaming at me not to be so naïve. I'd tried to push it down, hide it in the shadowy corners of my brain but it wouldn't let up. Over and over, it told me that it had nothing to do with movies or books, but I slammed the door on it, refusing to give it any credence.

The shocking result of the annoying lack of sleep, was two big black bags beneath my eyes and pallor so pale, I did look ill. There wasn't much I could do about the way I looked. I had tried to use some concealer, applied a little blush to my cheeks to try and hide the zombie face but I may as well have not bothered. It hadn't even taken the edge off and I still looked rough, but I refused to stay home and lay in bed all day. Other than a really bad night's sleep, there wasn't actually anything wrong with me – not physically anyways.

"I feel fine mum. I don't feel poorly or anything and I want to go to the library again. I promise, I won't be late though this time." I chewed my lower lip as her eyes met mine. I hoped she wouldn't make a fuss. She bit her lower lip too, something we both did when we were thinking, and it made me smile. We were alike in so many ways, it was probably one of the reasons we butted heads so much. She was still silent – thinking. I knew I could have stamped my feet and thrown out the 'I'm nearly an adult' card, but I hated arguing with her, so I tried to avoid it at all costs. She was all I had left, so it just wouldn't do to act like a brat and fill the house with a load of tension.

"Ok, fine," she relented. "But I mean it today Grace, home before nightfall!" I nodded in agreement and gave her a quick peck on the cheek, before snagging a piece of toast from her plate and heading into the hall. She didn't need to worry about me being late. There was no way I wanted a repeat of the night before; strange dreams and all.

My backpack was already full of my art supplies and as I pulled on my boots, I only hoped that the library had what I was looking for.

something. The joy of the internet means we see less, and less people visit." I felt myself soften at her words. There was a sadness in her tone, which suggested she shared not only my love of books, but my utter bafflement at people who didn't.

"I love libraries. There's nothing quite like old fashioned print; running your fingers over the pages of a good book. Running them over a keyboard and staring at a screen doesn't even come close."

"Exactly!" she said excitedly, extending her hand. "I'm Mia, by the way."

"Grace," I replied, taking it. It felt very formal to be shaking her hand, but I didn't want to leave her hanging and appear uncivil. She was, after all, talking to me, and it felt good to converse with someone who wasn't my mum.

"So, how're you finding life in the country?" She perched on the edge of the table, making herself comfortable. I glanced around the library. Apart from the people sat at the computers, we were the only others around. Was she bored? There wasn't much to do in a near empty library, perhaps that was why she was making the effort to talk to me. The fact that I was looking for an explanation was a good indication of the reasons that I lacked anything even remotely close to a friend. Hopefully, it was the London in me, and I hadn't turned into some sort of antisocial beast.

"It's certainly a lot different. I'll let you know when I decide whether that's a good or a bad thing." I hadn't particularly fallen in love with the village, but I wasn't about to share that fact. Mia had probably lived in Stonewell her whole life and I didn't want to insult her home. If you were willing to give it a chance, Stonewell was probably a really nice place to live, but I hadn't yet found myself very willing. I had hardly seen any of it, so I wasn't about to start passing judgement. God only knew what had drawn my mother to such a place, after living in the hustle and bustle of London for so long, but she had been adamant it was the right place to go.

"No drawing today?" she asked, lightly. I felt my brow raise. Had she been watching me? Was that weird? More often than not, I'd looked up from my pad to find I was the only person left. Not many people would sit in the library for hours, surrounded by books and pencils. When I thought about it, it would probably have been harder not to notice what I was doing. I smiled shyly and gestured to my backpack.

"I have my things with me – always come prepared." Mia laughed; a sweet, gentle sound that echoed around us. I couldn't help but smile. I liked her.

"Like a boy scout!" she chuckled. She tilted her head from side to side as she thought about speaking, unsure of whether she should. "Well, you know, if you ever want to do anything other than draw, you just let me know."

"Thanks," I nodded, feeling overcome with gratitude. She had not only taken the time to come and talk to me, but she was offering further opportunity to do something other than what had become, my daily routine. I admitted to myself, it would be nice to have something else to do. It would be nice to have a friend again. I was about to speak again when the front desk bell rang. Mia looked over before shrugging her shoulders apologetically.

"I guess I should get back to work," she said, nodding towards an impatient looking old man who was stood trying to balance an armful of books.

"Of course, I should go anyways," I replied, standing and reaching for the book. Tiredness was starting to creep in, blurring the edges of my vision. All the non-sleep was starting to take its toll and I could practically hear my bed calling out to me.

"Hey, that's ok, I'll get that for you. I guess, I'll see you tomorrow?" It was a question and I smiled, giving her a small nod. She picked up the book, gave me a small finger wave and headed to the front desk. Mia seemed nice, and I cursed myself for not making more of an effort sooner. As much as I enjoyed my own company, I longed to have someone else to talk to, to do things with. I waved as I walked past the desk, heading for the exit.

"Hey Grace." I turned as Mia called, my eyes meeting hers. "You know, my nan used to say that seeing an angel in your dreams, means that someone you lost is trying to visit, usually with a message." She gave me a knowing smile before turning back to the man, and I left, dragging my jaw along the pavement behind me.

a word to a soul.

So that was how I found myself, what felt like a million miles away from everything comforting, looking out across an old graveyard and wondering what life would have in store for me.

I ceased my scribbling and looked down at the sketchbook, dropping the pencil as my eyes roved over the picture upon the paper. I'd been so lost, so consumed in my thoughts that I'd assumed it would just be pattern upon scribbled pattern, but what I saw, couldn't have been any different.

It was a perfectly sketched outline of the angel headstone from my dream. I closed the book and threw it across the room, onto my desk. It was the very last thing I wanted to think about. Pinching the bridge of my nose, I knew there was only one thing I could do. I needed to immerse myself into a world that wasn't my own. I changed into my pyjamas, jumped into bed with my iPad and scrolled through my audio books until I found something suitably fluffy and mundane to listen to. Closing my eyes, I prayed for the first time in my life, that a dreamless sleep would come for me sooner, rather than later.

Six

Sleep had indeed come for me, soon after snuggling down into my duvet but it had been anything but dreamless. The same disjointed crap from the night before had disturbed my dreams, all over again. Leaves, angel headstone and trees, again and again like a record stuck on repeat. This lasted for an entire week and towards the end of it, there was even a new addition to the images – a shadowy figure, a dark outline. The images were scrappy, and nothing fully came into focus; it was like I was looking at them through someone else's glasses. Seven days of the same thing, night after night. Seven nights of weird dreams that made no sense; there was no rhyme or reason to them. It was annoying.

I'd thought a lot about what I'd read in the dreams book, and a lot about what Mia had said to me on my way out of the library. Something about the way her words cut so close to the bone, bugged me. Could she be right? Did she know more about me than she let on? No – there was no way she could possibly know anything about – well – anything. Yet the look she had given me, the one that I couldn't shake from my mind, suggested otherwise.

There was the possibility that she was just simply making a statement, saying the first thing that came to mind that could be seen as comforting. It would mean that she didn't know anything and was probably wondering why I had left looking so shocked and dazed. I closed my eyes and rubbed at my temples. The restless nights and odd dreams were making my brain ache and sending me in the right direction towards crazy. There was only one sure way to discover the meaning behind Mia's words – and that was to ask her.

I had avoided the library all week because I'd let my silly mind run away with me. It was daft and made me feel ridiculous; but worse than that, it made me angry at myself. Mia was the first person who had tried to talk to me, she was someone I could actually see myself being friends with, but I'd overreacted, gotten myself totally freaked out and ended up avoiding her like the plague. It wasn't like my absence wouldn't have been noticed either. I'd been visiting the library nearly every day since the move; I hoped that she thought I was ill, and she didn't take offense to my lack of visits.

I was starting to see weird things where there was none. The daft dreams and disrupted nights were beginning to consume me. I didn't like it, didn't like how it was ruling me. I'd let the nightmares do that for too long; I didn't want history to repeat itself. Dragging myself out of bed and getting ready was tiring. The house was cold, which meant my mother had already left for the day. She had been fussing over me all week, berating me for going to the library when I was obviously ill. I couldn't tell her that I wasn't in fact ill because that would mean telling her about the dreams and I didn't want to share those. It was good she was gone; I wouldn't have to face another morning of her forcing me back to bed. As I ran a brush through my hair, I scowled at my reflection. A little more colour had made its way into my cheeks and I looked less flulike but the pesky black bags beneath my eyes were still as prominent as ever. I turned away in disgust and headed downstairs.

The wind hit me as soon as I left the house, and it was still shockingly cold. I wondered whether the weather would ever change, if the sun would ever come out and shine down on Stonewell. Bring on the summertime.

As I walked through the doors of the red brick library building, I was shocked to find it was busy for a change. All the computers were taken and most of the desks were occupied. God only knew what had drawn everyone in, but it was typical. The one day I decided to make an effort to seek Mia out, to talk to her, and it could turn out that she was too busy to give me the time of day. I looked over at the front desk – she wasn't there.

A young boy, maybe a year or two younger than myself, was manning the crowd; at least – he was trying to. He was quite spectacularly failing at trying to calm down a woman who was refusing to pay her late fees. I smiled, before I tore my eyes away and glanced around the stacks. Could it have been her day off? I headed for a free desk and sighed, dropping my bag and setting out my pencils and sketchbook. Once the crowd died down a little, I would go and ask the boy at the front desk, but until then I would do what I always did to distract myself and pass the time.

I turned to a fresh page and started sketching the same thing that I had been trying to get down all week. The book was full of half-finished pictures of the great, hulking marble angel that flashed through my dreams, and weird shaded blobs that I couldn't get to remotely resemble the shadowy figure. The details were never right and I scrapped them before finishing, every time. Sketching had never given me any trouble before, I'd never failed to get down whatever I put my mind to, so this was a tad frustrating.

"Wow, you're really good!" My pencil flew across the page, as I jumped.

"You have a habit of doing that you know," I said, smiling and turning to face Mia. She had an armful of books, a look of awe on her face as she stared at my picture.

"Of what?" she asked, obliviously.

"Of sneaking up on people. That's the second time you've made me jump." She was still staring at the picture, taking in all the details and I felt my cheeks begin to burn. I was always shy when it came to my drawings. My art teacher at secondary school had raved to anyone that would listen about my abilities. She had told my mother that I had a promising future, but even with all that endorsement, it didn't make me any less nervous about sharing. Each picture I drew, was like a part of me, like a piece of my soul, stretched across the brilliant white page. It made me feel queasy, to expose myself to the scrutiny of others.

"Sorry," she laughed, her eyes finally meeting mine. "Occupational hazard. Being quiet becomes something of a habit when you work in a library." I smiled at her and took a deep breath, wondering how best to word my question without sounding like I had spent a whole week obsessing over, and trying to derive meaning from, what she had said. Conversation had never been a strong point of mine, but I knew I needed to try.

"Do you have a minute Mia? I was hoping to talk to you today." She didn't look surprised; she just smiled and took the chair opposite me.

"I can break for five," she said, without glancing across at her co-worker who was still embroiled in an argument about fees. "How can I help?" I rolled my pencil between my fingers, trying to find the right words. How could she help? Could she help at all? Could I ask, without sounding like a nutcase?

"You know when I last came in, and you mentioned something that your nan used to say about seeing angels in your dreams? What – what made you say that?" She couldn't hide her reaction, something flashed through her eyes, but as quick as it was there, it was gone again. She tilted her head and gave me a look of confusion.

"You were looking through a dreams book and I saw you were looking at angels – I didn't really mean anything by it. My nan used to come up with gems like that all the time. It popped into my head and I – I was just trying to make conversation with you." I laughed nervously as relief washed through me. I hardly dared believe it. I had spent all week, wondering whether Mia was right, whether she knew more than she let on. I'd worried that she wasn't who she said she was and that there was some big conspiracy, but it turned out – she just wanted to chat.

"Sorry, you must think I'm mad." I shook my head and tried desperately to suppress the hysterical chuckles that were threatening to escape. I'd been a complete idiot; wasted a full week fretting over nothing. Mia laughed too.

"No – I don't think you're mad Grace, but if I may be bold? I think you're bored, maybe even – lonely?" Her words cut through me, banishing the chuckles. I looked up and her eyes searched mine. She'd hit the nail on the head. I cleared my throat, swallowed back the emotion. It seemed books weren't the only thing that Mia was good at reading. She could read people too – or maybe it was just me, maybe I was easy to read.

"Sorry, you can tell me to piss off and mind my own business, but you seem to come here a lot. I'm guessing you're having a hard time with the move?" I expected to see pity in her hazel eyes, the thing that I was used to seeing, but was surprised to see nothing but sympathy.

"It's ok," I sighed. "You're right; it's been – rough."

"I thought as much. Do you think that's what the odd dreams could be about? Moving somewhere new can definitely be hard but fret no more – you have me now!" She bounced in her chair animatedly and smiled. "I bet you haven't even explored the village properly, have you?"

I shook my head. There was no point in lying. In a childish way, I'd hoped that if I didn't look around, didn't acquaint myself with the area, my mother might see how much I disliked it and move us back to London. Nearly three months had passed, and she still hadn't noticed my distaste. She hadn't noticed that I hadn't ventured far at all. She would probably be happy about that because it meant she knew I was safe.

"I made it to the library – and the cemetery," I grimaced. I hoped I wasn't coming across like the complete loner I knew I was. I hadn't always been so hell bent on being in my own company, and I was starting to resent it. I longed for friendship again – but I was scared. I'd learnt in the hardest and most horrible way, that the more you have to lose, the more it hurts when tragedy strikes.

"Wow – seriously? Well, we can't have that can we? Tomorrow just so happens to be my day off and I'm giving you a tour. It's a cool place to live – once you know the area." My heart skipped a beat. Was it possible that I had plans – plans that didn't involve running the hours down in the library with my pads and pen's?

My mother would be pleased. There had been a few occasions that she had nagged at me to try and meet new people, but I'd tried to explain to her that it wasn't easy when you'd already left school and you had no job. It was made even harder by the fact that I had grown up in London, the city where you don't ever talk to people you don't know unless you want to be shunned – or worse. It hadn't taken long for me to realise that being seventeen in a new place was hard work.

"That would be – fantastic actually. If you're sure? I don't want to waste your day off."

"Don't be silly Grace, it isn't a waste! You aren't the only one that could do with meeting some new people, you know? There's barely a handful of people our age still around here – most move away to college as soon as they're old enough."

"How old are you?" I asked, my mouth moving before my brain could register the words. Mia looked young, but I had assumed that for her to be running the library, she had to at least be in her early twenties.

"I'm nineteen, why?" she laughed. "Do I look old or something?"

"No, of course not!" I blushed, trying to backtrack. "Why didn't you move away?" It was baffling to me that she hadn't done the same thing she claimed others our age did and moved away for college or something. I knew I was being nosy but again, the question had slipped out without much thought.

"I like books – plus my family own the library. This was pretty much my destiny, but I don't mind – I love it. You thought I was some old fuddy-duddy, didn't you?" She laughed, which made me smile.

"Wait – hang on – what did you say?" Her words sank into my brain and I shook my head, confused as I looked around the building. How could her family own it?

"Ah – you didn't notice? Not many people do to be honest. We're a private library, we aren't funded by anyone but ourselves." She gestured round, sweeping her arm wide with a smile. "This all belongs to my family, it's why it's so big. We have books in here that have been passed down for hundreds of years. It stays in the family and every year, we just add to our collection." I was shocked and completely in awe; but it was soon outweighed by the excitement I felt, at the prospect of having a friend.

"Ok," I nodded, unable to wipe the smile from my face. "Should I meet you here tomorrow then?"

"No, it's fine. I'll grab your address off the system and come and pick you up. Ten sound good?" I nodded, not trusting myself to talk. I was overcome with emotion and didn't want to come across as some sort of overly enthusiastic, desperate person. Mia smiled before standing. "Until tomorrow then!" She walked towards the front desk, leaving me to slump in my chair. I'd made plans – I'd made plans with a friend. It was strange – but good.

When we had lived in London, there had always been something to do. You didn't have chance to be bored. Whether it was something exciting like wandering around the tourist sights and taking in a show in the theatre district, or something terribly normal like browsing in all the shops and visiting the local youth club. There was rarely an evening or a weekend, that I wasn't doing something.

It had been so busy and so exciting all the time. It was why it had been such a culture shock to move to a small village, that screamed quintessential English countryside – but I hoped that meeting Mia might mean I could go back to the days where I had plans, days where I laughed and made memories. I missed those days.

Maybe Mia could even help me find a job. I wouldn't need to wallow in my own self pity anymore, and I wouldn't have to live off my mother my whole life. I needed to start making plans for the future. Having Mia would surely make small town life a little bit easier to digest. With all these new possibilities running through my mind, I turned back to finish the picture that still eluded me.

Seven

I didn't stay in the library for long. After trying to recreate the images from my dreams for over an hour, to no avail, frustration had kicked in – along with my temper. I'd torn the page from my book, ripped it into pieces and snapped some of my charcoal. It wasn't too often that my temper got the better of me, but on occasion I couldn't help seeing red, and it usually bubbled over into some small act of mild aggression.

To save myself from spending any more of my mother's hard-earned cash on art supplies, I decided the only thing to do was to try and draw it from the source – if there was a source. Mia was at the front desk, wrestling with the unusually busy crowd, so I gave her a small wave as I passed by. I left the library and headed to the one other place I knew well – the cemetery.

I'd been right in thinking that the cemetery was a peaceful place, in the light of day. The village was small, but the graveyard was not. There were graves that spanned hundreds of years. It was beautifully maintained considering the sheer size of it. All the flowerbeds were vibrant and lush, with not a single piece of litter or a weed anywhere. As I walked between the stones, I wondered whether any of them belonged to Mia's family. If they had passed the library down through the generations, they must have always called Stonewell home.

There were lots of beautiful inscriptions, especially on

the older stones. Some of them were pure poetry, showing throughout the years how much people were loved by those around them. One stone caught my eye and I knelt before it. I ran my hand over the rough surface and tried to read what was written. It wasn't easy, the stone had taken a battering, beaten away by harsh weather and time – but I just about got the gist. It was the grave of a woman who had obviously been treasured by her husband. It was touching but also achingly sad.

I'd never been drawn to anyone in such a way. There had been a little interest at school, a couple of boyfriends along the way, but never anyone that I'd fallen for. Truth be told, I'd only even gone out with anyone at all to dispel the rumours that I was a weirdo. Kids were cruel and immature; I hated that I'd let peer pressure affect my decisions but that was just a part of secondary school. Wasn't it a normal part of being a hormonal teenager?

I wasn't worried about becoming a lonely, old spinster – not just yet. Being seventeen meant I was in no rush; but it did make me think of my mother. She wasn't getting any younger, she was growing older and she was doing it alone. I'd always wondered why she hadn't found herself someone to love. She was a beautiful woman; any man would be lucky to have her – and that wasn't just the bias talking.

I meandered between the stones slowly and took some rubbings of the ones that seemed too beautiful not to. There were many different types; great carved crosses, doves in flight, marble hearts – even one that looked like it used to be a giant tiger. It was hard to tell, time had not been kind to it. As I wandered round, the annoying voice whispered in the back of my mind that there was only one that I was looking for. There was only one that I wanted to find, but I didn't even know whether it existed or whether it was just a figment of my imagination.

The sun was starting to sink low and I realised I'd covered almost two thirds of the cemetery. I was surprised at how long I had spent walking between the stones, especially considering my last visit had seemingly sparked all the weirdness. I'd vowed that I wouldn't give Casper another chance to scare the bejeesus out of me, yet I was wandering around, looking for a particular headstone.

There were plenty of angel headstones but none of them matched the one that I had been seeing, every night when sleep crept over me. I couldn't explain my need to look for it – to find it. Maybe it was so I could tell myself that I had seen it before, even if I hadn't fully registered it, and that was why it now kept showing up in my bizarre dreams. Similarly, I didn't have an explanation for why I felt the need to draw it so much. Would getting it down on paper give me closure? Would it give me answers as to why the damn thing plagued my sleep? No – that wasn't it.

Inside, I had this mind-boggling need, this unexplainable urgency to find it. I had never felt anything like it, and I couldn't begin to understand where the feelings came from. There were no big questions I needed the universe to answer, no problems that I thought would be instantly solved – well – other than the obvious question of why I was having recurring dreams in the first place. Yet – when I thought about not finding it, of never seeing it other than in sleep, I was filled with a strange wave of panic and that worried me – a lot.

It had crossed my mind that I might be going a bit crazy.

What other explanation was there? It was all on the odd side. I'd half convinced myself that, after what had happened in London, I'd still been in shock and as that shock was slowly beginning to subside, this was the fallout – craziness.

The sun had completely sunk, the sky a gorgeous, dusky dark blue colour and the moon was already visibly brightening it up. I smiled to myself as I realised, that was something that I loved about the village. In London, the stars were rarely visible, their light not quite bright enough to shine through the light pollution that hovered over the city; but in the village, out in the countryside, the stars shone like tiny diamonds across the velvet blackness of the sky and the moon always looked so full and bright. It was the perfect time to head home. I'd spent too much time exploring the graveyard. I didn't want to get caught in the pitch black again.

I turned to head back down the small, gravel path that I knew would lead me to the main walkway and the exit – then I saw it. Tucked back into one of the farthest, shadowy corners, almost completely on its own, was the angel. Its wings were spread beneath a scarily familiar looking tree. I could hardly believe my eyes and my breath, when I managed to catch it, was ragged. I squinted into the shadows, struggling against my rising panic. There was something else – something that made the blood pound in my ears, made small lights dance before my eyes.

Stood before the angel was a figure; a figure that in the growing darkness, looked as familiar as the tree and the headstone. What was happening?

My legs had turned to jelly as adrenaline surged through me; they finally gave out and made me fall to my hands and knees. Hundreds of small, sharp stones cut into my skin, forcing a sharp cry from my lips. The pain was reassuring in what felt like a crazy, surreal dream.

I closed my eyes and squeezed them shut, as tight as I could. How could this be real? I tried to pull all the fragmented images to the forefront of my mind. Was this the figure – the one from my dreams? How could that be so? How could I be seeing something that I had so far, only seen in my sleep? Could it all just be a coincidence? Was there such a thing? Whatever was happening, I didn't want to continue contemplating it in the dark.

I took a deep breath and shakily pulled myself up from the ground. Trembles coursed the length of my body as I glanced tentatively towards the stone. My eyes widened in horror, my panic deepening. The figure was gone! How? There had definitely been someone there, but now they were gone.

I spun around, turning in every direction, trying to find the mysterious figure, but there was no one around; no one walking away, no retreating footsteps. There was just the sound of my rapidly beating heart and my shallow breaths. Where could they have gone so quickly? How could someone just disappear in the short time that I had been on the floor? My stomach churned as I turned and ran. No one could vanish into thin air, which made me question whether there had been someone there at all. Was I beginning to crack? Was it their presence I had felt before; were they the mysterious rustle that had started me down this line of madness? Could they still be around, lurking in the shadows? Why would they hide – unless they had some scary agenda...

My chest burned and my legs ached as I got to the gate,

but I didn't care. I needed to get out of the dark, out of the night and so I kept running and I didn't stop until I was through my front door.

Eight

By the time morning rolled around, I'd managed to calm down, almost completely. Did it matter if there had been someone there? People visited graves all the time. Did it matter that I'd found something that had so far, only appeared when I was unconscious? It wasn't beyond the realm of possibility that I'd seen the headstone before, on one of my many treks through the cemetery, but I'd been so wrapped up in myself that I hadn't properly noticed it. In the cold, harsh light of day, everything could once again be rationalised, and I felt like I could stop questioning my sanity.

In the middle of the night, during one of my 'almost asleep, not quite awake' moments, I'd vowed to myself that I would go back and check out the headstone, in the light. Now that I knew where to find it, I needed to prove that there was nothing to worry about, nothing scary about the old marble. But that was not today. Today would be a good day. Today I had the chance to feel like a normal teenager again; not one who lived with a big, black shadow hanging over her head.

I jumped up and showered early, making sure I had enough time to make my long, red mop presentable, taming it into semi submission with my straighteners. I'd not done it for such a long time, but I even applied some make up. I dug around in my cases until I found my favourite pair of jeans and pulled them on. My mother had lovingly hand sewn patches onto them and wearing them went a long way to making me feel like my old self.

It felt good to be excited about something, and to make an effort for it. Effort was something that had eluded me since the move. It was amazing, the power that a little sticky lip gloss could have on the soul. By the time I had finished faffing around, I had only fifteen minutes left to grab some breakfast.

I was just finishing the last mouthful of my cereal when I heard a knock at the door. My mother's sewing machine had been happily humming away all morning, the sound vibrating through the house, but it stopped dead at the knock. I could sense the wary confusion that seeped from her workroom. One of the reasons she had loved the house so much, was because of the number of downstairs reception rooms it had; one of which she had claimed. She often tucked herself away, especially if she had a difficult dress or a difficult customer. I wouldn't hear much from her, except the constant string of profanities, until she had finished.

Her footsteps echoed as she headed down the hall and I smiled to myself, glad for her to answer the door. I knew it would cheer her up to see me going out with someone, doing something other than sticking my nose in a pad.

"Grace – Mia is here for you." Her voice held a questioning lilt. Grabbing my jacket and small shoulder bag, I skipped down the hall towards her. I couldn't remember the last time I had looked forward to something so much; not since well before the incident and I couldn't deny it – I was incredibly excited. I felt like I had as a small child, waiting in line to see Santa.

"Thanks mum. This is Mia – she runs the library. She's

kindly offered to show me around." My mother glanced towards Mia and then turned to me with a smile. Her face was lit up; even though she had been really busy, I could tell in that one smile that she had been worrying about me. Mia was smiling graciously.

"Well, isn't that nice! Will you be out all day?" Her eyes darted between myself and Mia, but I could see that she never really met her gaze. Was she feeling nervous for me? A wave of affection crashed through me; she was so sweet.

"I'll have her back before dark, I promise," Mia said, her tone teasingly playful. I loved that she already felt comfortable enough around my mum to be that way. I knew that my mum would appreciate it too and if it made her happy, then it made me happy.

"You have fun girls! See you later Gracie Cake." My jaw fell open and I slapped my hand to my forehead. My mother headed back inside, and I groaned loudly. I had lost count of the number of times I'd asked her not to call me that, especially in front of people, but she never listened. I didn't know whether she did it to embarrass me, or whether she didn't realise she was doing it and it was just a way of showing affection. It was probably the former, seeing as all parents tried to embarrass their kids at some point or another. My cheeks blazed as I saw Mia's shoulders shaking.

"Don't laugh, it's not funny." I tried to look stern, but it wasn't a look I could really pull off and it didn't take long for me to start laughing with her.

"Hey, I'm not judging Gracie Cake. So – come on – spill. There has to be some amazing back story to this nickname!" I stared at her, trying not choke on the giggles that were escaping me.

"No, not really. I once smushed a whole cake into the carpet when I was a baby and it just – stuck." Mia started laughing even more and I giggled along with her, feeling freer than I had in forever.

The laughter was cut short, the chuckles dying in my throat as I took in the sight of Mia's car. It was a sleek and sporty red number, the roof rolled back and the sun beating down onto its cream leather seats. The wind had subsided at some point during the night, and although it wasn't quite warm enough to justify having the top down, I understood why Mia had. We lived in a country where the weather was as unpredictable as Mary Poppins handbag; the sun only deemed us worthy to shine on for a handful of days at a time, so you had to take every opportunity you were given.

"This is Minnie," Mia smiled, gesturing to the car. "She might look sleek and tough but don't let her fool you, she's my baby. Be nice to her." I was still gaping in awe. How did an eighteen-year-old afford such luxury on a librarian's wage? It seemed there was more to Mia than met the eye, and I found I was eager to learn all about it. I hadn't thought owning a library would be a lucrative business, but it would make sense if the family had generations of money. A rich family would certainly explain why Mia had taken on the running of it so young in the first place, why she had just accepted that it was her destiny. I slid into the passenger seat – it was already warm.

"Minnie is – wow." I didn't know what else to say. There were no words to describe all the multitude of feelings that were spreading through me. I was having an

Audrey Hepburn moment – I was only missing the scarf around my head. It was unbelievable.

Mia slid behind the wheel and reached into the glove compartment, slipping on a pair of sunglasses. She looked effortlessly cool, like an American movie star. She flashed her straight white teeth at me in a dazzling smile and the look was complete.

"I know, she is pretty amazing. Right – let's roll!" As we pulled away from the curb and the breeze took my hair with it, the free feeling returned, filling me with a warmth that I hadn't even realised I was missing. I was suddenly free from everything that had happened, free from my weird dreams and free from the loneliness that, up until that point, I had been trying to deny. I was beginning an adventure – all because of a new friend and her awesome car.

We weren't driving for long, but even the short journey was enough to get my adrenaline pumping. Excitement prickled at my skin; it was a stark contrast to anything I had felt for a long time. I wanted to cling to it with both hands and never let it go. I only hoped that Mia and I got along as well as we had done in the library, and it didn't end up being a day full of awkward.

Mia parked up and led me across a small bridge into the centre of the village. There was a wide river than ran through the heart of everything. Ducks, swans and geese glided gracefully over the glassy surface and schools of fish darted around beneath the ripples.

The sunshine had coaxed out plenty of families, beckoning them to the waters edge. The pathway that ran alongside the river was full of small children, their chubby little fingers clutching bags of bread; their heads covered in multi-coloured bobble hats of varying styles. They were all adorable; it was like a scene from a postcard. Their laughter tinkled through the air as they threw chunks into the water, watching as the ducks pecked it away to nothing.

"It's always like this on clear days," Mia said smiling, as we walked past the kids.

"It's so nice! There was a little pond not far from where we used to live, and it had a family of ducks, but it was nothing like this. I did used to like going and feeding them when I was small though." Being in the sunshine with Mia was having a profound effect on me. It was easier to reminisce without feeling so hard done to.

"Me too! My mum used to bring me down here and we would buy a bag of rolls from the bakery around the corner, then afterwards we would go and get ice cream." She nodded towards a van that was parked at the end of the path.

"Doesn't anything ever change?" I asked, surprised. Things in London had always seemed to change. Sometimes they had seemed to change on a daily basis, from the people to the buildings. What would be a block of flats one week, would suddenly be corporate offices the next. There was so much activity and buzz, you could blink and literally miss it all.

"The people tend to, but no – the things don't. Not really." She chuckled. "The ice cream van will always be there, come rain or shine. The weather can be downright dreadful, but he will still be there, waiting to sell to someone. People will always come and feed the ducks. We have a market too, and that hasn't changed my whole life. It's – comforting." I tried to imagine how different my life would have been, had I grown up somewhere like Stonewell. It would be easy to assume that living the same routine would get boring after time, but I could see what Mia had meant about it being comforting.

She led me into the village square and told me all about the Mayday Festival. Children from the local schools would gather and dance around a maypole, singing folk songs. It sounded charming and I knew it was something my mother would love to see. I laughed as Mia regaled me with the tale of her failed attempt at maypole dancing, where she'd gotten tangled in the ribbons and tripped several of her classmates.

"My mother still has a photo of me with my legs in the air. It's probably still on the mantlepiece. The whole village saw my knickers that day," she said, shaking her head.

"Oh my God, I have to see that picture one day!" I teased.

"Oh look – there's something you should see!" She grabbed my hand and pulled me towards a green fronted building, with old style leaded windows. It was the village bakery. There were yummy looking buns, pastries and cakes. Some of them looked more like pieces of art than something that was edible. I looked into the window in awe, my mouth watering. Mia's reflection was laughing – at me.

"Gracie Cake," she mumbled, covering her mouth to try and stifle the giggles.

"Oh, hilarious," I said, rolling my eyes playfully. I was enjoying the camaraderie.

We wandered down all the cobbled side streets, Mia giving me a running commentary of some of her favourite memories growing up in the village. She showed me some amazing vintage shops that I just knew I would revisit. Looking through old clothes had been one of my favourite things to do in London. Most of the old fashions were slowly coming back into style, so seeking out new thrift stores and discovering new outfits was something I loved.

She showed me the outdoor shops, of which there were many. Stonewell was located right on the edge of the Peak District, so it was a haven for walkers, and they were well catered for. She showed me a couple of art shops and some small bookshops, though I couldn't see myself buying any books when the library was so well stocked.

For a small village, it was packed full of shops and boutiques. I cursed myself for not exploring sooner, for acting like a baby and refusing to go anywhere but the library and home again – via the cemetery. I couldn't chastise myself too much though, because if I hadn't acted in such a way, I wouldn't be out exploring with Mia, so it was actually something to be thankful for.

Lunchtime crept up on us and Mia directed me towards one of the local pubs. It was very pretty; the walls were covered in climbing ivy. The small, attached garden had many picnic benches and despite the nip in the air, each of them was taken. There were hanging baskets that were crammed with colourful faux flowers; they brightened the place up, which meant that even on the coldest of days, you could almost believe it was summer.

It was only as we walked through the door, and the smell of food enveloped me, that I realised how hungry I was. My stomach grumbled loudly as we found a small, free table next to a big open fireplace. It was nice and cosy; the flames that burned and crackled in the hearth warmed my toes.

"What're you going to eat?" Mia asked as we perused the menu. There was so much choice and all of it sounded good. There were pies, Sunday roasts, fish and chips, hotpots, salads, sandwiches, burgers, fry-ups – it all made my mouth water in anticipation.

"What would you recommend?" I asked, knowing there were far too many things on the menu for me to make a choice. I'd never been great at making decisions, especially when all the options sounded so good.

"Oh, erm –" She blew her cheeks out and scanned the menu quickly. "I know! The homemade pie is to die for. The pastry is crispy, but it melts in your mouth."

"That sounds perfect," I said, salivating. My stomach gave another appreciative grumble and I blushed.

"I'll go order and grab us some coffees," Mia laughed. I pulled out my purse, but she waved it away, turning her back on me and heading towards the bar before I could protest. I felt awkward as I watched her weave her way through the tables and wondered if there would be some way for me to slip her the money for my lunch, without her knowing or being offended. It was highly unlikely. Even in the short time that I had known her, I had a good enough handle on Mia's character. She had a generous and kind-hearted spirit; she was the kind of person you instantly loved and that made me smile.

She wasn't gone too long, despite how busy it was in the pub and I laughed at the many faces she pulled as she made her way back through the crowd to the table, trying her best not to spill anything from the two, steaming mugs in her hands.

"So – what do you think? You reckon you might venture

a little further afield now you know the village better?" She blew on her coffee before taking a tentative sip.

"Definitely. I can't believe it's taken me this long. I guess I was just – scared. It'll take a while for me to know for sure where everything is but there is no way I'm going to be restricted to home and the library anymore."

"Or the cemetery!" she smirked. "I knew I shouldn't have shown you around, now you'll never come and visit me at work."

"I will I promise. Wild horses couldn't keep me away." I had enjoyed myself all morning, so much so that my mind hadn't once strayed to my past – but as I looked up at Mia, my stomach lurched. I recognised the look she was wearing, and I knew what was coming. I'd seen it many times before and I knew I would see it again, especially if I was going to start venturing out more. I braced myself, feeling extremely nauseous.

"So, where did you move from Grace? I know it must be somewhere down south because of the accent." My breath slipped out in a whoosh. It wasn't the question that I'd been expecting but I knew where it led to. It was understandable.

When you met someone new who had recently moved, it was reasonable to ask questions like where they had come from and why they had moved, so it shouldn't have surprised me that Mia would want to know, but – even though I was incredibly grateful to her for opening my eyes, for taking the time to show me the treasures of the village and taking me under her wing, I just wasn't ready to share the reasons behind our relocation – not yet.

"We lived in London." I picked up my coffee and took a sip. My mouth felt overwhelmingly dry, but the liquid was still scorching hot and it scalded as it slipped down my throat.

"That's cool. I spent a couple of weeks down in London, about three years ago, with my aunt and uncle. They've lived there a while now and I was doing a project on the capital, so they invited me down for the school holidays. It was nice for a change, but I must admit, I found it terrifying. Have you read that book, about the city mouse and the country mouse?" I nodded, raising my eyebrow curiously. Where was she going with this story? "Well, it was exactly like that. I was the country mouse and seeing the big city made me appreciate my little village all the more. I once said thank you to a bus driver as I got off, and he looked at me like I'd just announced I was going to eat his young!"

"Yea," I nodded, shaking with laughter. "Londoners aren't big on the whole 'talking to strangers' thing. It's more a kind of 'head down, mouth shut' kind of place. Generally, the only people that talk to others on buses and the tube and stuff are the crazies, and most people avoid them at all costs." I thought back to all the times I had avoided making eye contact with people, just so that I didn't have to talk to them; the times when I had stuck my nose in a book so that someone who thought they were from another planet wouldn't start spouting off in my ear about how they had come to take over the world. That was a surprisingly common delusion, it was strange just how many people shared it.

"Wow – well us northerners are a much friendlier bunch and I swear, we aren't crazy – well – not all of us are." She laughed. I'd never thought of myself as ignorant, but it hadn't passed me by that since the move I'd encountered people who were friendlier and more open to speaking to someone they didn't know. It had taken some time, but I was slowly getting used to it. It was different than what I was used to but – I liked it.

"So, what made you move?" There it was – the dreaded question – and although I had known it was coming, it still filled me with a sickening dread. I swallowed hard, my brain buzzing. I had two options. I could tell the truth, but I knew I wasn't ready to do that. I liked Mia, she was really nice, and I knew me and her were going to become good friends which meant at some point, I would probably tell her all about it – but this wasn't the right time. We were having an incredibly good day and I didn't want to spoil it.

Which left me option two – lie. A small, not completely false lie to deflect the attention and any further questions that she might have. I hated lying and I wasn't particularly good at it, but I hated reliving my past more.

"We needed somewhere bigger to live. My mum makes custom wedding gowns and our little house just wasn't big enough for how much work she has these days. Property in and around London is so expensive so she moved us here." My cheeks were burning with the heat of my untruths and I could feel it spreading across my chest. I hoped Mia wouldn't notice.

I was a terrible liar. My blushes always gave me away. I had no control over the way warmth would flood them and turn them scarlet. I stole a glance towards her. She was looking at me curiously, but then she smiled. If she thought something was off, she wasn't saying anything.

Our food arrived and I was grateful for something else to focus on. We chatted some more about school, what our favourite subjects had been and the friends we'd had. I found myself again, avoiding the conversation as much as possible, deflecting back to Mia. Talking about past friends was too difficult for me. I shovelled food into my mouth to keep myself quiet. She told me some more about her family; it was big – massive actually – and they were spread all up and down the country. Her mum and dad owned some farmland on the outskirts of the village, and they lived there with her favourite Aunt. It made me think again that she must come from a wealthy family – not that it mattered.

"Thanks to Facebook, I'm still in touch with most of my classmates, but I rarely see any of them. I have a couple of mates around here. You'll have to come and meet them. In fact..." She gasped excitedly and dug around in her bag, coming up with her phone. I popped the last forkful of my lunch in my mouth and watched her, wondering what she was planning. She had the excited look of someone on a mission.

"Yes!" she exclaimed loudly. A couple sat at a nearby table turned and looked at her, but she didn't notice. "I got this message this morning but didn't really get time to read it properly because I was on my way out to get you. One of my best friends Dan, regularly has these parties, they're amazing. It would be a great way for you to meet everyone!" I swallowed slowly. A party? I could feel the nerves creeping in already. Could I cope at a party, surrounded by people I didn't know? I wanted to meet more people, and if they were Mia's friends, they would have to be nice like her – wouldn't they?

"When is this party?" I asked tentatively. I'd been to parties before in London – not many – but generally speaking, I'd always known the person who was throwing them. If I attended this one, I would only know Mia, which could result in me being left alone to amuse myself for unknown periods of time, and that didn't appeal to me at all. The thought made my stomach churn so badly, the pie threatened to make a reappearance.

"It's this Friday and you have to come Grace; it will be awesome! And you should totally bring a bag – it's always a sleepover at Dan's." I felt my brow raise as I looked at her. First, I was going to a party thrown by someone I didn't know, and now I would be sleeping at their house? I didn't know if I was ready, plus there was my mother to contend with. Would she let me go, no arguments or questions asked – or would she insist that I head home and not stay over which would make me look uncool? I honestly didn't know the answer, and I wasn't sure I was brave enough to find out.

Butterflies rampaged through my stomach, but as the initial sickness began to subside, it was replaced with excitement. I could attend my first social gathering in my new hometown. I could begin to make new memories and start moving past everything that had happened. I was sure I could convince my mother to let me go, the only question was – did I want to? Only knowing Mia could be a problem, I would have to make the effort to talk to people that I didn't know. It wasn't necessarily a bad thing – it just terrified me.

"Ok," I said, before I changed my mind. "Yea – I'm in." There weren't any real, valid reasons not to go, but I could think of a whole load of reasons why I should. The silent butterflies continued their dance in my stomach, and I plastered a smile onto my face. Mia bounced in her seat as she quickly tapped away on her phone, replying to the message.

"Are you sure this Dan won't mind you bringing a stray to his party?"

"Don't be daft, he will love it! The more the merrier. You'll like Dan – trust me." There wasn't much else for me to do but trust her. I knew that she would look after me; she wouldn't just abandon me knowing just how long it had taken me to strike up a conversation with her.

"Dress to impress Gracie Cake – his house is ridonculous!" I gave her a nod as a shy giggle escaped my lips. Images of grand country houses with waiters and butlers sprang to mind. Did Mia and all her friends have lots of money? Would I fit in with them?

"How do I get there? And what time?"

"Don't worry, I'll come pick you up in Minnie." She gave me a warm smile before draining the last of her coffee. "Right, there's just a couple more places I want to show you and then I'll drop you home so you can start planning your outfit for your first ever Stonewell party!" Her excitement was contagious, but it was accompanied by sick nervousness. I hoped it didn't linger and spoil things for me.

She took my hand and dragged me from the pub. We jumped into Minnie, my mind already racing over the various, crumpled up outfits that I had, stuffed into my many suitcases. I couldn't shake the feeling that it was going to be a long three days till Friday.

Nine

Tick. Tock. Tick. Tock. Tick. Tock.

I growled at the clock, wondering whether my mother would miss it if I threw it from an upstairs window. Time was passing at an infinitesimal rate and I was running out of things to keep me occupied. I had already been extremely helpful and cleaned the house, from top to bottom. I'd scrubbed the skirting boards, cleaned out all the kitchen cupboards, mopped all the floors and cleaned the windows – inside and out.

I'd even taken the time to unpack several of the boxes that had been lying around, adding more of our personality to the house. There was still plenty more to do, but I didn't fancy myself as much of a handyman, so I wasn't willing to tackle putting up the shelves my mother had bought. Until she got someone in to do it, there was nowhere for the rest of the things to go. As I looked around at all the ornaments, trinkets and framed photos of us together, I wondered how we had fit it all into our tiny London home.

There was also a bit of an ulterior motive at play. I hadn't done all those things just to pass the time; I was hoping to sweeten the deal somewhat with my mum. She'd met Mia – albeit for a few minutes – and I could tell she liked her, but I didn't know how happy she would be about me going to a party at a boy's house, who I'd never met. Then there was the staying over.

I was only six months away from turning eighteen, so in the eyes of the law I was almost an adult. In her eyes though, I was still her baby and she found it hard to resist treating me as such.

It was Thursday morning before I finally managed to get hold of her. She had been manically busy all week, finishing off a tough dress design. She hadn't emerged from her workroom for more than the time it took to grab a quick can of cola and a sandwich. It was a good job I knew how to cook and didn't have to rely on her anymore, otherwise I would have starved a long time ago.

I'd gotten up early courtesy of a combination of the sun, streaming through my thin curtains, and the strange dreams that persisted to annoy me every night. I'd just poured her a cup of coffee when she walked into the kitchen. I needed to tread carefully if I wanted to make it to the party. One wrong move could result in her tagging along to keep an eye on me, and that wasn't happening. I was already going to be the new girl – I didn't need to be the weird new girl who brought her mum.

"You're up early," she said surprised, as she took the cup that I held out to her. My brow furrowed as I took her in. She looked exhausted. There were black bags beneath her pale green eyes, her skin looked thin and fragile and for the first time ever, I realised she looked – old. I would never dream of telling her that though. For one, I would never want to insult her like that, and for two – it would be more than life's worth. No one ever called Joanne Ayre old and got away with it – at least not to her face anyways.

"And you're up late. When was the last time you slept?" I was genuinely concerned. Sometimes, my mother laboured under the impression that it was perfectly acceptable to live on caffeine and very little sustenance, with next to no sleep. After the incident in London, she hadn't slept at all – not until we had moved. The first night in the new house, she had crashed; the highs of the many Red Bulls and espressos, finally wearing off. She'd fallen asleep and not woken up for three days straight. It wasn't a new thing, I'd seen it happen before, so it should have just been part of the fabric of our lives, but it was doubtful I would ever get used to zombie mum.

"You know me Gracie, I'll survive." She rubbed at her eyes and drank deeply from the coffee cup. "I haven't had the chance to ask, did you have a good time with Mia? Did she show you around?" I chewed my cheek nervously. This was it – this was the perfect opportunity, the opening I had been looking for to ask about the party. My lips felt dry as I ran my tongue across them, trying to build up some courage.

"Yes, I had a great time. It was amazing, actually. The village is much bigger than I thought it was. There are some really good shops I want to take you to when you aren't so busy, you'll love them. Also…" She looked up from her cup, guessing from the change in my tone that something was coming. She watched me carefully, and I could feel my cheeks brightening – those damn flushes! "Well, there is this get together, and Mia invited me along. She said it would be a chance for me to meet some more people my age. I'd really like that, and I can stay over too – as long as you're ok with it?"

I held my breath and tried to read her face, but she wasn't giving anything away. I knew that internally, she would be waging a war against herself. On one side would be her overprotective self, telling her that there was no way I could go staying out somewhere new, that it was an impossibility, and I should be locked up, never to be let out again so that she could keep me safe. On the other side, I knew there would be her old self, the part of her that still yearned for me to have a normal, teenage life, the part that wanted to forget everything that had happened and let me just – live.

"Ok," she finally said, squinting at me. I blinked, my brow rising towards my fringe involuntarily. Did she just say ok? Had I heard her right?

"Ok? Ok as in…"

"Ok, as in yes, you may go – but on one condition." I should have known it was too good to be true. I slumped into the chair and crossed my fingers behind my back, hoping to god it was something that I could agree to. "You must keep your phone with you at all times and if I text you, I expect a text back within half an hour. Otherwise, I'll be coming for you." A smile spread across my face. I leapt up and pulled her into my arms.

"Deal! Thanks mum." I was ecstatic. Nervous too, but mostly ecstatic. Finally, my life in Stonewell was taking a turn for the better, something I'd had a hard time believing could ever happen.

"I'm so glad to see you happy Grace. It's been a long time coming. I know things have been hard, but I told you it was all for the best." It was a statement, but I could hear the questioning in her words. She'd found it difficult, ripping me away from everything I knew, but it had been hard on her too. She had left behind all her friends, without a word to any of them. I gave her a reassuring smile.

"You did the right thing mum. Thank you." She pulled

me into another hug and kissed the top of my head.

"Well, you best sort yourself out for tomorrow then, and I best go and pack up that dress." She let out a massive sigh and headed back into her workroom.

I nibbled on my toast and thought about how easy it had been. Maybe it had been too easy. I'd geared myself up, mentally prepared myself as if I were going up against a dragon. I thought about it for a moment. Had a part of me wanted her to say no, to argue and make a scene so that I wouldn't have to go? There was a small part of me that was so terrified of messing up, that I'd half convinced myself it would be better not to go at all, and Mia wouldn't have been able to argue if my mother had been the one to stop me.

I looked up at the clock and groaned. Maybe mum was right. Getting my stuff together and picking an outfit was bound to pass some time. I cleared away my breakfast things, taking as much time as I could, before heading to my room. I was doing a mental run down on all my outfits, trying to think of which would be acceptable. What exactly had Mia meant when she had said 'dress to impress'?

My mind raced back to all the girls that had attended our leaver's prom, how they had been dolled up and dressed to the nines, wearing heels that made my calves go into spasm. I'd bought my fair share of pretty shoes and had even been known on occasion to wear them, but I preferred my converse – or Doc Martens if it was winter.

I closed my door and dragged the cases to my bed, opening and emptying them all out. The time had come to settle in and make the room more – me. I pushed the boxes around until I found one labelled 'hangers' and I dragged that over to the bed too. My old wooden wardrobe creaked when I pulled open the door. I half expected a family of bats to fly out, or at least some moths. It had stood empty and bereft of clothes for months, but the only thing that greeted me were dust motes; they floated out and danced across the beams of sunlight that shone through my window.

I'd always hated putting away laundry, but as I worked my way through my clothes, I found it oddly therapeutic. I folded, hung and rolled, filling my drawers and wardrobe. It took longer than I thought it would, but that wasn't a bad thing. It was well past lunchtime when I finally flopped down onto my bed. My back ached from heaving and bending but it'd been worth it. I looked across at the dress that hung on the wardrobe door.

It was a short dress – a summery, flower print number. Strapless and gorgeous; my all-time favourite. Memories of the last time I'd worn it floated into my mind, making me swallow hard. Flashes of that night hit me – answering the door to the police, hearing the news that would change everything. As it took over my mind, I was thankful I was already laid out on my bed. I shook my head, clearing the images away. It was about time me and the dress had some new memories – some good ones.

Ten

"Well, look at you!" I smiled shyly as my mum spun me around. Her eyes were glassy with the hint of tears, and her voice broke as she spoke. "Swit swoo Gracie moo."

"Thanks mum," I laughed. "You aren't going to cry, are you?" I wasn't sure how I would feel if she started bawling as I was about to leave. Would it make me stay?

"No, of course not. I'm happy for you – that's all. You look beautiful." She blinked rapidly, trying to ensure no tears slipped down her cheeks and made her a liar. I chewed the inside of my cheek as I looked down at my outfit for the umpteenth time. I'd found my favourite Converse out of my boxes, the ones that I'd hand painted flowers onto, and I'd gone to town and applied full make-up. The sparkly dust that shimmered on my smoky eyelids, along with the mascara and eyeliner, made my green eyes shine. I'd even put in maximum effort and curled my wild, red hair. It had been a pleasant surprise to look in the mirror and see something other than a washed out, tired teen. I was wearing my denim jacket; I had my canvas backpack thrown over my shoulder and I was ready – ready for Mia and whatever else the night would hold.

"Now, you just remember, if I text you…"

"I reply within half an hour, I know mum." She nodded and smiled. It was a tight smile, full of tension and I wondered how much she was holding back, how much of her wanted to stop me from leaving. A small toot sounded outside, and my stomach lurched. It was Minnie, and with her came Mia and my imminent departure. All day, I'd been a bag of nerves and I hadn't eaten anything since breakfast for fear of throwing up. I'd never nervously thrown up before, but there was always a first time for everything, and I wasn't willing to risk it.

"That's Mia. I love you, don't work too hard tonight; you need a break." I looked right into her eyes and gave her what I hoped was a stern stare. Either I didn't pull it off, or else she chose to ignore it because she didn't react.

"Don't worry about me. Go – have some fun! I'll be home late tomorrow, probably be after ten. Make sure you're home for then." She gave me a warning look and I nodded.

"Will be, I promise." I pressed a quick kiss to her cheek, before dashing out.

The sunshine hadn't lasted long, and the wind was once again icy cold. I started wondering if I'd chosen the right thing to wear. Thankfully, Mia had the roof up on Minnie. I dove into the passenger seat, the heaters blasting me in the face the moment my bottom touched leather.

"Whoa – wow," she said quietly. "Look who scrubs up all nice when her nose isn't stuck in a sketchpad!" I clicked on my seatbelt and turned to Mia. My eyes widened, my mouth falling agape as I took in her outfit. She was wearing a black leather skirt and a white, halter neck top. She had on a black leather jacket and spiky ankle boots. She looked stunning and – sexy. I couldn't believe how sexy she looked. It was a far cry from the person I was used to seeing; the one who walked around the library wearing casual jeans and jumpers. I inwardly groaned – I was going to be stood in Mia's shadow all night.

"Thank you, you look – well – you look gorgeous. Maybe I should go and change?" My mind was racing through everything that I'd unpacked and not a single other outfit came to mind. I didn't own anything that would even come close to what she was wearing. I smoothed my skirt down, self-consciously picking at an imaginary thread. If the good old 'girl next door' look was something to strive for, I'd definitely achieved it. Sitting next to Mia highlighted that fact.

"You're kidding me, right? Grace, have you looked in a mirror? No one is even going to see me once they get a look at you." She had a devilish grin, but before I could get worried about what it might mean, we were gone.

"So, where does Dan live again?" I asked, hoping conversation might help to ease the nervous knots in my stomach.

"Just outside the village. Well, about ten minutes outside. His family have a farm, lots of acres, horses, the works. It's an amazing house, you'll love it." I nodded along, half listening. My heart was hammering against my ribcage and my stomach fluttered, like someone had built an aviary inside it. This was madness. I'd never been overly confident, but I'd never been such a nervous wreck either. My fingers were crossed that Mia's friends would all be as welcoming as her.

She carried on talking about god knows what, and I watched as the village slipped by outside the window, opening up to lush green fields and dense wooded areas. Every now and then, a field would be dotted with little balls that looked like cotton wool – sheep. So many sheep. It was all very picturesque.

As she swung a turn, I noticed a small stream that ran alongside the road, cutting a little gully. If I closed my eyes, I could imagine what the soft, trickling noise of the water would sound like; how it would roar on days where the rain had fallen hard. There'd been nothing like it around where we lived in London – just another small thing to be thankful of the countryside for.

There wasn't much in the way of traffic on the roads and before I knew it, we were pulling up to a giant, black iron gate. I leaned forward, squinting through the windscreen to try and get a view of the house, the trees on either side obscured everything beyond the gate – something that spoke volumes in itself. Mia grabbed her phone and tapped out a quick message. No sooner had she clicked send, than the gates magically opened. The awe must have been obvious on my face because Mia silently laughed at me.

"You are too cute. I can't wait for you to meet everyone; they're going to love you." In one fell swoop, the fluttery wings of nervousness were back, playing havoc with my insides once more. I nibbled the inside of my cheek, watching as we pulled slowly up what seemed like a never-ending drive. I tried to calm myself, took a few deep breaths. The trees suddenly broke, revealing the most beautiful house I had ever seen.

It was a huge, stone structure that wouldn't have looked out of place on a show about stately homes. There were big bay windows and balconies to the first floor. Three big chimneys dominated the roof, and the front door was a dark, mahogany behemoth. You could have driven a tank straight through and not left a single scratch on the frame.

The driveway ended with a small roundabout that had a

massive fountain at its centre. It was like nothing I had ever seen before. Mia had been right – it was ridonculous. It was utterly breath-taking and left me speechless. How was I going to fit in with people that thought this was the norm?

"Please don't let the house fool you. Dan is real – down to earth." Mia smirked at me in the knowing way that she had. It was the same smirk she wore whenever she said something that seemed like she had just plucked my thoughts right out of my head.

"I'm nervous," I admitted, as she parked up and took off her seatbelt. I followed suit, but my hands were shaking so much, I couldn't release the belt. Mia took my hands and held them in hers.

"Don't worry. Nothing is going to drag me away from your side. I'll be with you all night – I promise." I nodded, praying she was right. I grabbed my bag and followed her out of the car.

The gravel crunched underfoot as I focused on making it to the door without my jelly legs giving out on me like they had at the cemetery. It was harder than you might think.

Mia didn't knock; she pushed her way straight into the house like she had lived there all her life. Music was playing somewhere, the sound of if drifted out to the foyer where we stood. I could hear people laughing and glasses clinking together. How many people were there going to be? Mia had said that most people our age moved away as soon as they could. Was this a reunion party of some sort?

"Dump your bag here, it'll make its way to a room." I dropped my bag beside hers, wondering how it could make its way to a room when I didn't even know where I would be staying. I didn't question it, just followed her through the hall, taking in the grand décor. The staircase spiralled up to the first floor, dark frames adorning the walls on either side. The carpet was plush and expensive, and I just knew it would feel like walking on a cloud if you were barefoot. I got the urge to take off my shoes, dig my toes in and see if I was right, but I was trying to avoid being the weird girl, so I resisted.

The hallway itself had wooden floors that reminded me of my primary school hall, instantly taking me back to a time when we had to sit cross legged and listen to the teachers drone on for an hour about something that no kid cared about. It was highly polished, and my shoes squeaked as I walked across it. End tables held vases filled with fresh cut flowers, the scent of them filling the air. It smelt like springtime.

Mia took my hand and pulled me towards the sound of the music. I hoped she didn't notice how damp my palms were. My lips were dry, and my heart was racing as we walked into what appeared to be a lounge.

All the sofas and other furniture had been pushed to the edges of the room, creating a dance floor. The windows were covered with black out blinds and the lights were dimmed to virtually nothing. A disco ball hung from the ceiling, casting thousands of tiny, shimmering squares into every corner of the room. It was possibly the most impressive house party I'd ever been to.

There were around twenty people in all. Some of them were dancing in the middle of the floor, others were stood to the side in small groups. They were talking and laughing, and all of them cradled drinks.

I glanced at Mia, still feeling nervous, and watched as

she scanned the crowd. She was obviously looking for someone in particular. The shaky feeling returned as I looked around at all the people. There were more girls than there were boys and all of them were impossibly beautiful. Their blonde hair shone under the disco lights and I grimaced. I stood out like a sore thumb, which made my already queasy stomach – worse somehow.

"There he is! Come on Grace." Again, I found myself being dragged, somewhat reluctantly, by an excited Mia. She weaved her way through the middle of the room to a brown-haired boy. He had his back to us as he fiddled with an expensive looking sound system.

"Dan – DAN! This is Grace." He turned around and my breath caught in my throat. He had the brightest blue eyes I'd ever seen; they were full of surprise as they met mine too. Then they were appraising me, the disco lights making them glint playfully. His mousy brown hair was perfectly quaffed – the front swept to the side. His nose had a small bump and as he smiled, I noticed his front teeth were slightly crooked, but it just added to his overall appeal. He was gorgeous – absolutely smoking hot, and I got the feeling he knew it. I felt like I was being scrutinised as his eyes made their way up from my feet. When they finally met mine again, he winked, forcing a blush to spread over my cheeks.

"Grace – I've heard so much about you," he shouted over the music. His voice was like runny honey and I wanted to melt, right in front of him. I cleared my throat, trying to shake myself up. There was no denying he was good looking, and he was obviously supremely confident – I could tell just from the way he was stood. He pulled me close and pressed a lingering kiss to my cheek. I stiffened, a little taken aback. My cheek felt like it was on fire where his lips had touched it. I had to pinch myself to snap out of my awkward silence.

"Nothing bad I hope," I said meekly. Was that the best I could come up with? I rolled my eyes internally, telling myself to get a grip. He was just a boy! He winked again and chuckled.

"Nothing bad. Maybe I exaggerated slightly. Mia has been awfully mysterious about her new friend. She hasn't really told us that much about you." He stared at me in such a way, it made me think of the way a starving dog might look at a steak. It was unnerving, yet exciting. I was thankful for the dim lighting, because I was sure my face was flashing like a red traffic light.

"There's nothing mysterious about me," I laughed nervously.

"He's just teasing Grace, he does it a lot." Dan stuck his tongue out playfully at Mia and she gave him the finger. It was an affectionate exchange, but it caused an unexpected reaction within me. Was it – jealousy? I shook myself and bit my lip to stop myself from loudly laughing and sounding like a loon.

"Well, I hope you enjoy your first party here in Stonewell, and may it be the first of many." He held up his glass in cheers.

"I'm sure I will, and thanks again for letting me tag along with Mia." He nodded, his eyes never straying from mine as he gave me a small, secret smile. Warmth spread through me, making my fingers tingle. It was a flirty sort of smile, which made me blush even deeper. He was incredibly nice, and he was so friendly and welcoming that it should have put me at ease, but I still felt on edge. I was very much the new girl, and though no one was looking at me, I still felt like a bit of a spectacle in my simple dress with my bright, slightly untamed hair. It was easy to feel like I didn't fit in with them.

"Let's grab a drink," Mia shouted. I followed her towards the other side of the room, sighing in relief. A drink sounded good. I glanced back but Dan had already turned back to the sound system to move some speakers. I considered asking Mia a bit more about him. Did he have a girlfriend? How long she had known him? Perhaps, whether she was interested in him? I stopped myself. What was I thinking? I'd only just met him, so it was none of my business. I didn't know what had come over me, but I needed to calm down. Anyways, I wasn't sure if I really wanted the answers. How would I feel if there was something between her and Dan? I shook my head, trying to convince myself I didn't care.

Mia walked through a door into a kitchen and all previous thoughts vanished. My eyes bulged as they swept over the magnificent room. It was a total contrast between old and new. There was a massive Aga with a brick chimney that dominated one wall and an old-style wash basin that was set low into the countertop. There was a double wide, American style fridge freezer that had an ice dispenser and what looked like a microwave, but there were so many complicated looking buttons on it that it was hard to tell. In the centre of the kitchen was an island, and it was stocked with almost every different drink you could think of. There were liquors, spirits, lager, beer, wine, cider, alcopops and bottle upon bottle of mixers.

The only time I'd had a drink, was one Christmas when

my mother had had some friends over and I'd been allowed a Babycham. It'd been weird; sweet and fizzy and I hadn't really liked it. In school, I'd known classmates that snuck spirits into the school discos in hip flasks and others who had an appointment every weekend with a few bottles of vodka on the local park, but I'd never been one of them – always leaning more towards goody two shoes than bad girl.

Now though, as I stood before the vast array of beverages on offer, I wished I'd experimented slightly more than never. I didn't have a clue what to drink. I didn't want to get something and not drink it, that seemed wasteful. I nervously scanned the bottles, trying to make a decision, when Mia handed me a glass of something very bright and very pungent. I could smell the alcohol from arm's length.

"What's this?" I asked cautiously. It looked appealing, and beneath the alcohol, I could smell something fruity. Its vivid red colour screamed additives and I knew it was probably lethally alcoholic, but it made my mouth water all the same.

"It's Dan's famous punch. He has it at every one of his parties, but he won't tell me what goes into it. You will love it though, it's amazing." She took a long drink, draining half the glass and then smiled. "Mmmm – yummy."

"Thanks," I said. I looked down into the glass. Should I actually drink it? Why the hell not? I apprehensively took a small sip. It was fresh and fruity, not at all how I thought it would taste. I'd expected it to be sweet and sickly, but it was tasty and refreshing; like it was made from real, freshly squeezed fruit juice. There was a slight tang, a burn at the back of my throat that I guessed what the alcohol, but it wasn't an unpleasant burn. It was nice, much nicer than I thought it would be. It made me feel warm, all the way to my toes. I drained the glass.

"Yea!" whooped Mia, laughing. "That's the spirit! Or more likely, three or four!" She laughed, refilling my glass before taking my hand and pulling me back into the darkened room to dance.

Eleven

Dancing with Mia felt silly at first. I'd gone to prom but even then, I hadn't danced. I'd stuck to the sides, sinking into the shadows in the hope I could stay invisible. I loved music, all types of music, but I often felt awkward moving around to it. Mia didn't have any such worry; she moved to the music like no one was watching and she didn't have a care in the world.

"Come on Gracie Cake, loosen up! This is meant to be fun, not a chore." She smiled encouragingly but I could only imagine the terrified look I had on my face. I was vastly aware of all the people in the room, and it made me skittish. It felt like the whole party was watching me – judging me.

I took another big drink of my punch and snuck a look at the other dancers. They were all around our age, and not even one of them was looking our way. Everyone was moving to the music, laughing and having fun. I began to relax and danced along with them. The punch was definitely helping; it gave me a braveness that I hadn't been able to conjure alone and a sense of freedom that felt liberating. It took a while, but I was soon enjoying it.

Mia's scream ripped through the air, making me and a few others around us, jump out of our skins. A boy with a black afro and skin the colour of cocoa swept her up from behind and swung her round. He was laughing and when she saw his face, all the anger left and she joined in, a flush creeping into her clear skin. He placed her gently back on her feet and she jumped into his arms, hugging him tight. He squeezed her back and she swatted at him playfully. As I looked between the two of them, I knew instantly that they liked each other. She hadn't mentioned a boyfriend and I hadn't asked, but there had to be something between the two of them.

"Grace, this is Tyler. He's a very good friend," she said, finally introducing us. "He seems to be under the impression that I am some sort of toy." She tried to look fierce as she glared at him, but she failed miserably. There was a whole sea of affection in her eyes. She liked him a lot, and I was willing to bet he felt the same way too.

"Hi Grace," he said, turning to me. "Enjoying your first party?" A small nod and a smile were all I could manage to give him.

My throat tightened, and there was a pull in my chest, a yearning that I'd never felt before, but that I knew had everything to do with the interaction I'd just witnessed between Mia and Tyler. I yearned for that closeness, that companionship. It was a strange thing to be experiencing; I'd never before been bothered by the whole dating thing. I turned away from them, looking across the room to where Dan had been stood when we had first arrived. I thought about the way he had smiled, how his eyes had twinkled in such a playful way. The blush returned to my cheeks as I thought about his lips brushing my skin. What if -? No – I cursed myself for thinking about him like that, I'd only known him a few hours. I just had to hope that this was the start of something for me, that perhaps one day I would be as close to them all as they were to each other and I would be part of their circle of friends.

"Stay away from him Grace, or it won't be long before he's lifting you and trying to crush your ribs too," Mia laughed, dragging my attention back to them. I looked at her in confusion – how did she not see it? The way Tyler was staring at her told me he wasn't like that with just anyone; this playfulness was reserved for her. She seemed completely blind to what was right in front of her. I smiled and drank some more from my glass.

"Hey, it's not my fault you got no meat on those ribs of yours." He took Mia's hand and spun her around. He was smooth and charismatic. His cocoa skin was flawless, his eyes a deep chocolate brown. They were framed by the longest lashes I'd ever seen on a boy and they were full of happiness and laughter. Even when his lips weren't smiling, his eyes were. As I looked between them, I could see the chemistry – it was hard to believe the pair of them were completely oblivious.

"Tyler is the comedian, can't you tell?" Mia shouted sarcastically. He gave her a small, playful push before turning to me once more.

"So, Grace, Mia says you moved from London. What brought you to Stonewell?" I froze with my glass halfway to my mouth. I'd not expected people to be interested in me, so Tyler's question threw me. Luckily, I didn't have to answer; Mia saved me.

"Her mum makes custom wedding dresses and she needed somewhere bigger to work, isn't that cool?" My chest swelled with gratitude towards her. She'd saved me from an awkward explanation whereby I would once again, have to omit a few details – even if she weren't aware that she'd done anything.

"Cool. Well, London's loss is our gain." He offered me

a warm smile before excusing himself and heading out to the hall.

"Come on," Mia said into my ear. "Let's go outside and get some air, I'm boiling." I followed her through the kitchen, out of some open French doors onto a gorgeous patio. Two big squishy sofas took up most of the space, centred around a square table with a firepit sunk into the middle of it. A fire was blazing away in the middle and I could already feel the warmth, tickling my skin. A wooden trellis glowed with tiny fairy lights and ivy climbed up the entire thing. It gave the whole place a magical aura. Mia flopped down onto a sofa and beckoned for me to join her.

"This house is amazing," I sighed, sinking back into the cushions. "I can't believe Dan's parents let him throw parties here. My mother would never let me, she'd be too scared we'd wreck the house." I drank the last of my second glass of punch and glanced around. It was having an effect; everything felt warmer and fuzzier. It was like I was experiencing everything through cotton wool – I enjoyed the sensation. Mia looked away and cleared her throat before speaking.

"Isn't it? I've never met them, but Dan's parents are cool. They buy him all the booze for the parties. He said the way they see it, he is better off having friends over and drinking at home than going out clubbing and getting into who knows what kind of trouble. They're great." She looked away, unwilling to meet my eye. That was strange. It was like she was hiding something from me, but she hadn't said anything weird. I shook off the unease and instead, concentrated on what she'd said.

"How often are they away?" With my mum working

away so often, I was no stranger to being in the house alone, but our farmhouse wasn't a fraction of the size of Dan's home. When the wind shook the windows and the whole house was cold and empty, the loneliness would creep in – so I couldn't begin to imagine how lonely Dan felt within the vastness of his home.

"Pretty often. All the time actually." She looked down into her glass, then turned and smiled at me.

"That's rough." My heart ached for him – no wonder he had so many parties. I bit my lip and considered asking about Dan and his status – but I wasn't brave enough.

"So, I've met Dan and Tyler – do you know everyone here?" I needed to change the subject before Mia spookily read my mind again, plus I was curious to find out what the other girls were like. Would they be as nice to me as Mia had been? My experiences of groups of girls had not been good ones. Not every girl is a bitch or a bully, but every group seems to have at least one and, in the past, I'd found myself their target on more than one occasion. My red hair and pale colouring were like a beacon, drawing nastiness to me like a moth to a flame.

"Nope – I know Dan and Tyler. I may have exaggerated the size of our group. It's pretty intimate. Dan more than likely doesn't know even half of the people in there. God knows how they find out about his parties, but he doesn't mind. As long as they don't make a mess or cause a riot." I nodded, taking it all in. Mia, Tyler and Dan – intimate was one word for it. I'd sensed there was something between Mia and Tyler, so could that mean that Dan was – free? Maybe we could double date?

I lifted my glass to my lips, swallowing back the urge to scream at myself that I'd only just met him, before remembering it was empty. Mia laughed.

"Come on my thirsty friend, let's get you another drink."

Twelve

My head spun, my eyes slipping in and out of focus. So – this was what drunk felt like. Everything was warm and fuzzy, and the world passed me by in an alcohol fuelled haze. I didn't really have a sense of time and the more I drank, the more confident I became. I'd wiggled my way onto the dance floor on more than one occasion, shaking what my mother gave me without a care in the world.

My mother – she had been cool with the texts, only sending a couple and I'd been with it enough to text back right away and avoid her hunting me down. I was glad though when she messaged, telling me she was heading to bed, because I was rapidly losing all coordination and my fingers felt too big to tap out any more messages. When I looked at my phone, the screen danced around my vision and wouldn't keep still, so yea – I was grateful.

Being drunk was a sensation like none I'd ever felt before. I was still undecided on whether it was one I ever wanted to feel again. It was exciting and I'd reached the point where I was comfortable, where nothing really mattered, but I wasn't sure I wanted to go much further.

It didn't matter that I was in a stranger's house, dancing the night away. It didn't matter that I didn't know anyone and had only spoken to three people the entire night. It certainly didn't matter what had brought me to Stonewell. All that mattered was that I felt good – I felt free. Though, all the excitement of my first ever drinks and my first social event in my new hometown, couldn't erase the feeling that when the party was over, I was going to pay – dearly.

After making another trip to the kitchen for yet another top up, Mia had excused herself to go to the toilet and I hadn't seen her since. So much for nothing tearing her away from my side all night. Other than standing at the back door for five minutes to cool off, I hadn't strayed from the lounge. I was dancing alone, but it no longer bothered me. I was having too much fun.

I had another cursory glance around, trying to spot Mia amongst the partiers, when a hand grabbed me from behind and spun me around. I found myself looking into the bright blue eyes of Dan. We'd crossed path's a couple of times throughout the night whilst grabbing drinks, and both times he had turned on the charm; he was funny and entertaining, intent on making me laugh. The look he now had in his eyes though – laughing was no longer his intention.

He didn't say a word as he pulled me closer. The music was loud, and the beat was fast, but we seemed to slow down – right down. Even with the faux confidence that the wicked punch had given me, I felt my stomach flop.

The nerves that had flowed through me at the beginning of the night, had been banished by the drink, but as he gazed into my eyes, they came creeping back – coursing through me. I needed to hold it together. It would be a shame to do something stupid like show myself up by puking on his expensive clothes.

His hands slid slowly down my back, settling on my waist. I inhaled sharply as he held me tight, his body pressed to mine. My skin tingled where his hands had trailed and it sent warmth, down through my stomach and colour straight to my cheeks. His eyes were intense; they never left mine. They drew me in, hypnotising me. I could feel the intense burn of embarrassment in my face and I wanted to look away, but I felt like if I did, I would lose something. The feeling was bizarre, and I didn't know where it came from. I swallowed hard as his fingers traced back up the length of my spine, coming to rest on my neck. His face slowly closed in on mine.

Shock kept me frozen in place. Was he going to kiss me? I wasn't sure I was ready for that. I'd never been kissed before and as sad as that may sound, I was ok with it. I didn't know Dan. Yes – I had been thinking of him in that way for most of the night, and I was obviously attracted to him – though it was a whole new feeling for me – but he was still practically a stranger. I wasn't sure I wanted my first ever kiss to be a drunken one with someone I didn't know. My body, it seemed, was not on the same wavelength. It thought very differently, pushing against him without me being able to do much to stop it. Panic began to set in. I couldn't see a way out of it. I closed my eyes and held my breath.

"There you are!" Mia shouted, grabbing my hand and dragging me from the weird trance. I'd never been so thankful to see anyone in my entire life. I pulled her into a drunken hug, my hands shaking.

"Thank you," I whispered in her ear. She gave me a warm smile and an almost imperceptible nod. She glanced at Dan with a serious look on her face, and I watched as he smiled, giving her a shrug. He backed away until he was stood, leaning against a speaker and watched as Mia pulled me away into the kitchen. She stood with her hands on her hips, her brow raised.

"Were you just about to kiss Dan?" she squealed giddily. My mouth opened and closed like a ventriloquist dummy, but no sound came out. Mia started giggling. "Honestly! I leave you alone to go to the loo and you end up in the arms of the hottest guy here!" I cringed, still trying to get my head around what had just happened. She wasn't wrong – Dan was incredibly hot, and my mind had strayed to thoughts of him in more than friendly ways, for most of the night. Should I have let him kiss me? Had I missed out on something – amazing? The idea both excited and terrified me.

"I don't even know how that happened," I said, finally finding my voice. "One second I was dancing and then…" I shook my head.

"Don't worry, no one will blame you. Dan is sickeningly good looking, and he tends to have that effect on people," she laughed. She winked and grabbed me a new glass of punch. I didn't know whether it was a good idea to partake in another one, but I disregarded everything my brain was screaming at me and took a long sip, hoping it would dispel some of the nerves. Mia watched me, but I didn't want to talk about it anymore; my mind was filling with regret and that created confusion.

"What are you talking about anyway, the hottest guy here?" It was time to change the subject to something more – juicy. "I've seen how you look at Tyler." My bravery was returning, and I wanted answers. Mia and Tyler gravitated towards one another; I'd witnessed it on more than one occasion during the night and from everything I'd seen, they would make the cutest couple. It was crazy that they weren't already together.

"Ah," she mumbled, her cheeks flushed. "You saw that huh?" So, she did like him!

"Come on – spill!"

"There isn't much to spill. I've had a crush on him forever and he's never noticed. That's all there is to it." She looked down into her glass and avoided my eyes, so she didn't see the look of incredulity on my face. Even a blind man would be able to see that the two of them cared for one another. It didn't take a genius to work it out. I shook my head in disbelief. How could she not see it for herself? The way he looked at her, like she was the only woman on the planet – it was hot enough to melt ice.

"Have you ever spoken to him about it?"

"No, I think it's pretty obvious I like him. I've hinted at it plenty in the past. He's never made a move, so I guess he doesn't feel the same way." She sighed, giving me a sad, little shrug. I couldn't believe what I was hearing.

"The only thing that's obvious, is that you've lost it!" I laughed. Her eyes widened in shock and I realised I'd been a little louder than I thought. "Sorry, that was the punch shouting. Seriously though Mia, Tyler is into you – he is SO into you! I don't know how you don't see it! I can't believe you aren't together already to be honest." Her brow furrowed in confusion, but I could see in her eyes how much she wanted to believe me; how much she wanted my words to be true.

"I…"

"Come on," I said, grabbing her hand and cutting her off. "Let's go and dance some more." I wanted to get back in the lounge where I could look for Tyler. Maybe I could help the whole thing along; it obviously needed intervention. I hadn't known them for long, but I was feeling bold and I wanted to help. Mia had helped me by talking to me – befriending me. She would probably never know how much that small act meant to me, so the least I could do, was try and repay the favour.

I held her hand as we made our way back into the middle of the dancefloor. People had started peeling off, disappearing to who knew where – bed probably. I didn't know what time it was, but I wasn't tired enough to care. Mia closed her eyes and smiled as she swayed to the music. I smiled too, scanning the room for Tyler. I couldn't see him, but I did spot Dan. He was still leant up against a floor speaker, but now he was talking to some blonde girl. A wave of emotion swept through me; emotion that I had no right to feel – envy. He must have felt my eyes on him because he looked up past the blonde, his eyes meeting mine. His stare was intense and leg-jerkingly hot.

It was a look that did things – strange things – to my insides. The heat returned to my cheeks and even though it was dark, and he was across the room, I swore he must have seen it, because he smirked like the Cheshire Cat. I averted my eyes and spun Mia around so that my back was to him. Then I clocked Tyler. He was stood on the edge of the dancefloor holding three shot glasses; each of them filled with an amber liquid. He held them up and winked. I smiled – this was my chance.

"Ladies," he said as he approached us. "The night isn't complete without a little help from my old friend Jack." He stood between us, glancing from Mia to myself. I didn't know whether it was the conversation we had just had or not, but she looked incredibly shy and her cheeks held the tinge of a blush. She looked adorable, and judging by the way Tyler watched her, I wasn't the only one who had noticed.

"I'm in," I shrugged. We both took one of the small glasses from him. I held it to my nose and gave it a quick sniff. My face contorted involuntarily. It smelt – strong.

"What shall we toast to?" Tyler asked.

"New friends," Mia said, gesturing towards me.

"How about – not so secret crushes," I laughed, wiggling my eyebrows at the pair of them. They both stood agog, neither one able to meet the others eye. I downed the shot, instantly wishing I hadn't. I closed my eyes and waited for the burn in my throat to settle.

"Holy crap, that's fiery!" I croaked. They both let out a laugh, Mia shuffling her feet and Tyler glancing at her nervously. I cleared my throat. "Well, I think you two have some talking to do, and I have to go pee!"

"Charming," I heard Tyler say, as I stumbled slowly away from them. "I like her."

I waited in the hall for a minute or two, before peeking back into the lounge. They were stood close together – chatting. Each of them had a look of adoration of their faces. I watched as Tyler held out his hand and Mia took it, leading them into the kitchen.

I sagged against the doorframe, a sense of pride washing over me. I'd done it. I was a drunken, matchmaker extraordinaire. It was a good feeling. I bit my lip and looked over to where Dan had been stood with the blonde, but he was no longer there. A lump formed in my throat and I frowned. What was wrong with me? Was I upset because Dan had gone off with another girl? I had no right to be – it wasn't my place. It wasn't like he was my –

"Did you just do what I think you did?" I jumped,

spinning around and came face to face with none other than the man himself. I choked back the lump and smiled shyly at him.

"It depends on what you think I did." My voice shook and I bit the inside of my cheek. He was stood so close – again. My hormones were having a field day, my body didn't know what to do with itself.

"Did you finally get those two to see how much they like each other?" I dragged my gaze away from his soft lips and looked up into the clear blue of his beautiful eyes. He had no regard for personal space, but I couldn't bring myself to be mad that he was invading mine.

"Yes – I think I did. I don't know how they didn't see it themselves though." I gave a nervous laugh and Dan smiled.

"Sometimes people just need a little – push -you know, in the right direction." I nodded. I was sinking into him again, just like I had on the dancefloor. "Have you had a good time tonight Grace?"

"Yes. Yes, I really have." It was barely more than a whisper, but it was all I could manage as his silky voice washed over me.

"Good," he smiled, his eyes glinting. He leaned down slowly – impossibly slow – taking his time to reach me. His lips touched my cheek in a soft kiss, and I found myself holding my breath. He pulled back and stared at me with incredible intensity. "I'm going to bed now. I just wanted to make sure you've enjoyed yourself."

"I have, and thanks again." He nodded before turning away from me and making his way up the stairs. My fingers brushed the spot where his lips had just been as I stared after him. He'd kissed me; a small kiss but still – it was a kiss. My eyes fell to the carpet, dazed. Exhaustion washed over me and I knew – it was time for bed.

Thirteen

My head spun as I walked across the darkened landing. Why had I drunk so much punch? And why had I decided that having a shot on top of all that drink, would be a good idea? It'd seemed like a simple solution to help banish the nerves, but I realised it was a silly mistake to make at my first ever party. I didn't even know what was in the mystery punch – it could literally contain anything. It had tasted all sweet and fruity, but I was fast discovering that it had concealed a deadly mix of alcohol.

After watching Dan retreat up the stairs, I hadn't hung around. I'd stumbled through to the entrance, trying to locate my backpack but it was no use. All the bags had disappeared. Mia had said that it would find its way to a room, but how did whoever moved it, know which room I would end up in? I didn't even know.

"All the beds are made up; just find a room and crash." Those golden words were the only wisdom I'd received from Dan with regards to where to stay. He'd said them quite early in the night, and I'd been so far away from thinking about bed, that I hadn't thought to question him any further.

So, I found myself wandering through a strange house in the near pitch black, searching for somewhere to sleep, silently cursing myself for letting the one person I knew out of my sight.

My heart had been in the right place playing

matchmaker, but I regretted it with every stumble and curse in the dark. My fingers found the handle of a door. I pushed on it, falling face first into the room.

"This one's occupied! Get out!" I squinted into the room and could just make out two shapes on the bed. My face burned as I watched them move together. I backed out quickly, a small squeak escaping me. Had they been doing what I thought they were doing? Had I just stumbled into two people – having sex? I was – mortified. The heat in my cheeks worsened as a hysterical, drunken giggle worked its way up from my chest and out of my mouth.

It was time to try something different. I listened at the doors as I crept along, not wanting to make the same mistake twice. There were muffles, moans and groans from almost every door I came to. When I'd walked into the party, I hadn't realised that most people would be staying the night; nor had I realised that most of them wouldn't be sleeping. I wouldn't consider myself prudish, but I was happy that at seventeen, my virtue was still intact. If I didn't find a room soon, I would end up bedding down in the big bathtub with the clawed feet, that I'd gushed over earlier in the night.

I reached the end of the landing – the last door. I stopped and listened but couldn't hear any noise coming from within. Finally – I'd found somewhere I might be able to lie down and stop the world from spinning so fast. I opened the door slowly, just in case.

There was a small lamp lit on the bedside table and the room was empty. I sighed heavily and smiled to myself, slipping inside and shutting the door behind me. I had a good look around.

The big, double bed in front of me looked incredibly inviting. It was made up with plain black sheets and as I ran my hand over them, I knew they were expensive. There was a pile of books next to the lamp. They all appeared to be travel guides of some sort. The far wall was covered from floor to ceiling in hooks and on each hook was a bag or backpack of some kind. All of them were different and all were in different states. Some were brand new and had never seen the light of day, while others were worn and looked like they'd travelled the world ten times over. It was a strange setup and would most certainly have a story; a story that I found myself wanting to know. My chest panged as my eyes roved over the bags, but I quickly dismissed it. How ridiculous to be jealous of a bag.

Mia had never said anything about Dan travelling, but it would make sense that he would go with his parents some of the time. They had to be his. Where in the world had he been? How many places had he visited? Who had he met on his travels? A sickening wave of envy filled me again, but I shook it off. I needed to slow down my hormones where it came to Dan, otherwise I would end up being swept away by them.

The room had a masculine feel to it, but as Dan wasn't in it, I wondered whether it was someone else's. I'd watched him go to bed, so if it were his room, he would be laid, snuggled under the lush, black covers – wouldn't he? Maybe he had two rooms, and this was a spare? It didn't seem likely, but stranger things had happened.

In the far corner of the room, stood a battered, old chest of drawers. From the way he had been staring at me all night, I was sure Dan wouldn't mind me borrowing a t-shirt to sleep in, especially seeing as my bag seemed to have disappeared and could have been put in any one of the rooms with copulating bodies in. I shuddered, praying it wasn't on any of the beds.

I pulled open the top drawer and was bowled over by intense scent of aftershave and clean linen. It was intoxicating and wasn't anything I had smelt on anyone before. It stirred something inside me, something deeper and stronger than I'd ever experienced, even stronger than the reactions I'd had to Dan. How could a smell do that? I squeezed my legs together, flushed at the reaction.

I grabbed the topmost t-shirt. It was white, with a faded Coco Cola insignia on the front. I stepped out of my Converse and pulled my dress off. When I pulled the shirt over my head, it had a profound effect. It almost felt like I was in the arms of someone strong and warm.

The bed was calling me, the sheets overwhelmingly inviting. My eyelids drooped, feeling very heavy. I slid beneath the duvet, inhaling its gorgeous scent. Within minutes, I was asleep.

Fourteen

I opened my eyes but instantly regretted it. The sun was beginning to creep through the curtains and it was evil and bright. I groaned and blinked a few times, my gritty eyes landing on a small clock on the bedside table. It was 6:45am. Why on earth had my body decided to wake me at such an ungodly hour when I'd drunk the earths weight in alcohol? I didn't even know what time I'd made it to bed. Late was all I knew – it was probably some time in the early hours of the morning.

My head was splitting, and my mouth was dry, like I'd been eating sand. My stomach was hollow; it felt cavernous and I realised that not only had I drunk like an Irishman, but I'd done it on an empty stomach. It wasn't the best idea I'd ever had.

I winced as I blinked at the clock again, my eyes falling upon a tall glass orange juice on the table, and beside it – a packet of paracetamol. I wanted to cry with happiness. I didn't know who had found me during the night, whether it be Dan, Mia or Tyler, but they must have left them for me, knowing the new girl would need them.

I tried to sit up, but the cover restrained me, held me tight to the bed. I pulled on the duvet, rolling over to try and free myself. That's when I saw him.

He was sat on top of the cover, nonchalant, reading one of the travel guides. I inhaled sharply; he was breathtakingly beautiful, more beautiful than any one person had a right to be. My stomach squeezed itself into nervous knots. I didn't recognise him from the party, and Mia had said she only knew Tyler and Dan – so who the hell was this?

He had wild black hair that curled at the nape of his neck, green eyes as clear as a jewel, skin that any woman would kill for and that scent – it was the same one that had hit me in the face when I'd opened the drawer, looking for something to sleep in. So – if this wasn't Dan's room as I had initially believed – whose was it? The corners of his mouth twitched up into a smile, but his eyes never left the book that was in his hands.

"Good morning, sleeping beauty." Was he talking to me? My tongue was stuck to the room of my mouth, so all I managed was a small croak. He turned to me, his eyes silently laughing. "Drink – take the tablets. I assume you drank the punch? That's never a good idea at one of Dan's parties." I could only imagine what I looked like; bloodshot eyes and a pasty complexion – nothing like a beauty, sleeping or otherwise.

My heart was beating madly in my chest. If I'd thought my body had reacted to Dan, then it was nothing compared to how it was lighting up for this new stranger.

I did as he'd said and popped two tablets from the packet, gulping them down with half a glass of the orange juice. His eyes were on me and the butterflies that had started dancing around my stomach threatened to throw the tablets right back out.

I felt ridiculous. I was laid in someone else's bed, in someone else's clothes and I was getting the sneaking suspicion that that someone, was the godlike creature beside me. I had no idea who he was, which made it worse. I moved my tongue around my mouth, running it over my teeth before I dared to try and speak.

"I'm really sorry," I croaked. "Dan said to crash anywhere. This was the only room that didn't have – um." I felt embarrassed as I remembered that every room had been occupied by couples, doing who knew what. My face felt hot, the warmth coming all the way from my toes.

"Ah – yes. I guess nothing is sacred at Dan's parties. I'll be eternally grateful that it was you that found my bed, and not them." He still had a faint look of amusement in his green eyes. I pulled his t-shirt and the duvet, closer around me, feeling exposed.

"I'll wash your shirt – and the sheets. I'm really sorry – again." This was beyond strange and beyond embarrassing. If I'd thought stumbling upon two people having sex had been mortifying, it was nothing compared to how I now felt, sleeping in someone else's bed and being caught by them.

"Don't be sorry. You can keep it. It suits you better than it ever did me." I looked into his eyes for the briefest moment but had to look away. They were a different colour, but they held the same intensity of Dan's, and in the growing morning light, they glinted just as playfully.

He had to be related to Dan in some way. I cursed myself silently for my stupidity. Of course, he was related to Dan, why else would he have a room in his house? My stomach was still doing back flips, front flips and roly polys. My heart was trying to escape through my mouth, beating so loudly I was sure he must be able to hear it.

"Thank you." It came out as more of a mumble than the clear, confident voice I pictured in my head. The spicy scent wafted to me as I fidgeted uncomfortably, sending my senses into overdrive. I had to stop it; this was insane.

"You're welcome.   Let it be a memento," he said, looking directly into my eyes again. "It's not every day I come home and find a beautiful girl in my bed." I swallowed hard. Was he serious? I ran a hand through my hair furtively, trying to assess the damage. It felt big, like a bird had nested in it overnight. A groan rumbled in my chest.   There was nothing I could do about it – he'd already seen it.

My hands shook as I lifted the glass to my lips again, taking a small sip of the cold juice. This was far beyond weird.   Not only had I woken in a strange house, but within that house I'd woken in a strange bed, with a strange man sat on it.

It hurt my head to try and fathom it. It was awkward and I didn't know what to do. I needed to leave, but all I was wearing was an old t-shirt – his old t-shirt – and my knickers.

I looked around the room and spotted my dress, folded neatly on top of my shoes. In the state I'd been in when I'd retreated up the stairs, I hadn't done that – I'd dropped it where I stood before stumbling into the bed. That had to mean – he had. I winced. Now it was definitely time to leave.

"Thank you, for the juice and the tablets – and for the shirt," I sighed. I sat up and swung my legs out of the side of the bed. I stood, hoping the shirt was as long as I remembered it being, but standing so quickly made me feel instantly sick. I was a fool. The room began to spin around me, and a pain shot through my head, like it was being hammered into a million pieces. It hurt so much, I cried out, squeezing my eyes shut tight to try and stop the pain. My knees buckled and I felt myself falling.

"Whoa there." Strong, soft hands caught me, pulling me upright. I leaned into him, feeling woozy. My head was still splitting, but I couldn't ignore the sparks that flew beneath the surface of my skin. I didn't care who he was; all I knew was that he was keeping me up and for that, I was grateful. Another wave of sickness passed through me and I willed it away. There was no way I was going to give in to sickness and vomit all over this gorgeous stranger.

My hands were splayed against his chest as I tried to right myself and rid my head of the banging. Breath caught in my throat. His skin beneath the black shirt was warm, his muscles hard, and I could feel the electricity where my hands touched him. My fingers tingled and my breath, when I let it go, was raspy. I looked up into his face. He was holding his breath too, his green eyes glittering as they squinted at me in confusion.

He looked exactly how I felt – completely baffled by the strange feelings that seemed to be passing between us. How could something so electric, so exciting, happen with someone I'd never met before? Someone who's name I still didn't know. He laid me back down and pulled the duvet up over me before kneeling beside the bed. The confusion was gone from his eyes, replaced with concern.

"I'm guessing you had a late night; you should rest some more. Go back to sleep, I promise you will feel better for it." I almost shook my head in protest, thinking it would be easier to get over the hangover than the mortification of going back to sleep in his bed, but a yawn escaped and betrayed me. I sighed, feeling sleepy again. Perhaps one more hour wouldn't hurt. I started to close my eyes, but then snapped them open.

"Will you – will you still be here? When I wake up?" My face was hot as the words tumbled from my lips, but I could do nothing to stop them. Why did I care whether he would be around when I awoke? It seemed silly, but something about that electricity, something about the feelings he had invoked in me, made panic rise at the thought he wouldn't be. He looked shocked, but smiled down at me.

"It is my room, isn't it?" It certainly did seem that way. I nodded and yawned again, snuggling back down into the pillows, unable to keep my eyes open for a moment more.

Fifteen

My eyes were sticky as I tried to pry them open for a second time. It took me a moment of squinting around to get my bearings and realise where I was. My head didn't feel as though it was going to explode anymore but there was still a dull ache there. The sunlight no longer made my eyes burn either, which was a good sign. I glanced at the clock – 11:30am. How had I slept that long?

The orange juice glass was still beside the clock, but it had magically refilled, and the tablets still lay beside it. I stretched, curling my toes beneath the soft cover. The bed was so comfy and cosy, I felt like I could stay wrapped up in the warm duvet forever, enveloped in that magical scent. That scent – I stiffened as everything came back into sharp focus. I closed my eyes and held my breath as I rolled over slightly in the bed, hoping it had been a dream. But no – he was still there, still reading his travel guide; just as he'd said he would be. My pulse picked up the pace instantly. He must have felt me move because he smiled into his book.

"Good morning again, sleeping beauty. Hope you're feeling a bit better this time around." A nervous laugh bubbled its way up my chest and out through my mouth. This was so surreal. "You'll probably need more of those tablets if you were indeed on Dan's punch all night. It's wicked stuff."

I sat up slowly, unbelievably grateful to this man that I'd

never met before. My head still span a little, but it was nothing like the first time. I washed two more tablets down with the juice and laid my head against the headboard.

"Thank you, for everything – really." I wasn't sure what else to say. No amount of words could do justice to the way I felt. He didn't know me; he would have been well within his rights to get annoyed and throw me from his bed when he'd discovered me in it – but he hadn't. Instead, he had been chivalrous and taken care of me. It made me feel all gooey inside, which in turn made me feel silly and nauseous. He closed the book and turned to me, giving me his full attention. His face wasn't that far from mine, and I became distinctly aware of the fact that I had yet to brush my teeth.

"You're very welcome. I'm going to hazard a guess and say you're either new to the joys of alcohol, or you just wanted to have a really good time."

"First time drinker," I winced. "Is it that obvious?" I shook my head, feeling utterly ashamed. Why had I let myself get in such a state? "It just tasted like juice." He laughed and it was such a loud, genuine sound; deep and rich and it filled the whole room, making the bed vibrate. My lips twitched into a smile.

"People only ever have Dan's punch once and then they learn to stay away. Unless you're Mia of course – she's a glutton for punishment." My ears perked up. He knew enough about Mia to know her drink preferences, yet he hadn't been at the party and she hadn't mentioned him. Who was this man?

My slow, punch addled brain was starting to piece a few things together. Though neither he nor Mia had mentioned it, Dan had to have a brother, and this had to be him. A room in the house and knowledge of Dan and his friends made it the only explanation. Apart from the disturbing intensity of their eyes, they didn't look remotely alike, but that had to be it.

"I feel terrible for sleeping in your bed – you don't even know me." He smiled, his eyes full of warm kindness.

"Like I told you before, I will be eternally grateful that you found it, rather than someone who had no intention of doing any sleeping. I would have hated to have to burn my bed – I quite like it." I laughed, blushing deeply as I remembered the noises I'd heard and the things I'd seen in the other rooms. "You're right, I don't know you – yet – but we can change that. I'm Nate."

As Mia had done when she first introduced herself to me, he held out his hand and I was once again surprised by the formality of it. The connection that I'd felt between us when we'd first touched, when I'd fallen into his chest, had shocked me so I was hesitant to take it; but he was looking at me expectantly and I couldn't deny those eyes. I slipped my hand into his, tendrils of electricity spreading up my arm, heat igniting deep in my stomach. He had the same surprised expression he'd had the first time the sparks had flown. I pulled my hand away and coughed, trying to cover my embarrassment.

"Grace – I'm Grace," I finally managed. My hormones needed corralling because this was now the second man to elicit such reactions in me. No – that wasn't entirely true. These sparks were far more intense than what Dan had made me feel – this was pure electricity, and it was freaking me out.

"Well Grace, I think this might be yours." He leant over

the side of the bed, producing my backpack. A grin as big as the Cheshire Cats spread across my face. I was so thankful it had materialised.

"How did you know this was mine?" I asked curiously. For a split second, colour seemed to flood his cheeks, but I blinked, and it was gone.

"I just figured – well – it matches your shoes." He nodded over to my dress and Converse and my heart fluttered. My backpack was covered in the same doodles as my shoes – and he'd noticed. "Don't worry, it wasn't among any bodies."

"Well, that's a relief!" I laughed again.

"You can get dressed in my bathroom if you like." He pointed to the corner of the room. Tucked away behind a row of backpacks, was a small door that I hadn't noticed in my inebriated state.

"Thank you so much – again." I rolled my eyes at myself. I sounded like a parrot with limited vocabulary. This time when I swung my legs out from beneath the cover, I did it slowly, not wanting to repeat the first time. I blushed as I recalled the feel of Nate's chest under my hands. No – I definitely didn't want to do that again. My legs seemed sturdy enough and the room didn't begin to spin wildly, so I took it as a sign that I was safe to walk.

I tugged at the t-shirt, trying to ensure it covered as much of my bottom and thighs as possible, but I needn't have bothered. A quick glance at Nate showed me he wasn't looking. He'd stuck his nose back into his travel guide. My heart filled with gratitude towards him. He had been nothing but a true gentleman.

"Feel free to take a shower if you'd like. The door locks." I saw the hint of a smile as I slid into the en-suite and I wondered whether my heart would ever stop racing.

The bathroom was incredibly masculine. It was more of a wet room than a proper bathroom – a manly wet room. The walls, floor and ceiling were covered in grey slate. The sink was modern and made entirely of glass, with a cabinet above it and there was a large chrome drain in the corner of the room, beneath the showerhead. The showerhead itself was huge, big enough to fit two people beneath it – easily. Images of Nate under the water popped into my mind and my cheeks burned.

I nibbled my lower lip, looking towards the closed door. It did indeed have a lock and I found myself trying to justify having a shower in this strange man's wet room. Only, he wasn't a stranger anymore, was he? He was Nate. I knew I would feel so much better if I no longer smelt like a mix of stale booze and the intoxicating scent of him that still lingered on the shirt. Who was I trying to kid? I was rationalising because I wanted to play with the super shower and all it's many settings. I locked the door, vowing to be quick. I just needed a few minutes under the jets to freshen up.

I stripped out of the shirt and my underwear and turned on the water, watching it run over my fingers as I tested the temperature. It didn't take long to warm up and as I stepped under the stream, I gasped. It was unbelievable. All my muscles were easing up, one by one as the water poured down my back.

When we had lived in London, we'd had an over the bath shower and in the farmhouse, we had shower cubicles – but they were nothing compared to this. I'd never been under something so powerful and soothing. The water soaked my hair and ran down my face, washing away the last remaining vestiges of the party. I knew it wasn't going to be as quick a shower as I'd thought, but I didn't care.

It was a shower that demanded to be enjoyed properly, so I didn't feel guilty for luxuriating under the hot jets, taking my time. Glass corner shelves held a range of bottles. They all looked the same and on closer inspection, I realised that it was all one brand – one type of shampoo and shower gel. It was a black bottle with no name, which told me it was expensive. I debated for a while about whether it would be weird for me to use Nate's stuff, but I'd just slept in his bed, wearing his shirt, so I decided that no, it wasn't weird.

As I popped the lid, I was overcome by that scent. I closed my eyes, inhaling it into my lungs, filling my senses. There was something about it, something dark and sensual. It made me go weak at the knees and did things to my insides that they weren't used to doing. I was sure I'd never smelt it before and yet it felt familiar somehow and strangely – sexy.

I took a lot longer washing myself and my hair than I should have, but I finally, grudgingly, shut the shower off. I felt a lot better, almost completely like myself again and not the hungover zombie that I had been before.

I grabbed a towel from the nearest rail. It was possibly one of the fluffiest towels I'd ever used. Would I ever get used to the luxuries that were normal to my new friends? I got dressed into my jeans and t-shirt, shoving the Coca Cola shirt into the bottom of my bag. God only knew how long I'd been stood under the water for, but when I walked back into the bedroom, Nate was gone. The room was empty.

A hollow disappointment settled in my chest, which was ridiculous because I'd only just met him. I couldn't be pining for him already. I stuffed my dress into my backpack and pulled on my shoes before roughly towelling my hair. I spotted a laundry basket in the corner of the room, so I dumped the towel in it and threw my backpack over my shoulder. It had been a morning full of surprises. I looked around the room, committing it all to memory. It might have been embarrassing but it was also one of the most exciting things that had ever happened to me, and the instant connection that I had felt with Nate, was one that I didn't want to forget.

Sighing, I pulled open the door. It was time to try and track down a familiar face. It was time to find Mia.

Sixteen

"Well, would you look at what the cat dragged in!" Mia laughed as I walked into the kitchen. She was sat at a small, round table cradling a cup. Her feet rested in Tyler's lap and Dan was stood against the counter. There was no sign of any of the booze from the night before; almost all remnants of the party had disappeared, like it had never happened. There was also no sign of Nate. I ignored the empty stab of disappointment in my chest.

"How long have you guys been up?" I asked, trying to sound breezy. I was nervous about the fact that I had slept in Nate's bed. I didn't want anyone getting the wrong idea. There was a part of me that wanted to keep our little rendezvous all to myself. I glanced at Mia. Other than her mousy hair looking a little on the bedhead side, she looked as fresh as a daisy. She showed no signs that she had spent all night drinking heavily.

"Only about a quarter of an hour actually," she grinned sheepishly.

"How did you enjoy the party then?" Dan asked. I lifted my hand to my cheek as warmth spread through it, the memory of his lips pressed against my skin flooding my mind. He watched me carefully and I was suddenly very aware that my hair was dripping, and I stunk of Nate – having used his shampoo and shower gel. I gulped, embarrassed.

"It was great," I squeaked. "I hope you don't mind that I

took a shower. I felt disgusting." I was trying to be sweetness and light, trying to act normal; like it was no big thing for me to jump in the shower at a strangers house the morning after the night before – but my heart was hammering in my chest as I spoke.

"I don't mind at all," he replied. His eyes glinted and the dark smile he wore on his lips, turned my insides to mush.

"You want a coffee?" Tyler asked brightly. He jumped up and gestured for me to take the seat he had just vacated. I plopped down and Mia put her feet up on my legs.

"That'd be great, thanks."

"Did you enjoy yourself last night then?" Dan asked again. His eyes were so warm, and that gooey feeling returned to the pit of my stomach. Boy was I in trouble. The way my body reacted to both him and Nate – you would think I'd never laid eyes on a man before.

"It was really good, thank you again for the invite." I gave him a small smile and hoped he couldn't see the way I was reacting to him.

"You'll definitely have to come to the next one then." His eyes were still on me, taking me in, burning a hole in my skin.

"Oh absolutely!" Mia said giddily. "She's part of the gang now." She grinned from ear to ear and I had to swallow past the lump that formed in my throat. I was part of the gang – it sounded so good, I found it hard not to tear up.

"You know, other than Mia, I have never seen anyone drink as much of Dan's punch as you did," Tyler laughed, handing me a steaming mug of coffee. It smelt amazing and as I took my first sip, it was like medicine, banishing the last of the hangover symptoms.

"Well, it won't happen again. That stuff was evil!" I'd really enjoyed myself and not once thought about the copious amounts of fruity punch that I was putting away, but I wasn't too keen on the aftereffects.

"What're your plans for the day?" Dan asked. I was desperate to get Mia alone so that I could ask about Nate, but she didn't look in any rush to leave. She looked curiously at Dan before raising her brow at Tyler.

"I don't have any," she said, stretching. "I always keep the day after your parties clear."

"Why don't we go into the village then, and have fish and chips by the river?" Dan suggested. Again, a look of confusion passed between Mia and Tyler, but they didn't say anything. My treacherous stomach growled loudly, making everyone laugh.

"Sounds like someone agrees!" Tyler said. "Let's grab coats and stuff and we can get going." Dan nodded and walked out into the hallway. I tried catching Mia's eye, but she kept looking at Tyler, casting him surreptitious glances. I narrowed my eyes. What was going on? Then it hit me – I'd sent them off to talk. I smiled; there was no way I was getting out of this lunch and I didn't want to begrudge Mia extra time with Tyler – no matter how desperate for a chat I was.

"I'll go grab my shoes and stuff," she said, leaving me alone with Tyler. He opened his mouth as if he were about to say something, but then closed it before he did. He was struggling with something, but then he smiled brightly.

"You know, I think you have an admirer." My eyebrows shot towards my fringe. How could he know that? He didn't even know that I'd met him, so he couldn't possibly know about the weird, instant connection we'd experienced. So, what made him think that? He took my silence as encouragement. "I've never seen him look at anyone the way he looks at you. Dan's a nice guy."

He was talking about Dan – not Nate. I let my breath go, relieved, but it only lasted a moment. Dan – liked me? He had been staring at me in that intensely dangerous way he had, and he'd kissed me tenderly on the cheek before he headed to bed, not to mention the more risqué kiss that he had attempted earlier in the evening, but I'd just thought he was trying his luck with new girl. Did he really like me – like that? My heart fluttered.

"I don't think it's like that," I said quietly, draining the rest of my coffee.

"We have been to many of Dan's parties; so many parties that I've lost count of them all. Not once, in all that time has he ever wanted to go out for lunch the next day. In fact, we don't usually see him – he's usually still in bed when we leave." Tyler looked at me pointedly. I bit my lip, letting the information sink in.

Dan was very good looking, and he seemed nice. He also made the butterflies in my stomach flutter around like they were doing the fandango. He made my knees turn to jelly and my heart race but – there was the problem of Nate. Although Dan was incredibly nice, when we'd touched, I hadn't felt the shocks and the connection that I had when I'd touched Nate. I blew my cheeks out in silent frustration. It was all new and confusing.

"Ready to go?" I jumped as Dan walked back into the kitchen. His smile awoke the butterflies, just like I knew they would. Could he really like me? I was flattered and the whole idea made me feel giddy, but as he stared it me, his eyes full of intensity, I felt my stomach drop. That intensity – it filled my mind's eye, but not blue – green. I shook myself. The only reason that Nate popped into my head at all was because he had been so kind to me, that's all. I almost snorted at myself. Yea right – because it had nothing to do with the fact that my body lit up like a Christmas tree at his slightest touch.

I jumped up, trying to clear my mind of him, and we headed out of the door. Dan and Tyler disappeared into a huge garage and Mia looped her arm through mine and led me to Minnie. We dumped our bags in the boot, climbed in and she took off, not bothering to wait for the boys.

I stayed silent all the way back to the village. My mind raced over the words that Tyler had shared about Dan, and as I ran through the night's events, I could clearly see that whenever we had spoken, he'd only had eyes for me. I shook myself, refusing to think about it anymore. I was tired and I was hungry, and somewhere in the village was a bag of fish and chips with my name on it.

Seventeen

"I can't believe you've never had alcohol before and then went so hard on Dan's punch. I'm surprised you're even alive after drinking all that!" Tyler chuckled, looking at me in awe. I laughed and nibbled on another chip. They smelt divine and I wanted to shovel them into my mouth to help soak up the remnants of alcohol that was swimming through my blood stream, but they were red hot. It was a good job; I didn't want them to think I was some sort of greedy pig anyway.

"And that awful shot you gave us," I grimaced, remembering how it had burned as I'd swallowed it.

"Hey now! That was Jack Daniels, Tennessee's finest – you wash your mouth out!" I threw a chip at him and he tried to catch it in his mouth, but he failed miserably and laughed as it hit the side of his face.

We'd grabbed our fish and chips and headed down to the river, finding an empty picnic table and settling onto it to chow down. Mia snuggled into Tyler on one side, so I sat beside Dan on the other, trying to stay cool. It was increasingly difficult because every time his leg brushed mine beneath the table, I jumped like someone had set me on fire.

Conversation was easy and flowed naturally. Nothing was forced and it was nice, peaceful to be around. I enjoyed it so much that I didn't even mind the headache that was slowly making a reappearance, nor did I care that

I was so tired, I could have fallen asleep at the bench. It didn't even bother me that I hadn't yet managed to have a word with Mia about Nate.

Dan had spent most of the time silent. It wasn't a brooding sort of silence, more a quiet, contemplative silence – enjoying the time spent with friends. I didn't need to look at him to know that his eyes spent in inordinate amount of their time on me, and any time I spoke, he was rapt.

It was exciting but also confusing, with a little bit of annoying thrown in for good measure. I'd never felt myself drawn to anyone the way I was drawn to Dan and I'd certainly never experienced the kind of connection that I'd felt with Nate. Seventeen years I'd managed to breeze through life without so much as a blip on the love life radar, and then bam – two boys came along at once. My brain was turning to mush.

We finished our lunch, my stomach feeling much better for being full of greasy chips. The night had been a great one, but I would never again make the mistake of falling for Dan's punch. I hadn't enjoyed the morning aftereffects – even if they did come with a side of gorgeous, scented Knight in shining armour.

"Who fancies some ice cream? We could go to the Vintage Parlour – my treat," Dan announced, standing from the table. Mia raised an eyebrow as she looked at him and Tyler smirked at me again with a knowing look in his eye. My cheeks bloomed with colour as they stood and whooped emphatically. It was a very kind gesture, but Tyler's words were playing on repeat in my mind. Was Dan trying to prolong our time together? Had he offered to take us for ice cream because he wasn't ready to leave me just yet? My heart raced at the thought.

Mia and Tyler led the way, walking ahead of us. The air was thick with tension, but I didn't know what to try and say or do to break it. I glanced sideways at Dan; he looked like he was struggling with the same thing. His hand kept twitching and my heart stopped. What was he doing? Was he trying to work up the courage to hold my hand? I bit the inside of my cheek to stop from smiling. He had been so cocky and sure of himself at the party and now, he was debating whether or not to reach for my hand. His nervousness was endearing, and I much preferred it to the cockiness.

In the end, he shoved his hands deep into his jacket pockets and I swore I heard him huff. Should I have taken his hand? Should I try and reach for it now, even though it was buried in his pocket? I wasn't sure what to do but my heart was telling me I needed to do something, so I slipped my arm through the crook of his. The surprise was evident in his eyes as he looked down at me, and he smiled gratefully.

"I hope Mia did a good job of showing you around. She said you hadn't explored much of the village when I spoke to her before the party." I nodded, trying to ignore the fact that my brain was screaming at me that touching Dan wasn't nearly as exciting as touching Nate.

"She did. There's quite a few places I would like to revisit when I get the time."

"Yea? Like where?" Again, his eyes were on me as he paid every bit of his attention to what I was saying. He was so in the moment; it made my stomach flutter.

"Some of the vintage shops, and the art supplies stores. I like to sketch and paint." He nodded, soaking in this information.

"Come on you two! There's a giant sundae in here with my name on it!" Mia yelled. I hadn't realised that we'd been falling so far behind. We hurried along and followed her and Tyler into the shop.

I gasped when I walked through the door. I loved it. I loved everything about the parlour. It was fitted to look exactly like a retro American diner, complete with jukebox, high stools lined up along a glossy counter and plenty of chrome. Everywhere you looked, there were signed black and white photographs of old movie stars and dotted along the walls were electric guitars.

"Grace is drooling, and she hasn't even seen the ice cream yet," Mia laughed. She walked across the parlour and slid into a red leather booth, tossing a menu my way as I sat down to join her. This wasn't just your standard ice cream parlour. They did glass bottled sodas, ice cream floats, pancakes, waffles and so many different types of pie and cake, that you could come every week for a year and still have something new and different every time. That was before you even reached the sundae section.

"How on earth do you choose what to have?" I asked in awe. The choices I'd faced at lunch with Mia now seemed like small fries compared to this monster menu.

"What sort of things do you like?" Dan asked softly, leaning into me and looking at the menu I held. His proximity set my pulse racing again, but I didn't let it distract me from the goodies I was faced with.

"Everything!" I moaned. He chuckled, his leg brushing against mine. I blinked rapidly, trying to clear the daze that I was fast slipping in to. Mia watched us closely and I looked at her, raising a brow in question. She smiled before giving me a shrug and going back to her menu. Had she planned this? Had she been beating me at my own game, playing matchmaker to bring me and Dan together? Had she known that I would like Dan and that he would return that affection? It was another thing I added to the list of things to ask her once we were alone.

"I recommend the Rocky Road Sundae, or if you would prefer something a little warmer, then the sticky toffee pudding with custard is amazing," he said. His voice was warm, like a caress and it drew my eyes to his face – to his lips. I licked my lips unconsciously and something flashed in his eyes that made my brain fog over. I blinked and turned back to the menu, trying to register what he had said to me. Rocky Road something or other – I looked down at the menu and saw the sundae.

"Yes, I'll have that," I mumbled. I couldn't believe how much I'd wanted to lean in, to see what those soft lips would feel like against mine. It was crazy.

"Are you getting the single or are you two going to share one?" Tyler asked. I narrowed my eyes at him and tried to work out whether he'd said it with some ulterior motive in mind, if he was trying to push us together. If it had come from Mia, I'd have no doubt, but Tyler looked genuine, like he was just asking a question. Dan watched me, waiting for an answer. I gulped.

"I don't mind sharing – if you want to," I said, looking up into his topaz blue eyes. The corners of his mouth twitched but he didn't smile. He didn't need to; I could see the amusement written all over his face.

"Actually, I was thinking of getting a big slice red velvet cake," he said. I sighed heavily, secretly grateful to him. The thought of sharing a sundae scared the hell out of me.

It held connotations – connotations I wasn't sure I was ready for – no matter how many times I'd thought of kissing him.

An overly friendly waitress came over and took our orders. What I mean by overly friendly – she was overly friendly towards Dan and Tyler. Me and Mia may as well have been invisible for all the attention she paid us. It made me chuckle, but Mia was deeply offended and ranted about it for a good ten minutes.

"Anyways…" Tyler interrupted, cutting her off as the same waitress placed our orders down on the table before us. Mia scowled at her but she either didn't notice, or she didn't care. I covered my mouth with my hand to hide the smile.

"Well," Dan smiled, picking up a spoon. "Dig in!"

Eighteen

"Bye! Thanks again for letting me come to your party!" I called, as Mia and I watched Tyler and Dan head back to his car. I was still buzzed from the atmosphere at the parlour. Once Mia had gotten over the fact that the waitress was only interested in the boys and wasn't aware of our existence, we had laughed and joked about the party. They told me plenty of stories about previous get togethers and I learned about the past antics of my new friends. It was so blissful. I almost didn't want to return home, knowing as I did that the house would be empty, but fatigue was fast catching up with everyone and the full tummies were making us all dozy.

We took a slow walk back to Mia's car. The weather was beginning to turn again, the sky full of rain, so it was nice to get into the warmth of Minnie. I still had questions that I wanted to ask Mia, but I wasn't sure how to begin. I waited until we had set off before speaking.

"Mia, does Dan have a brother?" I watched her reaction. It was only a brief moment, but I saw it – she physically stiffened. She glanced across at me, frowning as she shook it off.

"Yea, he does. Why?" I swallowed hard, forming the words in my mind before I let them out to make sure I didn't sound crazy, but in the end, I sort of spat them at her.

"I slept in his bed and then when I woke up this morning

and he was there and I met him and I was still drunk and I fell over and he caught me and he gave me some tablets and some juice and made me get back into bed and go back to sleep and then he was still there when I woke and I felt awful because I'd slept in his bed but the worst thing was – I stole one of his shirts to sleep in!" My cheeks were hot at the mere memory of waking up beside him, of the touch of his fingers on my arms when he'd caught me. I shivered.

"Holy shit – no way!" Mia laughed so much I almost reached out to swat her, but as she was driving, I didn't think it would be a wise idea.

"Don't," I groaned, covering my face with my hands. "It's bad enough that I had to live through it once. He must think I'm such an idiot." I was annoyed at myself. I'd had a wonderful afternoon. Dan had been charming and attentive, which made me think that Tyler might have been onto something, but I couldn't shake Nate free from my head. He was obviously older and there was no way he was still thinking of me, but every time I got a whiff of my hair or my head throbbed slightly, I thought about how nice he had been and how he had looked after me.

"Nate is a bit of an enigma. He travels a lot, and no one ever knows where he is or how long he will be gone for and then he'll just sort of, show up. Even then we rarely see him though. He's a bit of a hermit." Mia watched me curiously and I could feel heat spreading through my skin.

I chewed my lip, wondering whether I was brave enough to ask anything more about him. I didn't want to give Mia the impression that I was interested in him – even though I couldn't deny that I was. I was fairly sure I had a crush on him and even though I kept telling myself that it was because he was so kind to me, the connection I'd felt at his touch told me it could be something more. It was all made worse by the fact that I was sure I was also crushing on Dan. It wasn't anything as strong, but there was something there, and the way he looked at me – hot.

The couple of boyfriends I'd had in London were silly schoolgirl relationships and had only happened because I was tired of being called a prude and a weirdo – but this was different. Never had anyone had an effect on me like Nate had in such a short time. It was inexplicable and confusing – not to mention idiotic. I would probably never see the enigma of Nate again. My chest filled with a dread that I couldn't explain.

We pulled up outside my house and I turned to Mia to thank her. She was giving me a look; one of those knowing looks that made me grimace.

"What?" I asked, raising an eyebrow at her and trying to keep my cool.

"You've got it bad!" I felt my heart flutter, but I refused to pander to her, so I shook my head.

"I haven't got a clue what you're talking about, but thank you Mia; for an amazing evening, for introducing me to your friends and for nearly killing me with the punch." I grabbed my backpack, not wanting to meet her stare.

"Hmm – ok, if that's how you want to play it, you're welcome. But you know, if you did like him, or anyone else for that matter, and you wanted to talk about it, then I'm here for you. You can tell me anything." She waggled her eyebrows at me, and I couldn't help but laugh.

"Well, you know, if you ever wanted to talk about Tyler, I'm here too." I turned the conversation onto her. She hadn't mentioned where the two of them had disappeared to or whether they'd managed to talk. From the way they'd been around each other, I had a pretty good idea something had happened; then again, I'd been so wrapped up in my own morning's events, including what Tyler had said about Dan, that I could have been way off the mark.

"Actually…" she said, her cheeks turning pink.

"No way! What happened?" I bounced excitedly in the seat, momentarily forgetting all about Nate and the way he made my heart race, and Dan and the confusion he caused me.

"Maybe. We went outside after your toast, which reminds me, you need some lessons in subtlety!" She glanced sideways at me and I grinned. "Anyway, I was way past tipsy, so I took your advice and told him I like him."

"And – come on, don't keep me in suspense!"

"And – we kissed." I squealed excitedly. I was so happy for her. I'd only known her a short time, but I liked her a lot. She was easy to talk to, easy to be around and after spending so long as a loner, I was glad she'd pushed her way into my life.

"That is so exciting, are you going out again soon?" A pang of jealousy burned in my chest; not because I had any inkling towards Tyler, but because the feelings that were developing at an alarming rate for both Dan and Nate, meant I wanted the same.

"He's going to call me later and we'll chat. There's still a lot to talk about." She glowed with happiness which made me glad I'd given them the push they needed. New in town and I was already matchmaking – maybe meddling was more apt.

"Let me know how it goes ok?" I grabbed my bag and climbed from the car.

"I'll text you tomorrow," she called, as I stumbled my way up the small path. I waved her off, the sound of her laughter tinkling on the wind as she drove away.

It really had been an amazing night, a night where I had been myself and forgotten about everything. I'd even had a dreamless sleep, which was no doubt helped along by the strength of the alcohol I'd consumed, but it'd been nice to sleep and not wake up wondering why the hell I kept seeing the same things or what the hell they meant.

As I walked into my bedroom though, it was hard to forget the last couple of weeks. My desk was covered in half-finished pictures of the blobby, shadowy figure, the old, crooked tree and the angel headstone. Pictures that I kept scrapping because I was a perfectionist, and I couldn't get the details right.

It frustrated me but I wasn't sure how to fix it, other than sitting in front of the actual thing itself and sketching it – but did I really want to do that? If the past couple of weeks had shown me anything, it was that the cemetery liked to play tricks on my mind, and I wasn't sure I wanted it to do the same again after having such a good time with Mia and the boys. Maybe, if I went in the day though –

I walked over to my desk and ran my fingers over the most recent picture. Looking out over the cemetery, I found myself wondering what Nate would think of this craziness – then I cursed myself for thinking that Nate would give a damn – then I cursed myself more for not wondering about what Dan might think.

I laid down on my bed and tried to get the morning out of my mind, but it was no use. I could still smell him – on my skin, in my hair. My chest ached at the thought of not seeing him again, but there wasn't much I could do about it short of turning up at his door and asking for him. Even if I did know how to get back to his house, it wasn't something I would ever be brave enough to do.

It didn't help that every time I thought of Nate, I felt guilty. Dan had been so nice to me and he'd showed me a lot of attention. He was kind, funny and very good looking. I liked him, that much I knew, but just liking him didn't seem to compare to the feelings I had for Nate. I squeezed my eyes shut, feeling woozy as blue and green floated around my brain. How could I be such a fool and fall for two brothers?

It had just turned six o clock in the evening, so it was still moderately early, but I was tired. The late night, the drink, the excitement of the morning, the fun of the afternoon, the happiness I felt for Mia and the weird non sleep I'd been experiencing over the past couple of weeks, was all starting to catch up with me. I felt tired through to my bones. I yawned and snuggled into my pillow, the intense green of Nate's eyes the last thing I saw before I fell asleep.

Nineteen

It was the sun that woke me – again. It was streaming once more through the window. Only this time, it was my window, my curtains and I was in my bed. I looked at the clock on my desk. 7:30am. How was that possible? How had I slept for so long, without once waking up, not even to go to the toilet? I lifted the cover and found myself still fully dressed in the jeans and shirt that I had left Dan's in. Dan's – and Nate's.

I'd seen him – in my dreams. He had been there, wandering amongst the leaves. I'd barely recognised it was him as he had been such a distance away from me, until he had turned, and his emerald eyes shone like beacons in the dark. Beyond him I'd seen the angel headstone, but something had been missing this time. The figure – where was the shadowy figure?

I rubbed my eyes and groaned as I sat up. I had hoped that the fun of the party and the happiness at having new friends would banish the crazy dreams, but no such luck. Now it seemed they had mutated to include Nate.

My body was stiff from being in bed for so long. A hot shower and some breakfast were what I needed, and then I was going on a mission. As I stood beneath the spray, I thought about what I would need to take with me. I couldn't explain it; I just needed to do it. I didn't know what good it would do – probably none – but for some reason, I couldn't let it go. I had to get a complete picture of the angel, one with detail and definition rather than the half-finished, smudged failed attempts that littered my room.

When I headed downstairs, I was glad of the silence. I looked at the calendar and saw that my mum would be away again for most of the day. This was a good thing, because if she asked me what my plans were, I didn't want to have to lie to her. I couldn't imagine she would be terribly thrilled at the idea of me sitting in a cemetery, sketching a headstone that had been coming to me in my dreams. It all sounded absurd, but it was becoming my norm.

I grabbed my backpack, the sight of it again reminding me of Nate and the morning before, but I pushed him to the farthest recesses of my mind. Today wasn't about my silly crush – it was about getting the picture that had so far eluded me.

It was colder outside than it had been when I'd left for Dan's party, but thankfully the wind had died down and the sun was shining. Still, I pulled my hood tight around my face to shield my ears from the cold and to tuck away my hair.

Before I knew it, I was stood at the gate; the cold, iron gate whose creaks took me back to the weird night that it had all started – the night of the first of many odd dreams.

My heart fluttered as I wondered whether there would be anyone at the stone. I wasn't entirely convinced there had been someone there the first time around. My mind could very well have been playing tricks on me again, but I was torn.

Part of me hoped not – a massive part – the part of me that was girlish and scared, but there was also a tiny part of me that hoped the mysterious, shadowy figure would be there, if only to confirm that I had in fact seen them that night, that they were just visiting a relative that had passed, and I hadn't been seeing things or taking the crazy train.

No part of my mind could comprehend why I needed to see them, whoever they were. Perhaps it was my dented pride. Perhaps I just needed to know that there was nothing to fear. Something niggled at the back of my mind, a niggle that took me back to London and the reason we'd had to move to Stonewell in the first place – but I shut it down. I wasn't going there, wasn't opening up to that.

The angel came into view in the distance and even from far away, you could tell it was magnificent. I started towards it, but a noise stopped me in my tracks. I froze, instantly taken back to the night I'd taken the shortcut and the rustles I'd heard then. I spun around, determined this time to find out what was making the sounds, to find what it was that put me so on edge. I held my hand up to shield my eyes and scanned the headstones. Just down from the church was a small clutch of trees, and as my eyes roved over them, I saw the flash of someone duck behind one of the big oaks.

"Hey!" I called, my heart thumping loudly in my chest. They weren't scaring me away this time. I wanted to know who they were and why they felt the need to hide. I started towards the trees but froze again as I saw what looked like camouflage dart between them. Fear gripped me, stealing my breath away, even in the broad daylight. I couldn't explain the sudden danger I felt myself in. My skin was crawling, I needed to leave – now.

I span quickly, connecting with something hard and solid. My hands flew out, but it was too late. I landed with an unceremonious thud on my backside. Grunting, I blinked against the sun and tried to make out what I'd hit. Strong hands grabbed my arms and pulled me to my feet.

"Sorry, I think I got in your way slightly." I'd recognise that voice anywhere, and as I looked into his face, I knew those eyes.

"Dan?" I was surprised, but relieved as well. I stepped closer to him, glad of his presence, and turned back to investigate the trees. I couldn't see anyone and there were no more noises, no more flashes of camouflage, but my skin prickled – like I was still being watched. It was freaky.

"Grace – are you okay?" Dan followed my gaze, looking into the copse beyond me.

"I think – I think someone was there. Someone was watching me." I swallowed nervously; my heart still gripped by fear. I'd been so sure, but I could no longer see anyone there at all. I didn't want Dan to think I was losing it, but I told him in the hope that he might see something too and validate my suspicions.

"What're you doing here anyway?" he asked. He glared into the trees and the look on his face, the hard stare, was something I hadn't seen from him before. His expression was serious – not one to be messed with. He looked angry but there was also shock in his eyes. It put me on edge, and though he didn't say it aloud, he confirmed my fear. He moved and put himself between me and the trees. I exhaled slowly, grateful to him for showing up when he did.

"I was going to take some rubbings of the headstones,

you know, for my art." I wasn't going to bother mentioning my whole mission to draw a headstone that plagued my sleep. I'd only just found myself some friends, I wasn't going to push them away by letting them into my weird dreams and crazy past.

"Perhaps in future, you shouldn't come alone," he said quietly. Finally, he met my eyes and smiled. It was the easy smile I was more used to, the one he had worn for the majority of the day before. It was the one that made my knees wobble. I mentally shook myself.

"Duly noted. What're you here for?" I asked, trying to glance past him towards the treeline. I was loathe to admit it, but maybe he was right. With all the strange goings on I'd experienced lately in the cemetery, I was beginning to think the same thing, that maybe there was something for me to fear here.

"I was heading to your house actually. Mia gave me your address; I hope you don't mind. Then I heard you shout so I came running." He was grinning at me and my stomach was rolling. What did he want to come by my house for?

"Well – you found me," I squeaked. I was reeling, my mind going over and over the different reasons that he could have for hunting me down, and every one of them led back to what Tyler had said. Truth be told, I still didn't know how I felt about it. I'd fallen instantly in lust with him and his brother, one more than the other, and I couldn't shift that fact from my mind. I half wanted to shut myself away somewhere and scream. The whole thing was like a stuck record in my head, repeating over and over again, slowly driving me insane.

"Actually, it's about your art. There's a craft fayre in the village community hall. I don't know whether you've heard about it, but I thought you might like to go." He looked earnest and genuine. Part of me knew I shouldn't go with him because of how conflicted I was. I didn't want to do anything that might give him the wrong idea before I'd had a chance to work through all the crap in my head – but a craft fayre? It sounded amazing, just the thing to shake off the fear that still crawled just below the surface of my skin. Maybe he was just asking as a friend? Spending more time with my new friend couldn't be a bad thing – could it? My head hurt; it was too confusing.

"Yea, sure. That sounds great actually." In my mind, even with how scared and shaky I was, I knew I would return to the cemetery because I so desperately wanted to get that damn picture, but perhaps now wasn't the time. Dan nodded and held out his arm to me. I bit my lip, slipping my arm through his. I could hardly refuse after being the one to initiate it yesterday – even if I was trying to avoid complications.

"Whereabouts is the hall?" I asked as we made our way out through the gate. I was thinking back to the tour Mia had given me, but I was pretty sure she hadn't shown me any community hall. I took a deep breath, trying to quell the butterflies that banged against the sides of my stomach.

"It's not far, we can walk from here." It took around five minutes to get there. He hadn't been lying, it was close. From outside, the stone hall looked more like a house. It didn't look too big; it was on two levels and the windows were small and leaded. Once you entered though, it looked exactly like a large school hall. Tables were set up all the way through and there were lots of people milling around, chatting, laughing and browsing all the stalls.

"Wow – this is really great! Thanks Dan." I was touched by his thoughtfulness. He'd obviously listened when I'd told him about the vintage shops and art supplies stores that I'd said I wanted to revisit. He beamed at me and I smiled back. I pulled my arm from his and headed to the first stall.

Dan stayed quiet all the way round; following behind me like a faithful puppy might follow its master. He never complained once about how long I spent at the tables and he teased me playfully whenever I got excited about something and dragged him to see it. It was fortunate that I'd stuck my purse into my backpack because there were so many things I wanted to buy. After an hour, I was spent up and carrying several small bags.

"I'm sorry, I probably seemed a little manic in there," I apologised to Dan as we left. It was easy to lose myself in the moment when I was surrounded by crafty things, but most of the time it didn't matter because I was alone. Had I been antisocial?

"Don't worry about it. It's good to see someone so passionate about something. Plus, it was nice to get out of the house." I thought about what Mia had said, about his parents being away all the time and my heart throbbed for him.

"Anytime you need to get out, just let me know. It's not like I have a busy social life – or a social life at all really." I laughed, my cheeks blazing. My mouth had run away with me, caught up in the moment and I'd offered something that I was now unsure about. Was it a good idea to spend more time alone with Dan? Why did it feel like such a bad idea? It was too late to take it back, and I wouldn't have anyway because the way he was looking at me – filled with gratitude and affection. I felt very much discombobulated.

"Thanks Grace. I appreciate that. I'll walk you home." He needn't have bothered, it was only five minutes away, but then I thought about how someone had been watching me and I was grateful for his company. We arrived at the farmhouse and he stood, looking down at me. My stomach dropped and I shuddered with nerves.

"Thanks for taking me to the fayre," I said quietly, fiddling nervously with the handles of the bags. There was no one around, which meant that if he leaned in for a kiss, this time there would be no rescue. I took a step back from him, to ensure I wasn't within kissing distance. He had been sweet to me since the moment we had met, but I was still waging an internal war in the back of my brain between him and Nate.

"It was my pleasure. I'll see you soon then." His eyes were intense as he gave me one last look, then he turned and headed down the road, back towards the village. I was confused. He hadn't shown any ulterior motive, he'd simply taken me somewhere he thought I might like. It felt – odd.

I sighed and looked across at the cemetery, wondering whether I still had enough time to try and get a picture of the headstone. Then I wondered whether I was brave enough to venture in alone. It wasn't dark yet. Maybe if I were really quick – I could at least get a good look at it and commit it to memory.

I ran all the bags inside the house and then hurried across the road to the cemetery, heading straight for the angel. I glanced around nervously, checking for flashes of camouflage. I didn't want to come across my mystery watcher. I realised I'd been holding my breath, and let it go in a sigh of relief when I confirmed there was no one else around. There was no one around this stone or any other for that matter, and my skin wasn't tingling like it had before. I didn't feel completely safe, but I felt okay enough to stay.

I looked up at the marble. It truly was a breath-taking sculpture. Once upon a time, it must have cost someone a very pretty penny to have made. The sheer level of detail, the craftmanship – it was exquisite. I was in awe. The wings especially were something to behold; every feather looked unique.

As I looked into the face of the angel, all my worries dissipated, and I was no longer fearful of it. I was excited to sketch it. I opened my bag and pulled out a thick fleece blanket. Spreading it out on the cold, hard ground, I pulled out another to wrap myself in and spread my supplies out around me. I pulled my knees up to rest my pad on them and then – I was ready to draw.

Twenty

My ears registered the rustling before my brain had fully regained its function. I blinked, trying to remember what I'd been doing. I shivered, my fingers numb and my body aching from the cold. My eyes felt heavy and I groaned as I tried to focus. No – I couldn't have – could I? What was wrong with me? How had I managed to fall asleep in a graveyard?

"Oh good, you're alive then." I screeched, the embarrassing sound escaping before I could stop it. My whole body jumped backwards, and I cried out in pain as my head connected with the marble stone behind me.

"Shit," I winced, rubbing the back of my head furiously and preparing what I hoped was my best, most unimpressed scowl. I turned towards the voice, the scowl dropping from my face, my whole body frozen in shock. *Earth open up and swallow me whole.*

Not only had I fallen asleep in a cemetery and possibly drooled, but to add insult to injury I'd been discovered by the most attractive man I'd ever met – Nate. My neck burned from embarrassment, the flush creeping through every inch of my skin as I dragged my eyes to the ground. Not that it did me any good; even with my eyes shut I could see that face as clearly as if they were open. I squirmed uncomfortably. What were the chances that he would find me? First, I'm found by Dan, then his brother finds me in the same place, no more than a few hours later.

"Hey sleeping beauty. Sorry – I didn't mean to startle you." He held his hand out towards me, offering to pull me up but I didn't take it. His silent amusement irked me; then there was the guilty feeling that weighed heavy in my stomach, making me uncomfortable in my own skin. I'd spent the day with his brother and now he was here in front of me and all I could think about was the way my body ached when he was around.

How could he possibly have found me here? He wouldn't have asked Mia like Dan had and I doubted he had found out from Dan himself. I was annoyed with myself. Why could he not have seen me looking studious in the library or carefree in a coffee shop? Why, of all the places on earth, did he have to find me playing hobo in a cemetery?

"Like hell you didn't," I mumbled. I sounded like a bratty five-year-old, but it was only to cover the embarrassment I felt. "Why else would you disturb someone who was sleeping?" I tried to keep my temper down to a minimum and remember all the nice things he had done for me when I'd been in such a mess, however I was mad. Not at him – no – I was mad at myself. Why was I so hell bent on the stupid picture of the angel? If I'd just left it alone, he never would have found me asleep amongst the headstones. It shouldn't have bothered me what he thought – but it did. I shook my head. After Dan had walked me home, I should have just stayed in the house, then I wouldn't be in such a compromising position.

"Fair point. I suppose I'm just wondering why you would sleep here and not at home. Dan doesn't usually pick up vagrants for his parties so I'm assuming you do live somewhere around here?" His voice was warm and deep, and it made my heart quicken, but the mention of Dan's name also made me feel nauseous. It was all a bit too much to deal with after just waking up, especially after waking up somewhere I shouldn't. I thought of the dreams, the unfathomable need to sketch the angel – it was all crazy and probably not something I should share with anyone, least of all Nate, but – I wanted to tell him, wanted to at least try and explain myself.

"Would you believe me if I said I was waiting for someone?" I sighed. Until I said it aloud, I hadn't admitted to myself that really, deep down, it wasn't just about getting the perfect picture. I'd actually been waiting for the shadow in my dreams to appear. I desperately wanted Nate to believe me. I may have been questioning my sanity, but I certainly didn't want him doing that. I didn't want him thinking I was a nutcase who regularly camped out in graveyards.

"Strange place for a date Grace. I know we're out in the sticks here but there are a few places in the village that I'm sure would be more conventional." His eyes twinkled and I felt like my insides might melt from the heat he was stirring in my stomach. I ground my teeth together and tried to get a hold on myself. Him taking the mickey out of me was exactly what I didn't need.

"It's not a date; I don't really know who I'm meeting." I cringed, instantly regretting the words as they tumbled from my lips. I tried to stem the flow of verbal diarrhoea that seemed to have crept up on me.

"A blind date? This must be Mia's doing. Only she would pick you a candidate that wants to meet in a cemetery." He was enjoying himself far too much at my expense. I narrowed my eyes and glared at him viciously.

"Ha bloody ha aren't you just hilarious! I'm not going to sit here and explain myself to…" I stopped, my words catching in my throat. For the first time, I took in the entirety of Nate as he stood before me and an uneasy feeling settled into the pit of my stomach.

He was dressed head to foot in black and there was something so creepily familiar about the way he held himself as he stood over me, something I had failed to notice when I'd been suffering from a hangover and he'd been laid on his bed. The hairs stood up on the back of my neck. I closed my eyes, trying to pinpoint where the unease was coming from – and then it hit me. I snapped my eyes open and stood quickly, my sketches scattering to the ground around me.

"Were you here last week? Stood at this angel? Did you see me here last week?" I demanded. He tilted his head, the teasing smile gone from his face, replaced by shock and guilt. He shook it off quickly, but it was too late – I'd seen it. Waves of sickness passed through me, along with a whole horde of emotions; most of which I didn't know what to do with.

"So, it is some weird hobby of yours then, hanging around these old graves? How often do you partake in this peculiar habit?" I glared at him and he stared right back. His demeanour gave away nothing, but there was no way I was letting him get away with trying to turn it around on me.

"Don't change the subject, please Nate. I asked you a question." I couldn't conceal the hint of desperation that crept into my voice. His intense green eyes softened for a fraction of a second and his hand moved towards me, but then it dropped, and he shut me down – shut me out. I crossed my arms and tried to hide the fact that my hands were shaking uncontrollably.

I no longer looked fierce as I'd hoped – I was scared. What did it mean that Nate was the shadow from my dreams? What did it mean that I'd seen him in this very spot before? Were we destined to meet? No; I'd never believed that we all have a preordained destiny to fulfil. Our lives are our own to make, but this was a freaky turn of events.

I looked up to the darkening violet sky. I didn't want to be caught out in the dark again. I was still struggling to come to terms with the fact that I'd fallen asleep in a graveyard. Maybe I needed to see a doctor. It wasn't normal to sleep so much. I bit my lower lip to stop it from wobbling as I looked to Nate. He wasn't going to give me an answer, so I bent down and gathered up my things. A tidal wave of different emotions was still coursing through me as I stuffed everything into my backpack.

"These are really good Grace. What's with the leaves though? Wrong season for leaves falling." He trailed off, almost like he was speaking to himself. I stomped over and snatched the pictures from his hand.

"They're none of your business," I mumbled. I struggled to get the words past the lump in my throat. Hormones were the only thing I could think to blame – stupid teenage hormones. They had me in such a state.

The anger I felt for myself was slowly transferring to Nate. Why wouldn't he tell me whether it had been him? Why was it such a big deal, that he had to try and deny it? We hadn't known each other long, but I'd felt a connection, a draw to him that I couldn't explain, and he couldn't tell me he didn't feel it too. It freaked me out, as did the fact that I seemed to have dreamt him up before I'd even met him.

A million questions drifted through my mind as I rolled up my fleece, each one of them dying to burst from me, but my need to get home was stronger than my need for answers. I turned on my heel and headed towards the gate.

"Grace – wait!" I froze, my fingers inches from the metal. I should've just kept on walking, walked right home and ignored him – but his voice. I drew in a deep breath and prepared myself to face him, then I turned to see what it was he wanted. He was much closer than I thought he would be, and I stumbled backwards into the gate in surprise.

"Let me walk you home. You shouldn't be out alone at night. It isn't always safe." I looked at him through narrowed eyes. Hadn't Dan basically said the same thing? A shiver crept down my back as I thought of what I'd already seen, the feeling of being watched, the camouflage darting between the trees and that night, not so long ago, the night that had brought me to Stonewell in the first place. He was right – but I was still mad at him.

"And why is that Nate?" I spoke. My shoulders slumped as all the fight went out of me. I didn't want to be this way around him. I had a crush on him for god's sake, but I was coming across like some hysterical, highly strung teen. I wasn't sure whether I would be safer with or without him, but as I pushed through the gate, I didn't protest when he fell into step beside me.

We walked in silence, his closeness making my mouth dry and I rolled my eyes. He kept throwing glances my way, but I didn't dare look back to him in case he could see the effect he was having on me, like he might be able to hear the way my stomach did flip flops and notice the fact that I could hardly breathe.

Okay, so he was absolutely gorgeous, and his voice was warm and soothing, like hot chocolate on a cold night, but I didn't know him. I'd only just met him, and it hadn't been under the best of circumstances, so I didn't know why I was reacting to him the way I was.

It wasn't long before we reached the end of my messy driveway. I thought back to the mansion that Dan and Nate called home and felt embarrassed by our lack of grandeur. Perhaps he would find the rundown old farmhouse charming, rather than what it actually was – crumbling.

"Well – this is me," I said quietly, wishing I could still sound angry. I had reason to be angry, good reason in fact. He had teased me and hadn't answered my question, hadn't admitted to me that it was him I'd seen, but he had just walked me home and he had saved me from what would have been a killer hangover, so I couldn't find it in myself to be mad. "Thanks – for walking me home I mean. I know it wasn't far, but I appreciate it." I still couldn't meet the intensity of his eyes, but I gave him a small smile. He returned it with a dazzling one of his own.

"You are very welcome. You should get inside and warm up. The wind is picking up again." He nodded towards the house and then turned to leave. Was that it? Was that all he had to say to me? Panic bubbled up my throat.

"Wait!" I nibbled the inside of my cheek, already feeling stupid for asking, but I didn't like the idea of him disappearing and me never seeing him again. Especially now that I knew he was the figure from my dreams; now that the shadow had a face. "Will I see you again?" Shock crossed his face, but he shook it off quickly, a warm, thoughtful smile pulling up the corners of his perfect lips.

"Yes – yes I should think so Grace. I'll be around." He winked at me before turning and heading down the road. I watched until his silhouette disappeared, just as I had with Dan, and only then did I make my way inside.

Twenty One

I stretched out and wriggled my toes under the duvet. My clock told me it was 10am and the bright light told me I should be up, but I'd had such a peaceful, dreamless night that I was tempted to stay in bed all day. It hadn't even taken me long to get to sleep, which was very surprising given the amount of time I'd recently spent unconscious; plus, there was the fact that I couldn't get Nate out of my head. I closed my eyes, seeing the emerald green of his and the almost wild, unkempt black curls of his hair perfectly.

He'd gotten so far under my skin so fast; it was like an itch that I couldn't scratch. No one in London had ever come close to making me feel the way I now felt for Nate. A lot of it could probably be put down to the fact that no one had ever really shown me any interest; it had all been silly school stuff. I wasn't terrible looking, but I'd stuck out like a sore thumb. My red hair and green eyes made me different, and different was scary.

Something about Nate made me giddy and excited. I didn't have a frame for comparison, but I was sure I was crushing on him – hard. Wasn't this how all the books described it? Heart racing whenever I thought about him, his face filling my mind every second, a slight panic when I thought about not seeing him and a dull ache in my chest as I wondered where he could be now. My tummy was full of a warm, fluttery sensation and I could feel my cheeks glowing. I hadn't forgotten my suspicions that he was the one from my odd dreams, but it was pushed to the back of my mind.

I wanted to see him again, but I didn't have his number and I didn't know how else I would find him. For all I knew, he'd already left again on one of his jaunts that Mia had told me about. The thought filled me with dread and made it hard to swallow past the panic. But no – he'd said he would be around, and though I didn't know him, it felt like I could trust his word, so he must be planning to stick around for at least a little while.

I thought about wandering through the village in the vague hope that I bumped into him, but after my tour from Mia I knew it was bigger than I'd first thought so the chances were slim to none.

I sighed and rubbed my eyes, groaning at the dull ache that was starting to throb at my temple with all the overthinking. Dragging myself from my pit, I forced myself to get dressed and ready for the day. My stomach rumbled loudly as I brushed my teeth – breakfast was calling.

The house was silent again. The amount of work my mother was taking on was worrying. Not just because she was wearing herself out, but also because after everything that had happened in the cemetery, the unease that still made me feel queasy meant I didn't want to be alone for too long.

When I got downstairs, the chill in the air told me she'd already left, and the lack of milk in the fridge told me that it'd been early. I shoved my feet clumsily into my converse and headed outside, eager to get the milk and have my first coffee of the day. The milkman had left us four bottles. It was weird having a milkman; we hadn't had one in London. If we needed milk, my mother sent me to the shop, but now we got it delivered to our doorstep every other day. It was also weird that he kept leaving us extra milk. I thought it was because he was sweet on my mum – she said it was because he was old and senile. I smiled as I lifted the bottles into my arms.

"Want a hand with that?" I felt a bottle slip from my fingers, and I tried to catch it, but I'd never been any good at juggling and I jumped as the glass smashed, milk seeping into my shoes. I bent to start moving some of the bigger pieces from the path, flinching as I felt a sharp stab of pain. I'd sliced the end of my finger.

"Crap," I muttered, abandoning the glass and standing, blood running down between my fingers. After replaying near enough every word we had said to each other since the moment I'd woken in his bed, I would recognise his voice anywhere. It still didn't prepare me for the instantaneous butterflies that appeared when I met his gaze. He rushed forward and took a tissue from his pocket, wrapping it around my finger tenderly.

"It's clean, I promise," he smiled. He was so close, I could feel his breath on my face, warming my lips. It made me dizzy. I held my breath as the tingles that I knew were coming, spread through my hand where he held it. I knew from his reaction that he felt it too. "Hello Grace."

My memory didn't do him justice. He was wearing a black duffel coat, the collar turned up against the wind, black jeans and black boots. I let my breath go unsteadily. The stealth look suited him; it made my insides dance.

"Hello Nate. First my hangover, then the cemetery and now this. I'd say it's nice to see you but every time we meet, I seem to get hurt or be in some state." My voice was shaky, but I smiled, tightening my grip on the remaining bottles under my arm. The corners of his mouth turned up in a grin, his hand still clutching the tissue tightly around my finger.

"May I come inside? We should clean this up." My mind raced over the mess, all the unpacked boxes that were still lurking and my stomach dropped, but what could I say? I couldn't say no and leave him stood outside in the cold. Wasn't this what I'd wanted? To see him again? I nodded and stepped aside for him to enter.

"You'll have to excuse the mess. We've been a bit lazy – with the unpacking." Dizziness and sickness swept through me, and I didn't know whether it was because I was nervous or whether it was because I could still feel the blood pumping from my finger. Maybe it was because Nate was so close – in my house.

I stepped around a couple of boxes and led him straight through to the kitchen. Other than mums work room, it was the only other room in the house that was completely unpacked and as finished as it would ever be. I thought back to Nate's house; how massive and posh it had been, but he looked just as comfortable here as he had there. I opened the fridge and shoved the milk in, not wanting to drop another bottle.

"Do you have a first aid kit?" he asked. My breath caught again as I turned and saw him leaning casually up against the breakfast bar, looking every inch like he belonged. I reached into one of the top cupboards and pulled down the little white box that was almost as old as me.

"Sit," he said, taking it from my hands and gesturing

towards one of the stools. I was happy to oblige; I wasn't sure how much longer my shaky knees would hold me up.

He opened the box and peeled back the tissue. I turned away. I didn't have a problem with blood per se, but it was throbbing so much that I was scared to see how deep it had sliced. Nate took some kitchen roll and soaked it under the tap. He was incredibly gentle as he washed the blood from the cut itself and from in between my fingers. It was a moment of such tenderness, I struggled to breath normally. It was increasingly difficult to sit still, my nerves making me antsy. I hoped he couldn't see how nervous I was.

"There you go," he said softly, after he'd finished wrapping a small bandage around the cut. "It's a little deep but I think you'll survive."

"Thank you. God knows what you must think of me." I shook my head. He cocked his head to the side in thought as he looked at me, his eyes twinkling again as he maintained the silence. My babbling self felt the need to fill it.

"Would you like some breakfast?" I gasped, hardly believing the words that I'd just blurted out. Had I just offered Nate breakfast? What was I thinking? He grinned, flashing me his perfect teeth.

"I would love some, thank you." I jumped up and he sat down at the breakfast bar. My mind was in overdrive. What the hell was I thinking? I was a decent cook, but I didn't want to be cooking for someone who's opinion mattered so much to me. I hoped he liked omelette because it was all I was brave enough to try.

I didn't need to look at him to know that he was watching me; I could feel his gaze burning into my back. I stuck my head into the fridge to grab what I needed, letting the cold air wash over my skin in the hopes it would cool it down, but my reddening cheeks weren't giving up that easy. Maybe an industrial sized freezer would have shifted the glow, but I didn't have one of those to hand. I cracked eggs into a bowl, the silence slowly driving me mad. It was killing me – I was considering putting on some music when he spoke.

"So, when did you move here?" My hand froze over the bowl. This line of questioning – again. How was it still catching me out?

"Nearly three months ago now."

"Do you like it here?" I blew my cheeks out in a sigh. I wasn't used to talking about myself and to me, Nate was a much more interesting subject. All those backpacks in his room, the trips Mia had spoken of – he must have a million and one stories from all over the world and each one of them would be way more interesting than any one of mine.

"It's ok – I guess," I answered carefully. I didn't want to offend him, just like I hadn't wanted to offend Mia when she had asked the same. This was their home. If I was honest with myself, it was a nice place to live; especially now I was making friends. It had just taken a while to warm up to it. "It's different to London – quieter."

"Do you miss London?" I glanced at him. He was still watching me intently. I shook my head.

"When we moved, I didn't really have anything left there to miss." I closed my eyes and bit my tongue. It was too easy to talk to him, to open up. "I sometimes miss the familiarity of it, having grown up there. Everything here feels a little strange to me, but I guess it's just because it's new."

He thought it over as I plated up the omelette. He was silent as I poured us both some juice, the bright orange reminding me of how I'd woken in his bed to a fresh glass beside me. The butterflies were doing circuits round my stomach again; I tried to clear my throat.

"This smells good Grace," he spoke finally, as I sat down beside him. "So – can you cook as well as you drink? That's the question." He was teasing me again. His tone was playful. My hand shook as I lifted the glass to my lips. I needed to get a grip. He was just a man! I silently laughed. I could sit and tell myself that until I was blue in the face, but it didn't change anything, didn't change the fact that he was the best-looking man I'd ever met, and it didn't change the fact that my body felt charged whenever I was in his presence. He took a bite and I once again found myself holding my breath, hoping that he liked it.

"It seems you cook better than you drink, which can only be a good thing," he laughed. I exhaled happily, chuckling as the tension released its grip on me. "What other hidden talents do you have I wonder?"

"I draw too," I said absently, lifting a forkful to my mouth and chewing slowly.

"Yes, I did see that yesterday actually. You're very good too." He smiled, his fork halfway to his mouth. His perfect, amazingly kissable – I shook myself quickly.

"Thank you," I choked. God – I was out of control.

"Will you show me one of your sketches? Officially I mean, rather than me sneaking a look." What would my sketches of late tell him about me? Especially the ones that included dark figures that looked suspiciously like him.

"Maybe," I nodded slowly. I couldn't fathom his

expression. His eyes turned dark, stormy and brooding. It was enough to make my cheeks burn again.

"That was delicious," he said, standing suddenly. His plate was empty, and I'd hardly touched mine. He walked to the sink and I wolfed the rest of my omelette, hoping heartburn wouldn't make me later regret it. I picked up my plate and approached him. He was filling the sink with bubbly water.

"Hey, you don't have to do that." I reached out to take his plate, but he lifted it out of my reach. Not a hard thing to do with me being short and him being tall. His eyes teased me, playfully taunted me, daring me to try and take it from him. I made a grab for it again, gasping as I stumbled into him. I found myself once again pressed against him with my hands splayed on his chest. His muscles tensed. His breath tickled my lips; he was so close, if I leant in just a little – I could taste him. I stayed as still as I could, not daring to move an inch. The heat of his skin beneath his thin shirt made my hands feel like they were on fire.

"Ok, you win," he said quietly, dropping his plate into the sink and taking a step back. His voice wavered, confusion in his tone. He was like a panicked deer, not knowing which way to run. It was odd to see him so – vulnerable. He was broad in the shoulders and from falling into him, I knew that he hid some serious muscle beneath his black outfits. It made me think of him as strong and untouchable, so to see him look so lost was concerning. "I should go now. Thank you for breakfast."

He sounded so formal, not a hint of the playfulness I was slowly beginning to love. He didn't give me a backwards glance as he left. I heard the click of the front door and slowly slid down the kitchen counter to the floor.

What had just happened? What had I done wrong? The moment had fizzled with intensity, filled with such tension that my whole body was shaking from it. I'd slipped and fallen into his chest. I'd ended up with my hands on him – again. Ok, it had very nearly stopped my heart from beating, and ok, he had been close enough that I could smell his shower gel wafting from his skin in waves – but had it warranted such a change in him?

He hadn't reacted that way the first time. Unless – damn. How could I have been so stupid? Someone as amazing as Nate had to have a girlfriend and this was now the second time that I'd fallen into him. I pressed my hand to my forehead. It seemed like I'd literally thrown myself at him.

I groaned and stood, throwing my plate into the suds in utter frustration. Frustration that I hadn't guessed that he would be spoken for, and frustration that I even cared! With all his travelling, he probably had an exotic beauty stashed away in every country. I rolled my eyes. Now I was just being petty. Mia hadn't mentioned anyone, even after she had guessed that I had a crush on him, but perhaps even she didn't know. If he was such an enigma like she said, then he probably kept himself to himself and perhaps no one knew.

I didn't know why I had developed such instant feelings for Nate, but I needed to get my head on straight. The beginnings of a headache started to form behind my eyes, and I rubbed at my temples.

Nate was supremely good looking, and he had been nice to me every time we had crossed paths; and yes, it might be nice to imagine that finally, at seventeen years old, someone was interested in me, but I needed to face the facts and come to terms with the idea that he had probably done all those things out of a sense of duty. I was a friend of his brother after all. His brother – Dan – who, incidentally, did seem quite interested in me. Well, if Nate had a girlfriend, that was all I needed to know. Now I could stop pining for him like a sap and give Dan a chance. But why did that idea leave me – hollow?

Whatever the reasons, what I needed was the perspective of someone else, someone I trusted who knew them both and would be able to give me advice. What I needed – was Mia.

Twenty Two

"Well, look who it is!" Mia ran to me as I walked through the library doors, wrapping me up in a warm, vanilla scented hug. She pulled away and pouted at me playfully. "I was starting to think you'd moved back to London."

"It's been two days Mia," I chastised with a laugh. "I saw you two days ago." She dragged me to a table, pulled out a chair and pushed me into it. There wasn't anyone in the library as far as I could tell, but even if she'd had some customers, I doubt it would have stopped her from taking a break to sit with me and chat.

"Well, it felt like forever and I have so much to tell you!" She exuded so much excitement, she practically vibrated. I knew I had to push Nate from my mind, at least for the time being. It was obvious that she wanted to discuss her date with Tyler, and I wasn't about to rain on her parade and make the conversation all about me. I already felt guilty for not returning her texts. No – the whole Nate and Dan drama could wait.

"So, what happened? Where did you go?"

"He took me to a circus Grace! It was amazing. We held hands the entire time and he didn't even laugh when I got freaked out by one of the clowns." I smiled brightly, feeling lighter than I had since before Nate had stormed out of my house. Mia's happy enthusiasm was contagious.

"Wow, it must be true love," I teased. Her cheeks were

glowing, and her eyes shone bright as she talked me through the whole night. It all sounded wonderfully romantic and I hated that it brought back the dreaded pangs to pull at my stomach and at my heart. I wanted someone to do things like that with; I wanted someone I could fall for, someone who would fall right back. The obvious problem I was facing, is that there were two potentials. One of them I could absolutely picture going to the circus with, but he didn't illicit the same feelings in me as the other; but the other drove me crazy with flirty feelings yet ran off whenever things got remotely tense. It was hopeless.

"And then we kissed – again! It was such a great night." She sank back into her chair and gave a happy sigh. I was glad she'd had a good time, even if inside, I was fighting against the jealous urges brought forth by my raging hormones. My emotions threatened to well over, and I bit the inside of my cheek to stop myself from tearing up. I didn't want to bring down Mia's happy mood. What kind of friend was I? She tilted her head and gave me a look; I knew it was too late. She was good at reading people and she'd already seen something in my expression. Her eyes filled with concern.

"What's wrong?" she asked. I took a deep breath and looked into her expectant face. She was the only person I could talk to, so though I didn't want to bring her down, I didn't have much of a choice. My only other option was to go to my mother and that wasn't likely. When she had tried to have the sex talk with me, I'd run from the room screaming with my hands over my ears.

She watched me intently. I could trust Mia – couldn't I? She had given Dan my address in what was probably some attempt – albeit a misguided one – at matchmaking. Just as I had with her and Tyler. Although, it wasn't all that misguided, because I did have feelings for Dan – I knew I did.

She had guessed though that I had a crush on Nate, so why would she send his brother my way? Unless she knew he was taken? In swept the headache again; I cursed the steel band that had set up shop, drumming against my temples. It was a nightmare. We'd only just met but Mia already felt like a best friend, like I'd known her for years. She was someone I knew I could easily turn to and lean upon – and that was precisely what I needed to do.

"Oh god Mia – I need your help!" I told her everything. It all came spilling out; from feeling like I was being watched in the cemetery, to Dan coming to my rescue, taking me to the craft fayre, walking me home for me then to be found again in the cemetery, but this time by Nate, him walking me home and then showing up at my house this morning, causing me to slice my finger, fixing me up and then abruptly leaving after breakfast.

She sat rapt, hanging onto my every word. I left out the part about the dreams. Mia seemed open minded but even she would question my sanity if she knew about them. She raised her eyebrows and whistled when I'd finished.

"Holy crap Grace, that was intense! No wonder you're confused." She bit her lip and then spoke again. "You know, Nate never really spends a lot of time with anyone other than Dan when he's here, which is a rarity in itself." I shifted in my seat. What did that mean? Had he sought me out? But why would he do that, just to run away as soon as things got a little – heated?

"Does he have a girlfriend?" I asked warily. She

shrugged, avoiding my eye. It wasn't exactly the answer I was looking for.

"I wasn't joking you know Grace; he really is a total enigma. He's away so much that there are people who know Dan that think he's an only child. There's not really much I can tell you. He and Dan are close; they seem to stay in touch when he does go off travelling, so you might be best asking him." She looked away nervously, her jaw set. What wasn't she telling me? Why did it feel like she was putting a stop to the conversation?

My stomach was tangled in knots at her words. He and Dan are pretty close – how had I made such a mess of things so early in the game? Falling for two brothers who were close? The ominous, black feeling in the very depths of my stomach told me that this wasn't going to end well. There was no way I was asking Dan anything about his brother. He'd been so nice to me, taking me to the fayre, buying me ice cream. I closed my eyes and thought of his cute, crooked smile and those bright, topaz eyes. My heart fluttered, which made me want to slap myself. How the hell had this happened?

"I'm not going to ask Dan, Mia," I sighed, shaking my head.

"Not going to ask me what?" I jumped so much I nearly toppled backwards in the chair. My face instantly burned, and I knew it had turned a deep shade of scarlet. Mia looked as shocked as I felt. She hadn't seen him approaching either. He pulled out the chair next to me and I felt sick. How much of our conversation had he heard?

"Grace was wondering what you put in the punch," Mia said quickly, coming to the rescue. "She's felt funny since your party." I held my breath. Would he buy it? He laughed and put his hand on my shoulder.

"That's a trade secret I'm afraid Grace. Blame Mia, she knows how potent it is, she could have gotten you a beer. Anyway, how do you know it was the punch and not my sparkling personality?" Mia rolled her eyes and laughed but I could tell from the way she looked at me that she was as thankful as I was that disaster had been averted.

"Yea, yea – you keep telling yourself that Dan," she grinned. He smiled right back at her before clearing his throat.

"Actually Mia, would you give us a minute?" he asked. I looked pleadingly at her, trying to shake my head without him seeing. What did he want a word with me for? It could only be one of two things. He was either going to ask to take me somewhere again, or – my god – Nate could have told him to have a word with me.

Panic rose through my chest. I wanted to run away as fast as my legs would carry me, but then what would I do? I couldn't avoid Dan for the rest of my life. Especially as deep down, I knew I didn't really want to.

"Sure, I have some filing to do anyway. Give me a shout before you leave." She gave me a pointed look and I knew I was in for some serious quizzing once Dan had left. I bit my lip and turned to him. His topaz eyes held mine hypnotically. My pulse throbbed against my skin. He cleared his throat and leant in a little closer.

"I've been thinking about you a lot Grace. I can't seem to get you out of my head actually." He blushed, looking sheepish. Was he – embarrassed? It only made me melt more. "I've wanted to see you again." God – don't let me be too easy to read. Surely Nate had mentioned something to Dan, if they were as close as Mia said they were. I felt like I was holding my breath, waiting to hear his next words – but they didn't come. He stayed silent, his quiet eyes searching mine.

"Well – you can see me now," I said, trying to inject as much confidence into the cringe worthy statement as I could muster.

"So I can." His voice wasn't warm and soft like Nate's, it didn't make you feel all gooey and envelop you in a sense of safety. If anything, Dan's voice made me think of danger – danger of getting completely lost under his spell.

"Can I take you out one night Grace? On a date?" He looked directly into my eyes as he whispered the words. I was stunned, my mind racing. The minions in my brain were still dancing around the whole Dan vs Nate drama. How could I go out with Dan when I felt like I did about Nate? But Nate rushing out of my house was as good as him telling me no, as good as him telling me it wasn't going to happen – wasn't it? Dan was the stuff of many girls dreams and he was here, he was asking, he was – interested. As I gazed into his shocking eyes, I felt tingles spread through me.

"Yes." It was barely more than a whisper. I let my breath go, blinking several times to try and clear the Dan induced fug that had settled into my brain, making me feel drunk. He showed me his crooked front teeth as he smiled.

"Great! I'll pick you up tomorrow night at seven." There was no question, no checking if I was available. As he stood, he gave my shoulder a squeeze. Panic reared its ugly head, and I blurted the first thing that came to mind.

"Maybe we should double date! With Mia and Tyler, I mean." I had no idea where it had come from, but it felt

---

safer to have other people there. Mia would be a buffer against any awkward silences and if it started going horrendously wrong, she would rescue me.

"I think they already have plans. I'll see you tomorrow Grace." Every time he said my name, a shiver spread down my spine. It was equal pleasure and terror. I was still staring off into space, when Mia reappeared.

"Come on, spill it! What was that all about? Has Nate been spouting to him about you?" I shook my head, still feeling dazed by the whole episode. Had I done the right thing? And if I had, why did I feel so guilty? It was ridiculous, I had nothing to feel guilty about, yet I could picture how those green eyes would look if they knew.

"He asked me out," I mumbled.

"Get out! What did you say?" Mia was excited, much more excited than I was. I should be happy. I liked Dan and this was my first ever, proper date. So why couldn't I muster all the giddiness that should come with it?

"I said yes – then I suggested you and Tyler should come along too, to help with any awkwardness, but he said you already have plans." I felt queasy. The guilt was already eating away at me. A small, very stupid part of me, felt like I was cheating on Nate. Incredibly stupid, given he wasn't interested, we weren't together, and I'd only just met him.

"We don't have any plans," she said, looking confused. "I guess he wants you all to himself."

"Please god, don't say that."

"You don't seem entirely thrilled Grace. I know of at least six lovely ladies that would kill to be in your shoes right about now."

"I know, it's just…" I rubbed my eyes. How did I land

in this mess again? I blew my cheeks out in frustration and dropped my head to the table.

"Nate?"

"What, where?" I said, bolting upright. It would be too much of a coincidence if he showed up again, right after Dan had left.

"No," Mia said, hardly able to contain her laughter. "I mean, is Nate the problem?" I returned my head to the table to hide my embarrassed flush.

"Yes. I don't understand it Mia, I just can't explain it – this connection," I whined weakly.

"Well, you know, Nate ran out on you, but Dan – he just keeps on coming back. He's obviously interested; maybe you should give him a chance. You must feel something for him, otherwise you wouldn't feel so torn. He's a really nice guy Grace." I looked up at her. She was right. Dan was great, threw amazing parties, cared about my interests, treated me like any gentleman would and he seemed nice. I needed to shut Nate out of my mind and shake myself up.

"I will. It's just, I don't really know him." It was a feeble excuse and one that I knew she didn't buy.

"You don't know Nate either, but I bet if it was him walking through that door and asking you out, you would jump at the chance." She was right – I was being daft. I was going out – with Dan – on a date. My first ever date.

"Oh crap, what on earth am I going to wear?" I screeched. I looked at Mia desperately. Her face lit up like the bonfire night sky. It was like I could almost see the cogs, physically turning around in her brain.

"You leave that to me. I have the perfect thing in mind."

Twenty Three

I felt like a doll. Mia was busy doing who knows what to my hair and I sat in nervous silence, wondering what the night would bring. There was a sick feeling, deep in my stomach, that I couldn't shift as I ran over and over the whole thing in my mind. I still didn't know whether it was a good idea or a bad idea. Other than the fact that there was a tiny, idiotic part of me that felt like I was cheating on Nate, I couldn't come up with a valid reason not to go on this date with Dan. I could in fact, come up with quite a few good reasons that told me I would have a great time.

I tried to calm myself and just enjoy the feeling of being pampered. Mia had point blank refused to let me sit before my mirror, something about not wanting to spoil the surprise. She still hadn't shown me what she had brought me to wear either, but she was in her element, so I left her to it.

I was trying, and only slightly failing, to mentally prepare myself. I was trying to quash all thoughts of Nate that slipped into my erratic mind, as best I could. I wanted to have a good time with Dan; it wouldn't be fair to him to be thinking of someone else when he was taking me out and treating me so well.

"You're going to look killer when I'm finished with you." Mia was trying to tame my wild hair into submission with her straighteners. She was fighting a losing battle. My hair did what it wanted ninety percent of the time, regardless of what I did to it, what products I used or how much time I wasted; simple straighteners were not going to be up to the job.

"Thanks for this Mia. I'm really glad you're here." Truer words had never passed my lips. She was keeping me in a state of quiet calm. She talked freely, not needing me to respond, and it cocooned me in a safe bubble. Without her, I would have been a nervous wreck and I haven't a clue how I would have chosen something to wear.

"Hey, I'm glad I'm here too. Can't believe I get to see you off on your first date!" There was a playful teasing to her tone. "So – he really didn't tell you where you're going?"

"Nope. He said he'd been thinking about me, wanted to see me again, asked me out, I said yes, he said great and then he left." I'd been fretting about the venue myself. What if I was underdressed? What if I was overdressed? What if he took me somewhere that showed me a side of him I didn't like? What if he took me – I don't know – line dancing? There were so many things that could go wrong and naturally, my brain got caught on all of them. Was it normal to worry so much before a first date, or was I just a bumbling mess?

"Yea, that sounds like Dan. He likes to think he is a man of mystery. Maybe he's trying to be more like his brother." She froze behind me as she realised, she'd mentioned Nate. She'd obviously meant nothing by it, it was a simple slip of the tongue – but it clawed at me anyway. This had to stop. I didn't want to keep thinking of Nate. I just needed to focus on Dan – focus on Dan.

"Enough about me," I said. One sure fire way to

guarantee that there would be no further mention of him, would be to turn the tables and get Mia talking about her and Tyler. It wasn't that she was self-involved or anything like that, she was just incredibly excited about her new relationship and she was happy to share that excitement with anyone that asked. "I feel like all we've done is talk about me when what I really want to know, is how things are going with Tyler."

"Really good actually! He introduced me as his girlfriend in front of his mum and dad yesterday which was pretty exciting. It was a big step, you know? They've known me a while, but not as his girlfriend. I've met them loads of times before, but we were just friends. They seem happy that we're together which is nice. I don't know if I ever even thanked you but – thank you! For making me go with him. We text each other all the time and speak on the phone. Anytime he isn't at college and I'm not working, we're together. It's all very new and exciting." She sighed happily.

I smiled, glad that everything was going so well between them. Would Dan and I end up the same? Would we get to the point where I meet his parents? Maybe once we had been out on a date, Dan would agree to double date.

I was so grateful to Mia for bringing me into the fold and introducing me to what life could be like in Stonewell. It finally felt like things were picking up, like I was no longer stuck so deep in that rut anymore that had trapped me since London. For the first time in a while, I was genuinely happy. The shadows of the past were gradually dissipating.

"Right, keep still and close your eyes." I did as she said, flinching a little as the soft bristles from the make-up brush, dusted across my eyelid. It wasn't long before she declared herself finished, and she threw a bag into my lap. "Put that on and let me see my masterpiece." I groaned as I lifted the bag. I could tell from the weight of it that it was hiding some serious heels. I'd never been great with heels; I'd always much preferred my beloved Converse. I glanced longingly at my wardrobe.

"Don't even think about it! You need heels with this outfit; they'll make your bum look nice." Mia laughed loudly at my aghast face and settled herself onto my window seat. Did I want my bum to look nice? It wasn't a question I'd had to ask myself before. I shook all preconceived thoughts from my head and stripped down to my underwear while she wasn't looking. In the spirit of the occasion, I'd even made an effort on that front for once, wearing a matching, lacy black set that my mother had bought for me. I'd always been too embarrassed to wear it and so it had been hiding away in the darkest corner of my underwear drawer since the day I'd peeled back the silver tissue paper. It was a bit uncomfortable, but I couldn't deny the amazing effect on what little cleavage I had.

I peeled open the plastic bag to see what goodies Mia had brought for me. The fabric glided through my fingers as I pulled it free. It was a dress, but the skirt was made to look separate from the silky grey, leopard print vest. There was a chunky belt around the middle and the skirt looked like it fell to just below the knee. It was sexier than anything I owned, and a tremor of fear rippled through me at the thought of wearing it. The shoes were chunky and black, with diamantes running down the heels.

I slipped into the dress and eased myself into the heels,

taking a short walk across my room to try them out. They weren't as bad as I'd been expecting, but I still needed to be careful when I tottered around.

Mia turned her head at the sound of my footsteps clacking across the wooden floor, her eyes bulging and her jaw dropping as she took me in.

"Holy freaking mother of mercy!" She stood and circled me, whistling through her teeth. "Well, god help Dan tonight – he's going to need it."

"Do I look – ok?" I asked hesitantly.

"Ok? You look smoking hot! Look for yourself." She directed me towards the full-length mirror on my wardrobe door. As I looked at the girl in the reflection, my breath caught in my throat. It didn't look like me; it looked like someone who was hot and sexy, someone who was nonchalant about the whole dating scene because they did it so regularly. Mia had done my make up perfectly. My eyes were dark and smoky with alluring black flicks of eyeliner at the corners. It made my green eyes appear darker than normal. My hair was straightened and swept to the side, looking voluminous rather than its usual frizz fest. It was – beautiful.

"I – don't know what to say." Tears began to sting the corners of my eyes. I looked so – different. So unbelievably different that it was hard to recognise myself. Where had this sultry siren come from?

"Oh, no you bloody don't! Don't you ruin my artwork with pesky tears." Mia came up behind me and stood on her tiptoes, putting her head on my shoulder to meet my eye in the mirror. "You look beautiful Gracie Cake."

I laughed and rolled my eyes, unaccustomed to receiving compliments. The sound of a car door snapped my attention away from my reflection. I looked towards the window, my stomach churning.

"Crap," I uttered. There was no more time to prepare – this was it. I still wasn't sure what to expect and I didn't think I would ever be ready for this date with Dan, but it was too late to think about that now – he was here.

"Hey now, you just enjoy yourself. Dan is great." I nodded like a cheap, plastic Churchill dog, as she shoved a handbag into my arms. "I'll go down and let him in on my way out. Make him wait a minute before he sees you." She winked and then left.

I took a deep breath, steadying myself, and took one last incredulous look in the mirror. Tugging the skirt down, I walked carefully out of my room. Make him wait a minute – I was far too nervous and anxious to do anything of the sort.

As I approached the top of the stairs, I could hear Mia talking to Dan, and although I couldn't hear what she was saying, I could tell from her tone that she was giving him a warning. It made me smile. She'd know Dan and lot longer than she'd known me, and she knew he was a good guy, but that hadn't stopped her doing the best friend thing by looking out for me. I could imagine her telling him to be on his best behaviour, and I was grateful for it.

She called a final farewell and my stomach rolled right over. I was on my own now. I made my way, very carefully, down the stairs. The heels might not have been as bad as I had been expecting, but I was still new to the whole idea of them. It felt like I could fall over and snap an ankle at any moment. I didn't think Dan had planned our date in the Accident and Emergency, so I needed to watch my step.

He was stood, patiently waiting for me, and as I sneaked a peek at him, I couldn't help but smile. He looked gorgeous. His long legs were encased in dark jeans, a white shirt showed off his slim physique and a black suit jacket finished the look. I gulped – my heart was already going crazy. He looked at his watch and then turned – his eyes finding me as I made my way to the bottom step.

His eyes – the topaz blue instantly turned hungry, and I was fairly sure I heard something guttural escape his lips. My mouth was dry, and I was a nervous wreck, but in the best possible way, in an excited way. Finally – I was excited! I did a small spin, arching my brow in a silent question.

"You look – effervescent Grace." I wasn't entirely sure what effervescent meant, but with the way he said it and the look in his eye – I knew it could only be a good thing. He took my hand and brushed his lips lightly over my knuckles. Warmth spread through my belly.

"Thank you," I croaked. He interlaced his fingers with mine and nodded towards the door.

"Shall we go?" I nodded and smiled, trying to ignore the fact that although his hand was warm, it felt odd and out of sorts in mine. I'd never held hands with anyone before other than my mother, so I put it down to the fact that I wasn't used to it. He led me down the path, but I stopped dead before we got to the end. If I'd thought Minnie was flashy and amazing, she was nothing compared to the car that now sat at the end of my driveway. It shimmered two tone in the growing darkness and looked like it cost more than our house. Dan's family really did have money – and lots of it.

He held open the passenger door for me and I climbed

inside. It smelt of cherries and leather. I looked at all the gadgetry that adorned the dashboard and shook my head. If this was what Dan drove, what did Nate have hiding in that house sized garage? No – I wasn't thinking about him tonight – not a single thought. I rolled my eyes. Yea right – it was hard not draw comparisons when I was off out with his brother.

Dan was strong and controlled in the driver's seat. He didn't speed too much, never fully took advantage of the horsepower that was hidden beneath the shiny bonnet. I smiled, slowly easing into the evening. My pulse was gradually returning to somewhere near normal, and my stomach wasn't dancing around as much either. I licked my lips, trying to dispel some of the dryness.

"So where are we going?" I cursed my voice for shaking. People did this every day, went on dates, it was no big deal. At least I'd had the good fortune to meet mine beforehand, not like the poor souls who got set up by well-meaning friends and colleagues with someone they had never seen nor heard of, until the fateful night they met.

"I know a bar. It does great food, and we can dance. It's somewhere that outfit definitely won't be wasted." I looked down at the dress. Had Mia known all along where we were going, or had she just had one hell of a lucky guess? Maybe she knew Dan well enough to know where he would take someone on a first date; she had known him forever after all. His eyes slid sideways to me again before returning to the road. He couldn't disguise the longing and the desire. It was written all over his face, as clear as day.

Before long, we arrived, and I could feel the butterflies

starting up their routine again. The car park was full of cars just as flashy as Dan's. He jumped out, ran around the front of the car and opened my door for me, again holding out his hand. I took it, the touch warming my fingers. The gravel path was hard to navigate in my borrowed heels and I was grateful for his steadying hand. I let out a sigh of relief when we made it inside.

As I looked around, I didn't feel the same reaction as I had at the ice cream parlour. I didn't instantly fall in love with the place. The bar was black and shiny, the floor the same. The tables were black, the chairs were black – almost everything was black, like the whole place was slick with oil. There were massive mirrors behind the bar and shelf upon shelf of glasses. The music was playing just loud enough that some people were up dancing at one side of the bar, but not so loud that the people gathered around the edges at intimate tables, couldn't converse. It was dimly lit and girls in white aprons walked around, carrying brightly coloured drinks on silver trays. It was a nice place, if not a little – pretentious.

Dan led me to a table in a darkened corner, away from most of the other people who were gathered. If intimacy was what he wanted, he was certainly going to get it, tucked so out of the way as we were. Nerves shook my entire body again.

"What can I get you to drink?" I jumped as a waitress in a black dress and white apron materialised beside me. I didn't even see her coming, she'd appeared like some sort of stealthy ninja.

"I'll have a pint of Magners, and my lovely lady friend here will have…" Dan looked to me expectantly, but I just stared back at him in mild horror. Drink? What did I want to drink? I didn't have the faintest clue! I wasn't going to embarrass myself by ordering Babycham and Dan's punch was off the cards. He chuckled as he watched me struggle. "She'll have a strawberry and lime Kopparberg."

I sighed, smiling at him. I had no idea what he'd just ordered but strawberries sounded good, I liked strawberries. The waitress eyed me up and down, looking from me to Dan, before turning on her heel and stalking to the bar. Dan only had eyes for me, and I felt a punch of pride course through me. That's right ladies, the hottie is with me!

"Thanks," I grinned, looking into his eyes. "As you can probably tell, I'm not much of a drinker."   His knee brushed mine beneath the table. Whether on purpose or by accident, I didn't know, but it made me shiver, my whole body feeling warm.

"No problem," he chuckled again. "You liked my punch so I'm guessing you'll like this too, although it's not nearly as deadly."

"Well, thank god for that!" I laughed. "I don't think I would survive another punch hangover." I was starting to settle again. I knew the nervousness wouldn't entirely leave me at any point during the evening, but at least it wasn't as bad. I hated that I couldn't sit back and be confident, that instead I was a shaking ninny.

"Sleep, water and headache pills are the only cure," he laughed with me. The waitress returned, placing two glasses on the table. Dan handed her a card and asked her to open a tab, I raised a brow, but he just winked. "Speaking of sleep, where in my house did you end up crashing? We had a little look for you."

I stopped with the glass halfway to my mouth. Well –

this was awkward. The blush burned as it rose in my cheeks. Any sort of calm that had been settling, was blown away. How on earth could I explain to him where I had crashed? Should I be open and honest with him, tell him I'd met Nate? It was probably the right thing to do – didn't mean I was going to do the right thing.

"You know, I actually have no idea," I said, trying to sound breezy. It wasn't entirely a lie. When I fell asleep in Nate's bed, I'd had no clue where I was. If he thought I was lying or that something was off, he didn't mention it. He shot me another of his killer smiles. A knot of tension started to form between my shoulder blades, and every time I saw his eyes turn dark, it seemed to get worse. I took a huge gulp of the drink, hoping it would help me relax.

"Well, I'm extremely glad you came. Mia told us a little about you. She was as excited as a kid in a candy store all week. I think she was glad to have a girlfriend for once. I wasn't disappointed." I almost choked on the strawberry cider. The dimmed light was welcome – it helped hide my complete lack of control over my blushes.

"I'm glad too, I was beginning to think I'd never meet any friends."

"The move must have been tough," he said, taking a sip of his drink.

"It was – but it's getting better." His eyes glinted as I held them with mine, shivers spread through me. Had I just flirted with him? I almost giggled to myself. His knee brushed mine again, but there was no confusion this time – it definitely wasn't accidental. I coughed, clearing my throat.

"So, what do you do Dan, besides throw an awesome

party?" I asked, unable to sit in silence for any amount of time. I had lots of questions. If this was going to become something – more, then I wanted to know everything about him. He hadn't spoken much the day after the party, so I hadn't gotten much of an insight into him.

"How do you mean?" He put his glass back on the table and looked at me, his brow furrowed, as if he didn't quite understand what I was asking.

"Well, you know, Mia works at her family's library. Do you work?" I clarified. He laughed and it startled me. When he spoke, there was an edge to his tone.

"I guess you could say I have a job, but it doesn't take up much of my time. I'm not very high up so it's not often I'm needed. A couple of days here and there, and then I'm free again." There was a severity to his eyes that belied his calm exterior, and I got the distinct impression that continuing down this line of questioning, would be most unwelcome. He sounded – bitter, which only posed more questions, but I had to let it go.

"I should try and get a job." I tried to lighten the mood.

"Why bother?" He looked at me like the idea was silly, like it was a joke.

"Well – I could help my mum out with the bills and stuff, maybe save to go travelling, and it would give me something to do." A dangerous grin spread across his lips. My stomach felt like a tightly coiled spring. He leant in close, his knees touching mine.

"Stick with me Grace – I'll give you something to do." His breath warmed my face and his eyes held mine again. I was instantly taken back to the night I'd met him. What was it about that blue, why was it so – hypnotic? It was like he held me in a vice like grip, all with the power of his eyes. He leant in closer and his lips brushed against my ear as he whispered to me. "I'll take care of you Grace."

He pulled back and held his hand out to me. I shuddered as I took it, but I didn't know whether it was a shudder of pleasure – or whether it was fear. The fact that I was on the fence, couldn't be a good sign.

He led me to the dance floor, his hands pulling me in close and settling on my hips. All of a sudden, it was like someone had turned off the heat; my skin felt cold where he touched me. What had happened? Where was the fire and the tingles? What on earth was happening to me? A deep-seated unease had settled within me the moment he had sounded so bitter about his job, and I couldn't for the life of me think why.

I closed my eyes, taking deep breaths, trying to get a hold of myself. Dan was a nice guy, he'd shown me that in more ways than one, plus Mia said so. So why did I suddenly feel so on edge, why was he starting to – creep me out? My hands rested on his shoulders and it just felt – wrong. It wasn't like with Nate, whereby every touch sent electricity all the way down my spine and ignited a fire within my stomach like nothing I'd experienced before. I'd sworn I wouldn't think about Nate, but as I swayed in Dan's arms, as my unease built, I couldn't help wanting him to come and rescue me.

"Hey buddy, what're you doing here?" Dan pulled back from me and saluted to someone across the bar. I breathed a sigh of relief at the space now between us. I could take a deep breath and steady myself, try to figure out what on earth was going on in my head. I took a moment before turning and following his gaze, instantly wishing I hadn't. Any chances of steadying flew right out of the window.

Oh god – I felt sick – physically, get me out of here before I puke on the shiny floor, sick. Sitting at the bar, mirroring my look of absolute horror – was Nate.

"Come on Grace, there's someone I want you to meet." Dan's excited enthusiasm only made things worse. I hesitated – could I make some excuse and make a run for it? Dan's firm grasp on my hand meant that it wasn't an option. I tried to look everywhere but at Nate. I was starting to hyperventilate, my lungs struggling to take in the necessary oxygen to stay upright.

"This is my brother Nate. Nate this is…"

"Grace?" The question in the way he said my name, made my heart ache. I felt like I'd been punched in the gut. Dan looked surprised and extremely confused.

"You guys know each other already?" Suspicion crept into his tone and it worried me, only making things worse.

"We've met," Nate said steadily. I chanced a glance at him. Big mistake. His perfect lips were a tight line. His emerald eyes swam with a million emotions and unspoken questions. I felt like I was being crushed where I stood, and even though he had been the one to run out of my house, all the guilty feelings that had been plaguing me, felt justified by the pain on his face.

I was still finding it hard to breathe and the tight dress was beginning to feel constrictive. It was like the time I got stuck in a Chinese finger trap; the more I pulled, the more it stuck. The more I tried to breathe, the tighter the dress became. Small lights began to dance in front of my eyes, and I panicked. I tried blinking them away.

"Grace, are you okay?" Dan said. He was still holding my hand, and he'd felt it when I wobbled.

"She doesn't look so good," I heard Nate say. Their

voices sounded a million miles away. They were muffled, like I had my head stuck underwater. Then everything went black.

Twenty Four

"Should we call an ambulance?"

"No, I think she's coming around now. Maybe get her a bottle of water."

"Can we get some water over here?" The voices – those voices. One tender and obviously worried; one sounding ever so slightly pissed off. They were so familiar, but I was stuck in a haze. Music was pumping in my ears and through the lids of my eyes I could see lights; purple, pink and orange. Where the hell was I?

I opened my eyes, looking up through my lashes to try and decipher what had just happened. Two pairs of eyes looked down at me. Topaz and emerald. My eyes widened and I sat up, scuttling until my back hit something. I looked up. I was against the bar. My head hurt and I groaned as I felt the lump through the thick of my hair.

"Are you ok Grace?" Nate's voice was so warm and full of concern, concern that I didn't deserve. I could still see the hurt in his eyes that I'd registered before I'd passed out.

"I'm sure she's fine. It's hot in here, that's all." Dan was less concerned and was finding it difficult to keep the edge out of his voice. I felt like a deer in headlights. There they both were, knelt right before me. What were the chances? Mia was going to have a field day when I filled her in, if she even believed me in the first place. It was all too surreal. I swallowed – searching for my voice.

"I'm ok. Sorry – I feel so stupid." Stupid was putting it mildly. I felt like a Class A idiot. How could I have just fainted in front of the two hottest, nicest guys I'd ever met? "How long was I out?"

"Long enough," Dan said. My eyes flicked to his; I was stung by the callousness in his tone. "Let's go sit back down at the table. Care to join us brother?" Nate looked to me, debating whether or not it would be a good idea but whatever he saw in my face must have convinced him. He nodded slowly. They both held out their hands to pull me up and as I took them both, I could no longer deny what I'd really known all along. Dan could be the nicest guy in the world, but there was something stronger than mere attraction between Nate and me. I could feel his eyes on me as we walked back to the table. It wasn't a sensation I was enjoying much.

We sat down and Dan took the chair next to mine, slinging his arm over the back of my shoulder in the most macho move I'd ever seen. It couldn't have been more possessive or more of a warning, than if he'd dropped his trousers and pissed on me. It made my skin crawl. Why was he acting like this? I wanted to push him away, but I resisted. The situation was bad enough without me making it any worse. Nate sat down opposite me, but I still couldn't bring myself to meet his eye.

"Are you sure you're ok? Do you need to get checked out?" he asked gently. Dan's grip on my shoulder tightened, scaring me so much I shook my head and smiled.

"Nope – I'm good. Sorry again – funny turn and all that." I stayed quiet.

"So, tell me, how do you two know each other?" Dan asked, trying to sound polite and keep the venom in his voice to a minimum. My hands shook as I lifted my drink to my lips. Strawberry cider was not strong enough for what I needed. I needed the punch from the party, and perhaps a bottle of Jack. I would have gladly welcomed the oblivion it had given me after only a couple of glasses. I kept my eyes trained on the table. There was no way I was touching that question – it was up to Nate to explain how we'd met.

"I bumped into her the morning after your party," Nate said. His tone was flat – dead. "I gave her paracetamol." Dan's grip loosened. He sat back in his chair and laughed. The sound was cold and harsh, like fingernails on a blackboard. What was happening? I was confused and hurt, and I felt lost.

"She'd never had a drink before, and Mia gave her the punch can you believe that?" Dan pronounced. I felt like I was stuck in the twilight zone. Every inch of me was uncomfortable and my head was pounding. My skin was itchy, and I was still finding it hard to draw breath. I needed to escape before the blood pumping in my ears got too much again.

"I'm going to use the bathroom," I stated quietly. I needed space, needed to try and figure out what the hell was going on. Not just in my head, but between Nate and Dan too. The machismo crap wasn't sitting well. I stood and followed the signs for the ladies, not once looking back towards the table.

Once inside the bathroom, I let my breath go. It was ragged and uneven, and I could feel the tears of humiliation stinging the corners of my eyes. Even through the make-up, my skin was pale and washed out.

Seeing Nate had confirmed to me how attracted to him I was, and I hated that he'd seen me out on a date with someone else – his brother no less. It felt wrong on so many levels. I didn't even know if he felt the same way about me. Seeing Dan and I together had definitely had some sort of effect, but I was so unsure of myself, so unsure of everything, that I couldn't make sense of it.

I soaked a paper towel and dabbed at my forehead and my eyes. Luckily, Mia's make-up was still in place, so I was still passable. I didn't want either of them to know that I'd been stood snivelling in the toilet. Why hadn't I been with it enough to grab my bag? I could have sent a quick message to Mia. I cursed myself; I'd been too hasty, too desperate to get away from them both. I took a few more deep breaths. I couldn't stay in the bathroom all night, even if every fibre of my being told me it was preferable to going back out into the testosterone filled bar.

Dan's laughter floated to me as soon as I left the bathroom, but it wasn't the only sound. There was someone else too – a female someone else. I prayed she wasn't with Nate. I couldn't stand to see what calibre his girlfriend was, but as I neared the table, I needn't have worried. There was a small, pretty blonde – sat in my seat – with Dan's arm around her. How long had I been gone? Nate's eyes found mine before I'd even got to them. He looked concerned, like he was checking me over. He mouthed the word 'sorry' and gave a small nod towards Dan and the girl. Him being apologetic about it, made my heart ache more.

"Here she is look," Dan said bitterly. His voice was

alien to me. Gone was the nice guy I'd met, the gentleman who took me out for ice cream and followed me around a craft fayre like a puppy. This was someone else; someone new entirely. "Grace, meet Debbie."

"It's Donna," the blonde said. She glared at me, like she was daring me to sit down. My stomach churned; I felt sick. There was no way I was sharing my night with her – and sharing my date by the looks of things. It was time to leave.

"You know what Dan; I don't feel so good after all. I think I should head home." I chewed the inside of my cheek, waiting for him to say he would leave with me, waiting for him to say he would drive me home. It looked like I'd have to wait – he wasn't moving. He shrugged, looking right into my eyes as he spoke.

"Fine by me. I'm sure I can find something here to amuse me." I felt like I'd been stabbed, right in the chest. Tears threatened to spill over once more, but I refused to let Dan see me cry, refused to show him how much he'd hurt me. Not that I had any right to be hurt after everything that had happened, but still – it stung.

Why had he suddenly changed from being a nice guy to a complete jerk? Even if he suspected something between me and Nate, there was no way he could know for sure, so what made him act like a complete arse? I grabbed my bag and made my way outside. We were way past polite goodbyes anyway. He didn't deserve it.

Did Mia know about this side of him, the side that screamed douchebag? It was doubtful; she wouldn't have let me go on a date with him, wouldn't have pushed me so hard towards him if she knew. Then again, I had heard her warning him, so perhaps she had something of an inkling.

The more I thought about it, the more my head throbbed.

I sat down on a low wall with a sigh, my whole body shivering. It was freezing, but as I already felt like I'd had a bucket of iced water thrown down my back, it didn't make much difference. I pulled out my phone and stared at the screen. Should I call Mia? She would surely come and get me if I asked. But what if she was with Tyler? I didn't want to interrupt them. No – I couldn't put her out like that. I started searching for nearby taxi companies. The lump in my throat was getting harder to swallow past, and I just wanted to get home.

I didn't want to cry, but as I sat all alone, there was nothing I could do to stop a small whimper from escaping. A tear slid down my nose, dropping onto my hand, and I felt angry. I was angry at myself, at Dan, at Nate – at the whole damn world! My eyes blurred with more tears, and as I waited for the results to load, a shadow fell across my hand.

"Grace?" I swiped at the traitorous tears that had escaped my eyes and looked up to Nate. I didn't want to see him; I didn't want to see either of them. I felt vulnerable and I just wanted to get home and be alone.

"Go away Nate," I sniffed, trying to clear my vision.

"Let me take you home," he said gently, dropping down to squat in front of me. I couldn't cope with the warmth in his voice. It threatened to send more tears cascading down my cheeks, and I really didn't want to cry in front of him – any more than I already had anyway.

"I'll get a taxi thanks. Go back inside to your brother." My dented pride didn't want to accept the lift, even though I was freezing and wanted to get home so that I could hide away from the world. I couldn't help the venom that snaked into my voice either. Dan had made me angry; he'd hurt me with how quickly he had cast me aside on what was supposed to be our date. He reached out and touched my knee gently, making my breath hitch in my chest.

"Please Grace," he asked again. I looked into his eyes and melted. How could I deny him when he looked at me so? God I was a sucker. I rolled my eyes.

"Fine," I relented. His shoulders sagged in relief and he gave me a small smile. He stood and held his hand out to me. Did I want to put my hand in his and feel all that electricity? I blew my cheeks out, slipping my fingers into his. It fired through my arm instantly, making me feel warm all over. He pulled me to my feet, and I made sure to steady myself. The last time I'd fallen into him, he'd done a runner. It wouldn't do to throw myself at him for a third time. The second time was still too fresh in my mind.

"This way," he said, interlacing his fingers with mine, just as Dan had done. I bit my lip and hoped he didn't see the small smile that crept onto my lips. I couldn't hide it; it was inexplicable how different his hand felt. It cradled mine perfectly, like it was meant to be, and it didn't feel odd in any way, shape or form. It just felt – right. My mind was obviously conjuring all this up. A hand is just a hand – isn't it? Perhaps the cider had been stronger than I thought because I suddenly felt lightheaded. Nate walked slowly, helping me over the gravel.

"Mia loan you those shoes by any chance?" he said, looking down at my feet.

"You don't think I own nice shoes?" I asked snarkily, furrowing my brow at him. He chuckled softly.

"These aren't nice shoes. These were designed to break ankles. Your Converse are so much nicer." The fire in my belly ignited as I stared at him in shock. He'd paid attention to my shoes? I was gob smacked. But then, hadn't my dress been neatly folded on top of them when I had woken up? He had done that; he'd also found my backpack.

"Yes," I smiled. "They're Mia's. As is the dress and the – handiwork." I gestured to my face and hair.

"Mhmm. I thought so." He looked the dress up and down. What did he mean by that? Did he not approve? From talking to Mia, it didn't seem that he knew her all that well, and he certainly didn't know me well enough to know my wardrobe, so who was he to judge?

Before I could think too much more about it, we were stood beside a shiny black car. The badge told me it was a Jaguar and my awestruck silence told me it was expensive. What was with these rich kids and their cars? Was the village just full of them? It made me feel strictly mediocre by comparison. Nate held the door open for me, and it reminded me of how well the night had started out, with Dan doing the same and being a total gentleman.

"How old are you?" I blurted out. He cocked an eyebrow and smiled, his green eyes twinkling playfully.

"See if you can guess." I groaned as I slid into the seat. Guessing games? Really? I hated guessing games. I was never any good at them and always managed to offend one way or another. I snuck a look at him as he slid behind the wheel. He looked young, his face clean shaven yet his eyes looked like they'd seen so much, like they held so much knowledge. I knew Mia was eighteen, but I didn't know how old either Tyler or Dan was. I'd just assumed they were around our age, but Nate – he looked at least a couple of years older. He had to be if he had travelled as extensively as Mia made out.

"Twenty-two?" I hesitated a guess. He looked at me through his lashes and smiled.

"Sure, that'll do." I stared at him blankly. That'll do? What the hell was that supposed to mean? He either was or he wasn't. It was an odd thing to say.

"What do you mean, that'll do? Are you twenty-two or not?" My face screwed up in confusion. He laughed softly but didn't answer. Guess it was one to add to the bank for another time.

As he pulled away from the bar, I chanced a look back. My blood boiled at the thought of Dan inside with the blonde Donna, and the way he had basically told me to get lost. Would he be mad when he found out Nate had driven me home? A small part of me hoped so. I knew it was bitchy, but I didn't care – he'd been an arsehole.

"I'm really sorry I ruined your night Grace. I didn't realise you and Dan were – dating?" The question was evident, as was confusion. His voice wavered, and it damn near broke me.

"You didn't ruin it – HE did. And we aren't – dating I mean. It was the first and the last." It was all I could manage to say. It threw me that Nate was so bothered by the thought of me dating his brother, and it brought forth wave after wave of that ridiculous guilt again. I snatched a sideways glance at him, but his eyes were firmly fixed on the road and I couldn't read anything on his face. I turned back to the window and tried to get my heart rate to settle.

It was an increasingly difficult thing to do, as the car was filled with Nate's scent; that deep, sexy, spicy sort of smell that emanated from his every pore. I still hadn't washed his shirt because I didn't want to lose that smell. It reminded me of how nice he had been to me that morning and of the electric that had shook me to my core.

We drove the rest of the way in silence, but it didn't feel awkward. I felt completely at ease, totally comfortable with him. I should have been wary of it; that was how it had started out with Dan too, and look how that had turned out!

It wasn't long before we pulled up to the farmhouse. It was dark, every window looking black and sad. After the night I'd had, it looked so uninviting. My mother had left for another overnighter in Scotland, and I suddenly missed her terribly. We'd spoken on the phone; I'd told her I was going on a date. She'd been excited for me, if a little worried. I was dreading the moment I would have to fill her in on how much of a bust it had been.

"Is your mum away again?" Nate murmured. I nodded slowly, narrowing my eyes at him. How did he know about my mother's frequent absence? I racked my brains, going over every word we had ever said to each other. I was sure I'd never told him.

He got out of the car and ran round to open my door for me. The nerves were back with a vengeance. I didn't know what to do. Should I invite him in? Or should I just say thanks and send him on his way? It hadn't gone particularly well the last time he had been in my house; he had in fact made a hell of a hasty departure. My finger throbbed slightly, as if remembering the whole debacle. But would it be rude not to?

I shivered, the cold stinging my exposed skin. The warmth of Nate's touch and kindness had worn off, and now the wind felt shocking. Before I had chance to register what he was doing, he slipped out of his jacket and wrapped it around my shoulders tenderly. It oozed his scent and held all his warmth, so much so that if I closed my eyes, I could almost believe I was in his arms.

"You don't have to do this," I said with a small smile, gesturing at the jacket. "My door is literally right there."

"It's the least I can do." I stopped as we reached the end of the path. He was watching me, but I couldn't read his eyes. Did he want me to invite him in? Did he want me to give him a get out clause so that he could get as far from me as possible? No – that couldn't be right, could it? This had gone way beyond some sense of duty he may feel now – surely?

He'd once again shown me that there was a little more to the connection that existed between us. His concern for me wasn't just your normal 'hey look, someone fainted' concern. It was personal. Real. I leant against my front door, wincing as my head touched the wood. It was a corker of a lump that had risen back there. Nate reached out his hand, as if to stroke my head, but then thought better of it. He dropped it back to his side and I slumped.

"Well, thanks for the lift," I said, shrugging off his smooth leather jacket – even though every part of me was screaming to keep it. He stepped towards me. We were toe to toe and my heart could hardly handle it, picking up the pace and racing hell for leather like it was trying to escape the prison of my chest. I took a shaky breath. Hadn't I had enough excitement for one night?

"Grace," he said softly, his breath fanning my face. He lifted my chin, so I was looking directly into his eyes, and I bit my lip to stop myself from squealing. "Look, you can tell me to mind my own business, hell knows I've tried to tell myself that, but Dan – he's – well, you can do so much better." I narrowed my eyes at him. It was almost like he had been about to say something completely different and had thought better of it.

"Like I said. First and last," I mumbled, shrugging my shoulders. Anything that might have been between me and Dan was now gone, never ever to resurface after the way he had changed so quickly towards me. But what gave Nate the right to try and warn me off him? Did he think because he was his brother, because he knew what sort of person he was, he could stick his two penneth in? Or could there be some other reason – a reason that was purely selfish on his part? My stomach fluttered at the thought. He looked so sincere and serious – it felt like he was trying to protect me.

"Would you – would you like to come in?" I whispered, stumbling over the simple, yet loaded words. Nate didn't speak – he only nodded.

I turned to open the door and I could feel his breath on the back of my neck. It did things to my insides that made me blush. I closed my eyes and absorbed the feeling, enjoying the effect he had on me. My hand shook as I tried to get the key into the lock. I was fumbling so bad, it felt like the key had grown and was suddenly ten times bigger than the lock.

Nate's fingers closed around mine, and he guided the key smoothly into the door. I bit my bottom lip to stop the soft moan that I could feel in my throat. It was like I could almost feel him smiling behind me. I turned the key and pushed my way through, stepping aside for Nate to enter.

"Drink?" I asked, embarrassed by the huskiness of my

tone. *Whoa there – slow down girl.*

"Sure." His eyes were playful again, just as they had been the morning I'd woken in his bed. He followed behind me into the kitchen. I flicked on the lights and went straight to the fridge. There was an unopened bottle of wine, a few cans of beer, milk, juice and a couple of bottles of diet coke. I hadn't looked at Coca Cola the same way since Nate had sent me home with his shirt. It stupidly reminded me of him. Then again, I could probably find something in most things to remind me of him. It was becoming a bit of a habit.

"Wine, beer, juice, diet coke…" I looked to him apologetically. "Sorry, we don't have much."

"Coffee?" he asked, smirking. I sighed, giving him a small smile.

"Coffee – yes, I can do coffee." The heels clicked against the tile floor as I filled the kettle and clicked it on to boil. They were starting to make my feet ache, pinching at my poor toes. I wished I had just stuck with what I knew, what I was comfortable in. How Mia spent all night in them, I didn't know. I thought back to the beginning of the night, how taken aback I'd been to see myself looking so different, so beautiful. I'd liked what I'd seen, but Nate mentioning my Converse had reminded me that I wasn't that person – not really.

"Come here." Nate was suddenly behind me, guiding me to a stool at the breakfast bar. He sat me down, his fingers gently sliding the shoes from my feet. I gasped at the little bursts of energy that pulsed where his skin touched mine. It was overwhelming. How long would it take someone to spontaneously combust from sexual tension? Was that a thing? My skin burned; the fire lingering where his hands had touched me. "You sit and rest. I can do coffee."

He opened cupboards and drawers, searching for cups and spoons. I watched the muscles in his back flex as he reached up for two mugs. Something stirred so low down in my belly, it made the flush return to my cheeks. He was all in black again; black jeans, black leather jacket that I knew first-hand was soft and smooth, black boots and a black French Connection t-shirt. The whole thing screamed sexy.

"You take sugar?" he asked. I shook my head.

"I'm sweet enough." I cringed as the words slipped out before I could stop them. Oh, for gods sake! Why had I said that? It was hopelessly cheesy! Not only could I not control my body around him, but I couldn't control my mouth either.

"That you are," Nate chuckled, murmuring almost to himself. He came and sat beside me, waiting for the kettle to boil. I chewed the inside of my cheek. I shouldn't have, but I couldn't help worrying about what Dan would think of this little moment between us. Not so much because I cared about what he thought of me, especially after his less than gentlemanly behaviour, but because I didn't want to cause any friction between the brothers.

"Will Dan mind that you drove me home?"

"I don't particularly care if he does." He was barely able to hide the anger in his voice, and I nodded slowly. It was too late – there was obviously friction there already, and a frostiness that I knew was down to me. It made me feel uncomfortable.

"I feel like I should apologise," I said slowly, chewing my lip and feeling embarrassed. He looked confused, so I carried on quickly before I lost my nerve. "I should never have gone out with Dan in the first place. It didn't feel right when he asked me. I was so confused about – everything – but I couldn't seem to say no." It was a pathetic excuse, but I hoped Nate would understand.

"He can have that effect on people when he wants to." Again, his words seemed loaded, but I didn't know why.

"I should have called and cancelled when I figured…" I was mumbling, but I managed to stop myself before I admitted to Nate that I liked him – a lot.

"Then why didn't you?" he asked, his intense eyes boring into mine. I paused, my mouth agape. Why hadn't I? It was a good question. I could tell him; I could tell him that I didn't cancel because I wanted what Mia had, because I wanted that closeness, that romance, someone to get excited about and Nate had made it very clear to me that he wasn't that guy. I could tell him that, or I could avoid the question altogether and go on the defensive.

"What the hell do you care?" I snapped. My heart hammered against my ribcage as I watched the green of his eyes turn a stormy grey. They turned dark; not like I'd ever seen them before.

"I shouldn't," he murmured. His words hung in the air, catching my breath. He shouldn't? What did he mean he shouldn't? Could this mean?

"But – you do?" I asked. Did I want a definitive answer? In such a short time, I'd become attached to Nate in a way that made me sure my heart would break if he were to cast me aside – like his brother had. His voice was low and husky when he spoke.

"I think you already know the answer to that." His eyes held mine. The tension between us was thick and palpable. My heart was beginning to race again.

"Do I? I seem to remember you making quite the exit the last time we were alone." He jumped down from his stool and spun mine around from the counter. I was startled by his quick movement, even more so when he leant in close. I bit my lip hard as his hips parted my legs, the skirt riding up my thighs. His hands were balled into fists, his knuckles white on the counter behind me. There was no more than a hairs breadth between us. I unconsciously licked my lower lip and he groaned.

"It's – complicated."

"So – uncomplicate it." I don't know where my bravado was coming from; it was a new side to me that Nate had brought about. There was a fierce fire in his eyes and the muscles in his jaw were strained.

He pushed himself away from me and away from the counter, letting out a frustrated shout as he turned his back to me. I jumped; the atmosphere was so thick; you could have sliced right through it with a knife. I watched as he ran his fingers through his black curls, feeling desolate. He'd been so close to me; I'd smelt the toothpaste on his breath and the provocative scent on his skin. His warmth had radiated to me and now, I felt cold and empty without him nearby.

He was pacing back and forth, and for the first time in Nate's presence, I felt scared. Not scared of him but scared that I'd done something that meant I might lose him, something that would push him away from me. I swallowed hard and went to him, pressing my hand to his back. It took every ounce of strength I had in me not to go weak at the knees.

"Nate…" It was barely more than a whisper. He turned sharply, his lips coming down onto mine before I even had time to think. They were soft and tender, yet the kiss felt hard and urgent. His hands skimmed down my back gently and I pushed myself closer into him, the contours of our bodies a perfect fit. My hands found his hair and I sighed. It was even softer than I'd imagined. As my lips parted, so did his, his tongue touching mine for the briefest of seconds. And then it was over. His breathing was raspy and hard and mine mirrored it. He closed his eyes and laid his forehead against mine.

"Don't hate me," he whispered. Why would I? How could I ever hate the man that had given me my first kiss? A kiss that had ignited a passion within me that I wasn't fully aware I had – not until I'd met him.

His hands dropped from my back and without a word, he walked out. I stared after him, frozen in shock. Ah – so that was how. The kettle clicked loudly in the empty kitchen and I was stunned as I heard the front door close, the lock turn and my keys hit the floor. He'd locked me in and posted my keys? What the hell? I slumped onto one of the stools and laid my head against the cool counter. Whatever it was that was so complicated, it was really starting to piss me off.

Twenty Five

"Grace sweetheart, there is someone here to see you." I rolled over and closed my eyes. I knew who it was going to be. Mia had been calling and texting me for just short of a week, trying desperately to get in touch, like any good friend would. I however, had been wallowing in a pit of my own despair and had therefore ignored every attempt she'd made. How could I explain to her what happened? How could I possibly tell her that I thought her friend was a complete jerk? How could I tell her that I never wanted to see him again? And how on earth was I supposed to tell her that I'd started out the night with one brother, and ended it being kissed by the other?

There was a small tap at the door. I opened my eyes in time to see Mia walk in with Tyler following behind her. They were holding hands and my eyes suddenly filled with tears. Stupid emotions. Tyler pushed the door closed quietly before the pair of them took a seat on the edge of my bed. Mia didn't look angry, which could only be a good sign. Dan must not have told her about our date. If anything, her face was full of concern, which did nothing to assuage the sickening guilt that I now felt for ignoring her. She rested a hand on my leg.

"Come on – tell me what happened." Damn her and her concern. It made my heart ache. Traitorous tears slipped down my cheeks. It was a good thing she was worried; perhaps it meant she would stay friends with me after I'd filled her in.

"Where do I start?" I sniffed.

"The beginning is usually the best place," she said softly with a smile. "You were so excited to go out with Dan, then you go out and I don't hear anything from you in like six days! Dan has nothing to say about the date either. And then we saw him at the movies, with some blonde bimbette!" So, she had seen Dan and he hadn't said anything about me. Why was that? Was he protecting his fragile ego? Was he keeping quiet because he didn't want to affect the friendship I had with Mia? No – after the way he had acted, I couldn't believe it was out of any sort of remaining affection he had for me. They'd been friends for a long time; I'd been expecting him to bitch about me behind my back.

"Her name's Donna," I choked miserably.

"I don't give a shit what her name is Grace! How the hell did she end up at the movies with Dan instead of you? Did the date not go well?"

"Nate kissed me." I slid my eyes sideways to look at Mia. Her jaw nearly hit the floor. Tyler had a look of complete disbelief on his face, mixed with a little bit of awe.

"What the – when – wha – eh?" She shook her head around like a crazy person, trying to grasp at words that didn't fully form.

"Yea – that pretty much sums up how I feel right about now too."

"Ok, you need to rewind and tell us everything." So, I did. I told them about how Dan had driven us to the bar, about how excited I was and how nice he was being, about how flirty he'd gotten and how I'd even started flirting right back. About how we started to dance, how we saw

Nate and I had a complete panic attack and fainted, about how possessive and creepy Dan had become when I'd finally come round, about how, after coming back from the toilet he'd replaced me with Donna, about how Nate had driven me home and then the rest – I told them everything.

"Whoa," Tyler uttered. I nodded, although whoa didn't quite feel big enough to do the whole scenario justice. It was more like a script from a new Netflix series than my life.

"Whoa is one word for it," I said. Mia took my hand and offered me a small smile.

"I am so sorry Grace. I really don't understand why Dan would treat you in such a way. He was so interested in you; I could tell how much he liked you. I've known him so long and he's never behaved like that. I really thought he would treat you right. I just don't understand..." She trailed off and looked down at her hands, confusion clear on her face. She had known Dan so much longer than I had; it can't have been easy to hear that there was another side to him.

"Nate knew," I shrugged.

"Come again?" She looked to me questioningly.

"Nate knew about Dan's other side. He said that I could tell him to mind his own business if I liked and he said that I could do so much better than Dan, but – it felt like he was going to say something else, maybe something more." She was as speechless as I had been, lost in some deep thought. Did she know more about Nate than she initially let on? Something that I'd said, had sparked something in her mind; I could almost hear it working furiously through it.

"I guess if anyone were going to know he's a bit of a

dog, it would be his brother. Though, I'm still finding it hard to believe he was so uncool. Like Mia, I just don't understand," Tyler said, shaking his head.

It had been a long six days. I'd waited and hoped that Nate would come back – but he hadn't. For all I knew, he'd escaped to another continent. The pain worsened with every day that passed.

"Have you heard from him? Nate, I mean?" Mia asked. I shook my head, my eyes stinging from the tears as they started to well again. "Oh honey." She pulled me into a hug and held me, whilst silent tears slipped down my cheeks. I didn't even care anymore that I was crying in front of Tyler, all I cared about was that Mia wasn't mad at me for ditching her friend, and she was here, giving me a hug when I needed it the most.

"He was good for something though," I sniffled, wiping my eyes with the sleeve of my cardigan. "The weird dreams have stopped."

"What weird dreams?" Tyler asked puzzled.

"I'll tell you later," Mia said quietly, her eyes never leaving mine. It was true – the headstone, the leaves, the tree and the shadow had all disappeared. Now my dreams were just full of Nate, of the kiss, of the way his hands had felt as they'd slid down my back. I woke up every morning with a pain in my chest so sharp, it almost hurt to breathe.

"He'll be back." Mia said it with such conviction, I almost believed her. "Really Grace, he will be back. He obviously has some stuff to work through. Whatever it is – he won't stay away too long." The look she gave me, and the convincing tone almost gave me hope, but I hardly dared to. It felt silly and childish, but it really hurt that he'd kissed me with such passion, such feeling and then just walked out, not to be seen again.

"Right, you need cheering up. You can't stay cooped up in here like some morbid Miss Havisham type. You can come out with us and have some fun." She said it like it was the best idea in the world, but I wasn't convinced that playing third wheel on a date with her and Tyler was exactly what I needed. Then again, the thought of spending another day in bed moping and thinking about Nate wasn't so appealing either.

"What did you have in mind?" I asked cautiously.

An hour later, I was lacing up blue plastic boots and finding out exactly what Mia had in mind.

"Ice skating is so much fun!" she squealed, making her way out onto the ice like some sort of gold medal pro. She glided across the surface like an elegant princess and I could only watch on in awe. I turned to Tyler.

"Don't go too far, I'm going to need you to keep me upright." He laughed and helped me to my feet. We stepped out onto the rink and I smiled. Mia had been right; it was fun to get out and do something that I'd never done before, even if I was convinced I was going to fall and break my neck.

It took me a while to get used to it, but eventually I felt confident enough to skate round without clinging to Tyler for dear life. He still stayed within grabbing distance just in case I took a nosedive towards the ice. Mia kept lapping us gracefully, laughing every time she did so. It seemed the perfect opportunity to grill Tyler; something that would help take my mind away from my own failed attempts at romance.

"So – you and Mia huh?" His chocolate brown eyes

smiled.

"Yea. I guess we have you to thank. Your not-so-subtle toast and Mia said you told her to talk to me." I shrugged, blushing a little.

"What took you guys so long? It was so obvious. I knew right away, and I'd only just met you." He thought for a moment before answering.

"Mia and I have been friends for a while. I've always liked her, but I never realised she felt the same way until she drunkenly confessed that she's always liked me too. I'd always been too scared to make a move in case I ruined everything, ruined the friendship we have and lost her altogether. I couldn't have lived with that, so we stayed friends." I stared at him, but he was watching Mia, adoration obvious in his eyes.

"Wow – that's so…"

"Sickly?" he laughed.

"No!" I laughed too. "I was going to say sweet and romantic. There aren't many good guys like you." I felt the familiar burn at the back of my throat and the sting in the corners of my eyes. Tyler skated closer and put his arm around me comfortingly.

"You know Grace, you're a really cool girl and if Dan can't see that, then it's his loss." I nodded, sniffling pathetically. I wished his words would make me feel better – but they didn't, because it wasn't Dan I was bothered about.

"I don't care about Dan, not anymore," I mumbled stroppily. There was a part of me that still stung from his rejection, a part that had really liked him, but I was never going to admit that to anyone, especially not to his best friend.

"No, you care about Nate, right?" I glanced sideways at him, keeping my lips sealed. I wasn't going to confirm, nor deny it. "You know, I've only met him once, one morning after one of Dan's parties and we talked for a while. He seems like a really stand- up guy. Mia is probably right; he'll come back as soon as he can."

"I hope you aren't stealing my Tyler, Gracie Cake," Mia said playfully, skating to a perfect stop in front of us. I shook my head, chuckling.

"No, we were just chatting. You know, you two should start some sort of couple's advice service. He's just as good as you are at dishing it out." She smiled at him warmly and I excused myself, giving them some time on the ice together.

Maybe they were right; maybe all I had to do, was wait.

Twenty Six

Waiting sucked and as it turned out, I wasn't any good at it. After we got back from skating, Mia had sent Tyler on his merry way, so that we could have a girly night in at my house. She was still on some sort of mission to cheer me up, whilst also distracting me. I was more than happy for her to try; I'd had enough of feeling miserable over something as ridiculous as boy troubles. She'd stayed over and we had watched movies whilst eating junk food all night long. I kept thanking my lucky stars that she hadn't thought badly of me for mine and Dan's horrifically failed date. She was exactly the pick me up I needed. I hadn't had a close friend since Emily, and that hadn't turned out so well. I shuddered, pushing all thoughts of her from my mind. My heart ached too much already without picking the scab off that wound too.

We hadn't spoken once all night about the boys – any of them. Instead, we chatted mindlessly about our favourite films and books, about my art, about her job. It was just the stuff I needed to make me forget, even if only for a short time, about the agony I was in.

It had now been a full week since the terrible date. A full week since Nate had kissed me. Within an hour of Mia leaving, boredom had begun to set in again and I was getting antsy. The skating had been fun, but other than that, I hadn't left the house for six days; and staying inside for six days was enough. I needed more than Mia to help lift the funk that was settling within me. I needed to draw.

I bagged a new sketchbook, not wanting to see any of the pictures in my current one and shoved all my pencils into my bag.

"I'm going to head out for a bit mum," I called to her.

"Okay baby, don't stay out too late. You have your phone, right?"

"Yes mum." If I had been in a better mood, I might have rolled my eyes at her. As it was, her concern for me made me feel loved, which in itself seemed pretty stupid. I headed out and tried to remember the way Mia had shown me to get to a small picnic area in the woods by the large river that ran through the centre of the village.

It was a beautiful spot and had been teeming with wildlife when we had passed through; ducks, fish, butterflies, bees, swans, squirrels and Canadian geese but to name a few. It was just what I wanted to sketch.

It took longer than I expected and a few wrong turns but finally I found it. It was quiet and peaceful. There were a couple of fishermen sat beside the river, but other than that, I was the only one around. I sat down at one of the wooden picnic tables, breathing in the fresh air. It was a truly picturesque place.

I pulled everything out of my bag and set it all up on the table, angling myself so that I could sketch one of the many small, stone bridges that arched over the river, along with all the little ducks below it. Art was one sure fire way to take my mind off everything and cheer myself up. To lose myself in all the details and just concentrate on getting the picture right left no room for anything else; so I could forget for a while that it still felt like my heart was breaking.

Half an hour; thirty very short minutes. That's all the time I got before the little hairs on the back of my neck began to prickle. Half an hour before the uncomfortable queasy feeling settled deep within my stomach. Half an hour before I glanced up and saw Dan stood on the bridge staring at me; staring at me in such a way, my blood turned to ice within my veins and I shuddered. He walked towards me, his expression flat. I couldn't tell whether he was angry, happy or sad and I didn't really care. All I knew, was that I didn't want to be alone with him, especially somewhere as secluded as this.

"Well, if it isn't Grace herself," he said, his words full of that dangerous edge that I now knew Dan possessed. I refused to meet his eye. There was something about his eyes that always captured me, and I was powerless to stop it. I started gathering my things together. He stepped towards me and snatched the sketchbook from my hands.

"Hey! Give that back, what are you, twelve?" I was loathe to admit it, but Dan scared me, and I didn't want to play his game. I stood and reached for the pad.

"Nuh-uh, what's the magic word?" he said, smirking. I took a deep breath, trying to control my temper, but it was becoming increasingly difficult with the disgustingly smug look upon his face. It was so – slimy. How had I ever thought I liked him? Really?

"Please can I have my pad back?" I said through gritted teeth. Bending to his will and saying please made me cringe.

"Come and get it." He winked at me, instantly making my skin crawl. Seriously, how had I ever thought that I could be attracted to him? I knew how – because whoever this was, whatever twisted persona he was now portraying, it was a very different entity to the one that I'd first met. That guy had been genuinely sweet, kind and caring.

"That's not going to happen." I held my hand out for the pad, placing my other on my hip impatiently.

"Aww, come on Grace. Where's the fun in that?" He stepped towards me and I took a step backwards – right into the table. I had nowhere to go and he knew it. I cowered away from him feeling trapped. He was enjoying the chase, like a fox that had cornered a rabbit.

"Dan, this isn't like you," I whispered. "Please – you're better than this." For a moment I saw something in his eyes that almost reminded me of the Dan I'd first met, but then it was gone.

"Don't pretend to know me Grace; you don't know anything." He crushed his hips against mine and held my chin in his hand. His face was so close to mine that for a moment, I considered biting him. "You know, you shouldn't have left the other night, the fun was only just starting."

"Dan, please – you're hurting me," I said shakily. I was close to tears and I felt helpless. He liked how vulnerable I was and that terrified me. Who was this guy? Surely this couldn't be the charismatic Dan that Mia had talked about and introduced me to. This couldn't be the same guy that had rescued me in a cemetery and taken me to a craft fayre. Could it? It was like he was possessed. How could he have changed so quickly? How could he be so different from his brother? Nate was warm and caring, even if he did have an annoying habit of bolting every time things got a little heated. He would never hurt me, not like this. I blinked, wishing he were here, wishing he could see what his brother was doing to me.

"Please," I whispered again, closing my eyes as a tear escaped down my cheek.

"Get your hands off her Dan – now." My eyes snapped open. I hardly dared to believe it. The sob that had been building in my chest, finally released. I looked over Dan's shoulder and sagged in relief as I found his green eyes. I'd know that voice anywhere.

"Mind your own business Nate." Dan turned back to me. I could feel his fingernails along my jaw. It felt like they were cutting into the skin, but within seconds his hand was gone from my face, instead twisted up behind his back. Nate pushed his brother away before turning to me.

"Are you ok?" I shook my head. I was not feeling one bit ok. I was trying to quell the panic that had filled me with terror, but I couldn't speak. I didn't want to look at Dan; I couldn't let him know how scared I was.

"I said mind your own business Nate. We aren't done here." Dan glared at me. What had I done to deserve this? I didn't understand. Could he really know how I felt about Nate, and could it really make him hate me so much?

"Yes – you are." Anger rolled off Nate in waves. He was furious and he was fierce. I might've been mad at him for being AWOL all week, if I wasn't so ridiculously grateful to him for being here. Dan spat on the ground and shook his head laughing.

"I'll see you again soon Grace." It wasn't just a parting farewell; it was a thinly veiled threat, and we all knew it. He left, his chilling laughter echoing around the small clearing.

"Sit down Grace," Nate said softly. I wasn't in the mood for fighting, plus my legs felt like jelly, so I did as he said. He knelt before me. He ran his fingers over the places where moments before Dan's had been, but his touch was feather light and gentle. I could feel the bruises purpling beneath my skin already. I looked into his eyes. They were filled with fury as they took in my damaged skin, the usually emerald green turning stormy grey once again. It was all too much – a fresh wave of tears sprang to my eyes.

"He hurt you." He ground his teeth together in a feeble effort to portray some semblance of calm. Part of me wanted him to go after Dan so that I could make my escape without him, but an even bigger and probably more stupid part of me, just wanted to be close to him. I wasn't going to let him off easy though.

"Yes, he did, but – he's not the only one. It seems you both have a propensity for it." His face twisted in pain and guilt. Watching him crumple as the emotions struck him made my chest burn. I hated making him feel bad, but he needed to know that I wasn't some toy he could play around with. He couldn't kiss me and then disappear for a week.

"Look Nate, I know you said things are complicated. I have absolutely no idea why or what you have going on, but I get it, ok? But you need to know, I've been through enough heartbreak in the last year to last me ten lifetimes so please, don't mess me around. Don't add to it."

"You were hurt by a boy before? In London?" I almost laughed aloud. I wish it had been something as simple as a boy who broke my heart. That I'd be able to get past. I shook my head sadly.

"No, it's nothing like that. It's a long story." His hand closed around mine.

"I've got time." I looked to him. Did I want to tell him,

him of all people, the one that kept running away from me every time we got close? Could I trust him to listen to the worst thing that had ever happened to me, without finding some excuse to run away and turn his back on me – again?

"It's not a very nice story. You sure you want to hear it?" He settled down in front of me, his hand squeezing mine encouragingly.

"You should only tell me if you want to. I'll understand if you can't." I stared off into the trees, thinking it over. I'd been avoiding it for so long, so desperate not to split old scars that had barely healed and open myself up to all that tragedy again. I hadn't spoken to a soul about it since all the questioning had ended. I knew Nate wouldn't push me if I decided not to tell him anything, but as I looked into his serious eyes, I decided that perhaps, it was time. Perhaps he was the one I'd been waiting for to open up to. Perhaps now was the perfect time to lean on someone.

"There was a reason we moved from London and despite what I told Mia and everyone, it had nothing to do with my mums work or the need for a bigger house. I had a friend there, a best friend in fact and she – she died." I swallowed past the fast-forming lump in my throat and squeezed back the tears. I'd not even gotten to the worst part yet; I needed to hold it together if I were going to tell him everything.

Nate pulled on my hand and it took me a moment to realise he was trying to pull me into his lap. I obliged, wanting to be close to him, as close as I physically could. I rested my head in the nook of his shoulder. It was comforting; he was comforting and strong, he made me feel safe and gave me the strength to carry on.

"I'm so sorry Grace." I'd heard those words so many

times but never had they felt so genuine, so heartfelt. I absorbed the condolence, taking a deep breath before continuing.

"Her name was Emily." I closed my eyes, smiling sadly as an image of her floated into my mind. "There was only two weeks between our birthdays. Our mothers knew each other well; they became friends after meeting in an antenatal class for single mums. They were actually amazed at how we stayed best friends all through our childhood because we were polar opposites. Emily was older, but more often than not, she was a lot more immature than me." For the first time in a long time, I threw open the doors in my mind and let all my memories of Emily flood through. Polar opposites we might have been, but you wouldn't ever find two girls closer than we were. We loved each other like sisters.

"What happened?" Nate asked cautiously, his fingers running soothing circles over the back of my hand.

"She was attacked." His arms stiffened around me, his fingers ceasing movement. "A few days before it happened, she told me and her mum that she thought she was being followed. Her mum called the police, and she was warned not to leave the house or travel anywhere alone. She didn't listen though. Her boyfriend was having this big, fancy dress party and Emily being Emily, she completely disregarded everything she had been told. She came by my house, wanting to borrow an outfit that I'd worn on Halloween – it was a Poison Ivy costume, and she thought her boyfriend would get a kick out of it because he was a massive comic book fan." I thought back, my eyes burning with unshed tears. I should have told her no. I should have told her mother what she was planning. I should have gone with her. I had so many regrets and so much guilt that I carried around daily.

"I don't fully know what happened to her. My mum wouldn't tell me anything, not one single detail, so I know it must have been bad. She was already dead when she was discovered." The tears flowed freely now, hot and thick as I choked out the last few words. Nate gently took my chin in his hands and kissed the tears from my cheeks.

"I really am so sorry Grace, truly I am." His voice cracked and my heart ached. He was so full of emotion. I sniffed, swiping at my eyes.

"It's ok, you weren't to know."

"So – is that why you moved? Your mum didn't want to be around where it happened?" I thought about it. It'd be easy to nod, to leave the story there, but then I would be lying and that was something that I didn't ever want to do to Nate. I'd started, so I needed to finish. I needed to tell him everything, even if it was going to stir it all back up again.

"Partly," I nodded. "But there was another reason, a bigger reason. Afterwards, when the police were going over the scene, they found a screwed-up piece of paper, thrown on the floor not far from where Emily was. On the paper, it had our year of birth – and my address – with my name on it. Do you see? Emily left my house, wearing my outfit. She was wearing a red wig Nate – do you know what that means? It was meant to be me."

He couldn't hold back the horror that shone in his eyes, but there was also something else – something I couldn't quite put my finger on. It was almost like it wasn't news to him, wasn't that big of a shock. It was almost like he already knew – which was strange. I shook it off.

Obviously, it was a shock to him; it would be a shock to anyone. I'd tried to lock down my emotions as soon as the police had shared that detail with us. I'd not been entirely successful; living in fear and weighed down by uncontrollable guilt for a long time. My best friend was gone – but it should have been me. The nightmares this had caused still haunted me, still made me pale and shiver. I closed my eyes, trying to absorb some of his warmth. We sat in silence for what felt like an eternity.

"I told you it wasn't a very nice story," I whispered quietly as I sat up. Nate pressed his forehead against mine, but it was as if the contact wasn't enough. He crushed his lips to mine in an urgent, emotional kiss. Shock was the first thing I felt, and a small voice in the back of my mind was telling me I should be pushing him away, especially as he'd left after our last kiss, but as his lips moved against mine, I could feel an anger radiating through him to me and I didn't have the willpower to stop him. He pulled back and we both gasped for air.

"Are you going to run away again now?" I asked softly. The question had formed on my tongue long before my brain had caught up enough to stop it. He looked into my eyes and shook his head slowly.

"I swear to you Grace, I will never let anyone hurt you – ever." He was so deadly serious, it made stomach twist into knots. A cold finger of fear ran down my spine at the conviction in his voice. Did he think there was still someone out there who wanted to hurt me? We'd moved away and not told a soul where we'd gone. My mum ran her business through PO boxes and all sorts to hide our whereabouts, doing everything in her power to keep me safe, but – what if I wasn't safe? What if there was still someone out there who meant to cause me harm? What if whoever attacked Emily had realised their mistake, and tried to correct it? I didn't even know why I was a target in the first place, but could it be that they were out there looking for me now? I thought back to the cemetery, to the feeling of being watched. Dizziness overtook me as dread flowed through every part of my body, worrying thoughts swimming through my mind. I leant against the one thing I knew for sure; Nate was here, and I wanted it to stay that way.

"Are things still complicated?" Did I really want the answer? He tilted his head and a sad smile settled on his lips.

"More than you could possibly know." I pressed my palms flat against his chest, my fingers taking in the hard contours of his muscles.

"So – enlighten me." He struggled and for a nanosecond, I thought he was actually going to open up, but he shut it down again just as fast.

"In time – I'm sure you'll find out in time." He looked tortured, so much pain hiding in the green sea of his eyes. I didn't want to push him, for fear of pushing him away.

"But you're sticking around? For now?" Opening up to him about Emily, about the real reasons behind our move to Stonewell, only made the connection between us more potent. I was fighting a losing battle with myself. I could push him away now and save myself more obvious hurt, save myself from losing someone else because a little barely there voice in the back of my mind was telling me that eventually, I would lose Nate. Or I could take what I could get and just enjoy whatever time we did have together, no matter how short that time might be. I'd learnt to live with the tragedy of Emily – could I do the same with Nate? I was at least willing to give it a go.

"For now," he muttered. For now, seemed about all I was going to get. I stared at his mouth. It was set in a grim line. I leant forward and brushed my lips softly over the top of his, as light as a feather falling from the sky. He closed his eyes and smiled.

Footsteps sounded behind us and I jumped, my heart leaping into my mouth. Had Dan come back? I turned, cold fear soaking through me, but it was just one of the fishermen leaving. I exhaled slowly. I was still shaking from everything that had happened; Dan hurting me, telling Nate about Emily and from his kiss.

"Nate – what's going on with Dan? He wasn't like that when I met him, he was so lovely. Why did he – change so quickly? Why does he want to hurt me?" My jaw throbbed, reminding me of how close he had been, how tightly his fingers had gripped me.

"He doesn't – not really, at least not how you think. Don't worry about him. I'll sort it." His mind was obviously elsewhere as he said it and I watched the muscle in his jaw tense again. He looked down into my face. "You want to get out of here?" I nodded. I thought he'd had never ask.

He helped me pack away my things and then took my hand in his, leading me over the bridge. I followed him blindly. We weren't going back the way that I'd come in, but I knew I didn't need to worry; I was with Nate now.

I saw his Jaguar as we broke through the trees. It was parked at an odd angle; right at the side of the road, almost like it had been dumped there. Nate opened the door for me as we approached and I looked to him, my brow furrowed.

"Did you know I was here?" I asked. Had he known Dan was coming to see me? Had he followed me? Followed Dan? He pinched the bridge of his nose between his thumb and forefinger and smiled.

"Jump in Grace." He never answered any of my questions straight, if at all, which always brought to mind more questions. Mia was right; he was an enigma.

"Where are we going?" I asked as we reversed into the road.

"I'm taking you home. I need to sort something out." The beginning niggles of panic started setting in at the thought of him leaving again. Was that something Dan? What was he going to do? Would he come back, or would he leave me for another week, alone and scared? I stayed quiet. I didn't want the fear to creep into my voice and give me away; I didn't want Nate to know how scared I was of him going again.

Before long, we pulled up outside the farmhouse. He walked round and opened my door, just as he always did, taking my hand in his and walking me down the path. I leant against the door and he stood in front of me. He was trying to say something but whatever it was, he was struggling to find the right words.

Instead, he leant in and kissed me, so tenderly that I thought my heart might melt. I might not have kissed anyone before Nate, but I was fast learning. I had a great teacher. I ran my tongue slowly over his bottom lip. He gasped and pushed himself against me. I knotted my hands in his hair hungrily; I couldn't get enough of him. He chuckled.

"Slow down Grace," he rasped. He took both my hands

in his and gave me a look of pure sincerity. "This isn't another goodbye. I promise you; I'll come back and see you tomorrow."

I smiled; it was music to my ears. I was about to lean in for another kiss when the door opened, and I stumbled backwards. If Nate hadn't been holding my hands, I would have fallen backwards and landed rather embarrassingly, on my bottom.

"Grace?" My mother looked at me with a mix of annoyance and intrigue. My face was burning. I felt like a naughty child that had just been caught drawing on the walls.

"Mum – this is Nate," I squeaked. He was still holding my hand in his; a gesture that didn't slip my mother's attention. I could feel my palms getting damp. It was gross and I only hoped Nate didn't notice. My mother looked to him and for a second, I swear I saw her eyes widen. It was as if – it was as if she recognised him, but it was just a flash and then it was gone.

"Nice to meet you Nate. I'm Joanne." She looked directly into his eyes and I felt mortified. Catching us stealing kisses on the doorstep was not how I envisioned my mother meeting the first man that I'd ever had a connection with, but there wasn't much I could do about it now.

"Nice to meet you too." He gave her his most dazzling smile and I hoped it won her over as much as it had me. She was still watching as he turned to me. "I should get going."

My lips felt like they were glued together, and I couldn't do anything but nod. My mother finding us at the door had nigh on robbed me of speech. I stood with her and we both watched Nate head back to his car. We didn't go inside until he had turned off the road. I cringed; I didn't really want to answer the barrage of questions she was sure to have. I turned to her; she was watching me with a raised brow.

"Care to explain?" she asked slowly. I rubbed my eyes. How could I even begin to explain Nate? I had no idea what he was to me – really good friend? One that always seemed to come to my rescue, one that made me feel things I'd never felt before, one that kissed me in a way that perhaps a friend shouldn't? I couldn't call him my boyfriend because I still wasn't sure where I stood with him; plus, it didn't feel right, didn't feel – enough.

"That's Nate." I chewed the inside of my cheek to stop from smiling. The past week of feeling miserable due to his absence was gone, wiped away in a moment of heroism. Mia had been right after all. He had come back.

"Yes, I got that part." She was still looking at me and I knew she wanted answers, but I was struggling to come up with a way of filling her in on what Nate meant to me.

"He's – a friend," I shrugged, nonchalantly. The word didn't feel right, but it was all I could offer her for the moment.

"A special friend?" She was giving me that look; that look that mothers give their children when they know they're withholding information.

"You could say that."

"He seems – nice," she said, sounded guarded. What did she mean by that? He was more than nice; he was amazing, beautiful, he was kind, he was a gentleman, he was strong, he was – everything. Why had she said it like it was a bad thing? A giggle burst from me. I couldn't help it; this was such a surreal conversation to be having with my mother. She smiled and rolled her eyes.

"Are you hungry?" she asked. My stomach grumbled in response and I realised I was starving. I hadn't eaten all day, in fact – I couldn't remember the last time I had eaten.

"I am actually," I grinned. She led me into the kitchen and sat me down. If I'd thought she was done with the inquisition – I was wrong.

"You know, you never did tell me what happened on that date – and I'm sure his name wasn't Nate." She eyed me curiously as she flitted around the kitchen. I blushed heavily. I'd been hoping to avoid discussing the whole debacle with her. I especially didn't want to fill her in now that I knew Dan had a dangerous side and he didn't seem scared to hurt me. She'd obviously known something was wrong, she wasn't blind, nor was she stupid, but when I'd taken to my room and moped for a full week, she hadn't pried or probed too much. What she hadn't known was that I wasn't moping over my failed date; I'd been moping about Nate's kiss and run.

"His name was Dan, and nothing really happened," I said, treading carefully. "I realised on the date that I don't like him in that way."

"But you like Nate in that way?" she asked, watching for my reaction. I nibbled my lip, my face hot enough to fry a steak.

"Yes."

"Are Nate and Dan friends?" She tried to keep her tone light and not accusatory, but I could hear the unspoken question there. Was I coming between two friends? Well – this was awkward. What would she think when I told her the truth? Did I care? Yes – I suppose I did care a little bit, but not enough that if she disapproved, it would keep me away from Nate.

"They're brothers," I said quietly. I looked at her and she stopped what she was doing, her composure slipping for just a second. She realised she was staring at me and looked away, continuing to chop tomatoes.

"Dan? Nate's brother Dan? They're brothers." She was mumbling so quiet; it was almost to herself. "That's – different. It's not going to cause problems between them is it?"

"No," I lied. I never lied to my mum. Never. I hated it, plus I wasn't particularly good at it, but I didn't want to put up with any speeches about how I should be careful, how I shouldn't come between family and so on and so forth. "Dan doesn't like me in that way either. The date proved that."

"Ah, well then, that's sort of nice then isn't it. You have Nate and Dan; two strapping young men to protect you." She smiled at me. I hoped she couldn't read what was going on in my head. Dan – protect me? Maybe once, I could have believed he would, but not now. If anything, it seemed I might need protection from Dan. I sighed, before realising what she'd actually said. Exactly what else did she think I needed protecting from?

I was about to ask, but then thought better of it. I didn't want to dredge everything up with her, especially not when I was feeling so happy from seeing Nate, kissing him and having him promise he would be back to see me tomorrow.

My mother didn't question me any further and I was grateful. We sat in comfortable silence, her cooking something yummy, and me daydreaming about Nate's lips.

Twenty Seven

I tipped my concealer bottle, watching the creamy coloured liquid seep into the small, black sponge. I'd not been wrong when I'd said I could feel the bruises rising beneath my skin. I'd woken up to clear fingerprints all the way along my jaw and every time I looked in the mirror and saw them, I shuddered. I hadn't slept well. I'd felt completely drained, both mentally and physically, but when I'd headed to bed, my mind had been full of Emily and I was wracked with guilt from finally opening up.

I realised that I'd locked away all my feelings for such a long time, that even I didn't know how I was feeling about the whole thing half the time. I never spoke about it with anyone and sometimes, on a few rare occasions, it really felt like it'd happened to someone else.

I could still remember how I'd felt when they knocked on the door. I'd been wearing my favourite dress, the one that I'd worn to Dan's party. The police were sombre, asking to speak to my mother alone. I remember wondering what they'd come for, panicking that I might have unknowingly broken the law; but no – no, it was worse – much worse.

After they'd left, my mother had sat me down, explaining everything to me; how Emily's body had been found, how she'd been attacked and how she was – gone. I'd been stupid, immature almost, as I'd asked, 'gone where?' When it finally sank in, I'd been devastated. I could pinpoint the exact moment my heart had broken.

I'd cried for days, wondering how someone could do such a thing. It was made worse by the fact that Emily's mum had been so nice to me, like I was the one who had lost the most, like she hadn't just lost her one and only daughter. That's when the nightmares had started.

They were always the same, always filled with the same, gripping fear that would make me wake up screaming. Emily was being attacked in front of me, she was screaming my name, screaming for me to make them stop and all I could do was stand there and watch. In the end, it got to the point where I avoided sleeping for as long as I was able, because I couldn't stand seeing the absolute horror on Emily's face.

The day of the funeral my mother had finally filled me in on some of the details that the police had told her; about the note and the danger they believed me to be in. They had no explanation as to why I was a target; all they knew, was that Emily's attack no longer seemed as random as they first thought. We'd moved the day after the funeral. I didn't get a say in it; my mother had packed everything up right under my nose and I'd barely noticed a thing.

The shock of finding out it was supposed to be me and then the wash of guilt that swept through me, had made the move easier. I was too preoccupied with hating myself for the whole thing. It was only when I'd begun trying to unpack, that I'd finally snapped out of it. It had taken a massive amount of effort to lock away all the anger and the guilt, but I knew if I didn't, then it would rule me and my life. A life that I was lucky enough to still have, a life that should have been taken instead of Emily's.

There were still plenty of boxes to unpack as I looked

around my room. They were filled with memories, precious things like photos and scrapbooks that even now, even after leaning on someone with my past, I still couldn't unpack and look at.

I sighed and tried to push Emily from my mind. I missed her everyday and when she died, a little piece of me died with her, but I didn't want it to get the better of me today, not when I knew Nate was coming back to see me. I turned back to the mirror and brushed the sponge along my skin, trying my best to hide the marks. I didn't really want anyone to see them but least of all my mother. It would raise questions that I wasn't prepared to answer. She hadn't asked anything more about Nate or Dan whilst we had eaten, in fact, she had been unusually quiet. I stared at my reflection. If you looked closely, you could still faintly see them, but it would have to do.

I headed downstairs, only to find that I needn't have bothered. There was a note attached to the fridge telling me that she was away and would be back around 11pm. I was alone in the house again. There were times when I wished I could ask her to stay, times when I didn't feel like being alone and this was definitely one of those times. Dan knew where I lived, so now I felt exposed. I could head to the library and see Mia, fill her in on what had happened, but Dan had found me there too. I was beginning to feel like there was nowhere I could go without fear of him showing up. At least in my own home, I could lock the doors and make sure I was safe.

Nate had promised he would come and see me, but he hadn't specified what time. I slumped onto the sofa and ran my fingers over my lips. If I closed my eyes, I could almost feel him, and I was beginning to think the smell of him was ingrained into every fibre of my being, because no matter where I was, his scent seemed to surround me. The warmth and spice of it made me dizzy with desire. My heart raced when I thought about him, and my chest ached when he wasn't around.

Thinking of the conversation I'd had with my mother only served to give me a headache. Special friend – it seemed such a silly, juvenile description for someone who was more than that – so much more. In the short time I'd known him, I'd felt things that I never had before, but it was way more than a teenage crush, it had to be. When he was around, it felt like my soul was on fire, and the empty feeling that I'd been carrying around since losing Emily, dissipated the moment he showed up. I suddenly felt like all my life, I'd been missing something and then Nate showed up and now I was – complete.

I inwardly groaned, cringing at how stupid that sounded. How could he make me feel so whole? How could he make me feel like anything was possible? Like I could be the happiest girl in the world, as long as I had him? I'd barely known him two minutes and already it felt like I couldn't live without him. How could I like him so much already? How could I be so – in love? I was shocked to admit it, even just to myself, but I knew, without a shadow of a doubt, I was in love with Nate.

I covered my eyes, frustrated with myself. There was no denying it, Nate was my first love – but what was I to him? I still didn't know what was so complicated, other than the fact that his brother seemed hell bent on hurting me for reasons that were beyond my comprehension. It was all too much to take in. I needed a distraction. I needed – a movie.

It didn't take me long to pick the one I wanted. I grabbed a couple of fleece blankets, made myself a coffee and got ready to immerse myself in the hope that it would make the time fly until Nate eventually arrived.

I was just getting to the emotional part, where Shadow comes limping over the hill to Peter, when I heard the knock at the door. I jumped up, dropping my fleece blanket to the floor and practically ran to the door. My hammering heart and the dancing butterflies in my stomach, told me who it was before I got there. Even through the distorted glass, I could tell it was him. I smiled, taking a moment to compose myself before sliding the chain and opening the door.

His smile lit up his whole face, his green eyes sparkling in the cold sun. That warm, complete feeling that I'd only this morning acknowledged, flooded through me. I wanted to reach for him, but I was still feeling a little apprehensive on where I stood with him.

"Morning Grace." Heat spread through me every time he said my name. The way it rolled off his tongue. I didn't think I would ever get used to it, or the sparks it seemed to ignite in my belly.

"Morning Nate." With the pleasantries out of the way, I stepped aside, gesturing for him to come in. His eyes darkened as he took in the small bruises along my jaw. I turned my head, letting my hair fall over my shoulder to try and hide them. Closing the door, I leant against it and looked at him. God, he was beautiful. He stepped towards me and brushed his fingers lightly over the blemishes, making me shiver. My cheeks flooded with colour and the hint of a smile played at the corners of his mouth. He could see the effect he had on me.

"Do they hurt?" he asked quietly. Even if they did, I wasn't going to tell him. The last thing I wanted was for him to be in a bad mood and brood over something that he couldn't change. Shaking my head, I cleared my throat.

"I'd offer you a drink but last time you did a runner before the kettle had even finished boiling," I said playfully. Nate laughed. It was a deep, genuine sound and it made my stomach do back flips.

"I promise, I won't go anywhere until you kick me out." Internally I was dancing around doing a happy little jig, but outside I just smiled as graciously as I could.

"So, did you sort it?" I asked, leading him through to the kitchen. He didn't answer straight away, but then nodded, taking a stool at the counter.

"I'm getting there."

"Coffee?" I asked, filling the kettle. He cocked a brow, a seductive smile on his lips and I could tell he was thinking about the same thing I was – our first kiss.

"Coffee sounds good." I turned away from him, not wanting him to see the flush as it crept up my neck and flooded my cheeks. I'd be lying if I said that it was the kiss that started everything, because it wasn't. It had certainly helped things along, in the way dynamite helps a building explode, but no, it wasn't the beginning. By some stroke of luck, I'd managed to find myself in Nate's bed and I knew from the moment I fell into him and he steadied me, putting me back to bed and looking after me, that I liked him. The kiss was just the beginning of the fall – and I fell fast, and I fell hard.

"So, what are your plans for the day Grace?" There it was again, my name rolling from his mouth like something sexy. My hand shook as I spooned coffee into two mugs.

"I don't really have any plans." Other than spend as much time with him as possible of course.

"We could make some." I turned, arching my brow.

"Careful now Nate, next you'll be asking me out on a date." I bit the inside of my cheek, gob smacked. I spun back around to the cups. I didn't even know where it had come from, but the brashness of it made me feel dizzy and flustered. I seemed to lose all ability to filter my words when I was around him. I could feel his eyes on my back, but I didn't dare look at him. I was too embarrassed.

"A date? You want to go on a date?" Nate asked slowly.

"I – um – a…" I stammered, placing a hot coffee in front of him as carefully as I could. I didn't know where to look. I smiled at him sheepishly and he laughed.

"Grace, I…" I shook my head and shrugged my shoulders.

"I know, I know, it's – complicated!" I snarled in frustration. I just wanted the floor to open and swallow me. What was I saying? I wasn't usually so bold, but Nate really did remove all the filters that usually existed between brain and mouth, so my thoughts just spewed out without any way of me stopping them. Tingles spread down my spine as his hands rested on my shoulders. He turned me slowly to face him. I hadn't even heard him get up.

"Sorry," I mumbled. "I – I didn't mean it." His eyes were full of amusement and his mouth was turned up in a grin.

"Yes, you did." I opened my mouth to speak but I had no words. He was right – I had meant it. "If I ask you out, will you say yes?" I blinked. Had I heard him right? He seemed nervous and I was stunned. Surely, he knew how I felt about him? Maybe not to the extent that I'd admitted to myself, but he had to know I liked him?

"I think you know the answer to that," I replied, throwing his words back at him from the night of our first kiss. He leaned in closer, and I held my breath.

"Grace – will you go out with me tonight?" He was so close, his breath whispered across my lips. His lips were mere centimetres from mine, and I could think of almost nothing else but leaning in and touching mine to them. It was intoxicating.

"Yes," I whispered, closing my eyes. He stepped back and when I opened them, I saw he was smiling at me. He returned to the stool. I swayed on the spot and heard him chuckle. He knew exactly what he was doing. Finally, I let my breath go, exhaling loudly. Well, if he hadn't known how I felt about him, he sure did now. His eyes were glinting, teasing me.

"How much time do you need?" Amusement was etched into his every feature.

"Um – what are we doing?"

"Going on a date, aren't we?" I smiled as he teased me again, finally regaining some semblance of composure. It was good; it was nice for the atmosphere to be more flirty than full on heavy.

"No, I mean, where are we going? What's the plan?" I glanced at the clock on the microwave. It was already 4pm. Where on earth had the day slipped away to?

"I know a place. Wrap up warm." He stood and stuck his hands in his back pockets, rocking back onto his heels. "I know I said I wouldn't leave until you kicked me out, so – can you kick me out please? I need to get a couple of things for our date."

I gulped and dipped my head in a nod. What sort of things was he talking about? A dark side of my mind gave a dirty little laugh, and my cheeks grew instantly hot. I coughed, shaking those thoughts away. He stepped towards me and pressed his lips to my forehead, his eyes still lit up with playfulness.

"I'll be back at six."

Twenty Eight

Warm – warm – wrap up warm. That's what he'd said. I pushed the clothes back and forth in my wardrobe, chewing on the inside of my cheek as my mind raced. I was going on a date with Nate. It was unbelievable. It was what I had fantasized about and dreamt of since I'd realised how I felt about him, but it had still felt unattainable – until now. Nate had been my first kiss and a big part of me wished that this were my first ever proper date, then he could be my first everything, even –

I abandoned the wardrobe and ran to the bathroom to splash cold water on my face. It should have sizzled with the heat that my cheeks were amassing. Perhaps a cold shower was what I needed. I didn't want Nate to think I was a horny mass of hormones – even if he did seem to bring out that side of me.

I stripped and jumped under the spray. It was cold, refreshing and shocking – just what the doctor ordered. It couldn't be more different to the shower I had taken in Nate's bathroom, but that was probably a good thing. I was trying to calm myself down, not work myself into more of a frenzy.

I stood beneath the water until I was shivering. It did the job. I wrapped myself in a towel and stood before the mirror. As I stared at my reflection, I noticed that my skin had a glow to it that I'd never seen before and my eyes looked different somehow. Was this what love looked like? Love – it was such a big word and one that I still wouldn't be admitting to Nate in a hurry, but I was absolutely sure I was in love with him. It was terrifying; I was scared of opening myself up to the kind of rejection that a word as big as love could create.

I carefully plaited my hair and put on a sweep of mascara before heading back out to my room to decide on what to wear. None of my clothes were as sexy as what Mia had brought me to wear for my first attempt at a date, but Nate had said to dress up warm, so I doubted he was taking me somewhere like the pretentious club.

Finally, I settled on a soft cream V neck jumper over a vest, my black skinny jeans and my black Doc Marten boots. I looked at myself in the mirror, spinning slowly. It was a vastly different outfit to my last one, but I felt just as beautiful. Perhaps it was because this was the real me; this was who I really was, not the heels and skirt type. It was nice to step out in something different every now and then, but I loved my creature comforts.

There was still some time to wait before Nate would reappear at my door, so I sat in my window, looking out over the cemetery. It felt like an age since I'd last been in there. I smiled as I remembered how Nate had found me, how he had seen a couple of my sketches. My fingers itched to pick up some charcoal and sketch him, his beautiful features, but I didn't want to get covered in black dust after just showering.

The sun still seemed very high in the sky and I realised the date – it was almost time for the clocks to go forward. Soon the days would feel longer, and the sun would shine brighter, and it might finally feel like summer was just around the corner.

Movement in the corner of my vision made me turn my head sharply. I squinted out across the cemetery. Icy fear swept through me as I saw a dark figure. They were some distance away, but I was fairly certain they were wearing camouflage gear. They were just stood – staring up at my window. They couldn't possibly see me – could they? I was too far away, surely? It was unnerving. I jumped up to grab my phone from the bed. I dialled Mia's number, needing to speak to someone, anyone, but when I turned back to the window, the figure was gone.

"This is Mia. I'm obviously super busy right now so leave a message and I'll call you back – probably." I hung up before the beep of her answering service kicked in. I was making something out of nothing again, seeing things where there was nothing to see. It was a public place and public generally meant people – it was nothing to be worried about. Even if it did make my skin crawl and it wasn't the first time I'd felt like I was being watched. Didn't mean I had to sit in the window and freak myself out any more than necessary though.

Nate had said to wrap up warm, so to distract myself from the uneasy feeling that clung to my skin, I headed downstairs and began rifling through a couple of boxes, looking for a scarf and some gloves. I knew from experience how the chilling wind could numb your fingers to the bone, and frostbite was not attractive. The only pair I could find resembled something from The Muppets. I grimaced but they would have to do. At least they were black and not some obscene, fluorescent colour. I pulled my favourite scarf from the box. It was soft cotton and had tiny candy skulls printed all over it. There was nothing left to do now but wait.

The clock ticked loudly as I sat on the sofa, watching the second hand move at what felt like an infinitesimal rate. Time was dragging, and the more time dragged, the more tense I felt. I was excited and I was finding it hard to contain it.

I almost got whiplash as I spun my head towards the knock at the door. 5:45pm. He was early. I jumped up, nearly tripping over my own feet in my haste to get to the door.

"Hi," I said breathlessly as I swung it open.

"Hi," Nate replied warmly. His hair was damp and the way it curled around his ears made me want to reach out and touch it. He pulled his arm out from behind his back and held out a single white rose. My heart skipped a beat.

"Thank you," I said, softly surprised, taking it from him and holding it to my nose. I could feel the prickle of tears behind my eyes, but I refused to let them spill.

"l know red is more traditional…"

"No!" I said, louder than I'd intended. I smiled, clearing my throat. "No, this is perfect. I'll be right back." At Emily's funeral there had been red roses everywhere, as they were her favourite flower and seeing them always brought back all that pain and the memories of her. I couldn't stand the sight of them anymore, they reminded me too much of death. But Nate couldn't have known that – could he? He was a mystery for sure, but a good one.

I ran inside quickly, shoving the rose into a pint glass of cold water. It would have to do until I could dig out one of my mum's old vases. Looping my scarf around my neck, I shrugged into my winter coat and shoved the Muppet gloves into my pocket. Nate was stood, patiently waiting where I had left him. I drank him in one last time, before skipping out of the door.

Twenty Nine

"This place is incredible!" I stared out over the green valleys and the craggy hills of the Peak District. It was simply stunning. Everything felt so lush and alive. There were pheasants wandering around us, and flocks of sheep with their spring babies by their sides. It made me want to paint, which was something I hadn't done in a long time.

"I thought you might like it." I turned back to Nate. He was smiling easily as he laid out boxes on a thick picnic blanket. He pulled out two flasks, two small cups, two small bowls and two plates. I watched him in awe. He must have been some sort of Tetris master because there was no feasible way he had fit everything into the small backpack that he'd brought. It was like Mary Poppins handbag, stuff just kept on coming.

I was glad he had warned me to wrap up warm, as we'd settled on the top of a hill and it was definitely a few degrees below chilly. It was ok though, because all I had to do was look at Nate's lips and the blankets he had brought, let my imagination run a little wild and I instantly warmed up. I could always blame the flushed look on the wind. He patted the ground beside him, so I joined him.

"I know this is no fancy bar." I looked at him with a stern expression. Talking about that night and Dan, was the last thing I wanted to do.

"Did you have to mention that? I was hoping to live the rest of my life without ever thinking about that night again." His eyes glinted lightly, showing the playfulness I so loved to see shining in the green.

"You want to forget about that night? About – all – of that night?" Realising what he was getting at, I smiled.

"Oh – ok, I guess I don't want to forget all of that night. There were some – high points." His eyes stared into mine fervidly as I recalled the taste of him and the feel of his hands on my back.

"Let's eat," he said huskily, breaking his lustful gaze. There was so much food, I hardly knew where to start, and it all seemed so – posh! There was Italian bread stuffed with prosciutto, olive and feta salad, tiny chicken skewers that smelt like lemons, bite sized pork pies with a rich, dark pickle, little chilli crab cakes, not to mention the sweet stuff – chocolate dipped strawberries, tiny Battenburg cakes, chewy meringues filled with cream and fruit. It all looked so delicious and my mouth was watering.

Nate opened his legs and patted the space between them. I swallowed, my heart pounding out a happy little beat as I shuffled over and sat with my back against his chest. He smelt amazing and I closed my eyes, committing the whole scene to memory. I never wanted to forget this moment, how it felt to be on a date with Nate, wrapped in his arms and looking out over the beautiful countryside. It was perfection.

He grabbed one of the cups and poured us out coffees from one of the flasks. It was gorgeous, rich and more expensive than anything I'd ever drunk. He filled the plates with a little bit of everything from the boxes and then we sat and ate in silence, absorbing it all.

"You didn't have to go to so much trouble you know," I

said, as I chewed my last mouthful of crab cake. It had all been yummy, but it felt like Nate had gone to a lot of expense. I would have been just as happy to sit on top of the hill with him, eating a jam sandwich. I didn't want to sound ungrateful, I was far from it, but just being with him was enough for me. He didn't need to go to so much effort on my behalf.

"You're worth it," he murmured quietly against my ear. Shivers ran the length of my spine, my body instantly reacting to him. He lifted a chocolate dipped strawberry and held it out to me. I felt a little self-conscious as I bit into it, the juice running out of the side of my mouth. I licked my lip and felt the groan emanate from Nate's chest against my back. I gasped, closing my eyes as his lips closed on my jaw, gently sucking the juice from my skin. I squeezed my legs together, embarrassed by how low down the tingles were spreading.

He brushed my plait aside, gently nuzzling into my scarf, his lips pressing to the soft skin of my neck. I'd never felt more alive and less in control of myself as I did, right in this moment. His lips were by my ear again, his hands around my waist.

"I could sit here forever," he whispered wistfully. After the way his lips had set fire to my insides, I felt like doing a lot more than just sitting! I didn't trust myself to speak, so I just nodded, laying my head back against him, my hands on his legs.

We ate some more of the strawberries, and I laughed when Nate bit into one and the juiced sprayed up into his eye. We polished off the meringues and I even managed to squeeze in a couple of the little cakes. I was stuffed to bursting.

The sun was setting by the time we'd finished, and the sky had started to fill with dark clouds. It looked like the heavens were about to open up and empty themselves all over our perfect picnic. Nate must have sensed the same, as he began shoving everything back into his backpack. I stood, folding the blanket, casting wary looks to the sky. *Please don't rain. Please don't rain.* I didn't want to resemble a drowned rat in his presence.

"You ready?" he asked, after everything was packed away. I took a last, sweeping look out across the hills and the rocks. England was so full of beautiful scenery and living in London, being a city girl, I'd never given much thought to just how majestic the countryside could be. I wasn't really ready to give up on the fun I was having on our date, and I wasn't ready to be away from Nate again, even if it was just for the night, but the clouds were rolling in and we couldn't stay any longer.

"I'm ready," I nodded. He took my hand in his and we started our descent down the hill. I was glad of his hand as the ground was difficult to navigate at times. Rocks jutted out at odd angles seemingly everywhere, ready to claim their next broken bone. We were a third of the way down when the clouds began to empty.

"Holy shit, that's cold!" I squealed. The raindrops felt like they were the size of fists, and every one of them soaked me through. It was like being under the cold shower again, only this time fully clothed.

"Jump on my back," Nate called, through the thunderous drops. I wasn't about to stand and argue. If a piggyback was what it was going to take to get me out of the rain, then I was all for it. I pulled my hood over my head and nuzzled into his neck as he carried me.

Suddenly, the loud pounding of the rain on my head stopped. I could still hear the rain, but it was no longer hitting me. Nate dropped me to my feet, and I looked around. We were in a cave. I looked out of the opening; the downpour was ridiculously heavy.

"Where are we?" I asked, squinting through the dark.

"A cave, about halfway down. I figured we could wait out the worst of the storm." I shivered. It was cold and every single part of me was wet. My jeans clung to me, and even my jumper was damp beneath my so-called waterproof coat.

"I didn't even see a cave on the way up," I murmured. I could hear water dripping at the back of the cave, where it was pitch black. It sounded far away, which made me wonder how deep it went. I heard the strike of a match and turned to see Nate's face lit by a small fire. I stared at him, astonished.

"Come and sit, get warm." My mouth was gaping.

"How – where did you – how did you do that?" His face gave nothing away. "Where did you even get the wood? Everything is drenched."

"Grace – come and get warm." He was laid on his side on the blanket, propped up on his elbow. He was a sight to behold. Another question I wasn't going to get answered it seemed. Just another thing to add to the long list of mystique that was Nate. I shook my head, baffled as I sat cross legged beside him. He rested a hand on my knee, so I took it in mine, running my fingers across his palm.

"I'm sorry about the date," Nate said, staring into the fire. "It probably wasn't what you had in mind."

"No, don't you dare do that, don't you dare try and take it from me and belittle it. It was perfect." How could he think he had any reason to apologise to me about it? Couldn't he see how much I had enjoyed it? He gave a snort of derision. "Seriously Nate, it was better than anything I could have imagined. You know me so well already, and I – well, I'm just happy to be with you."

He stared at me, that same look in his eyes that I was fast becoming used to. It was also the one that scared me the most because it was the look he usually gave me just before he bolted. There was a desire, deep within the green, but it was tinged with sadness. He had a tortured look that just about broke my heart.

"I never accounted for this." He stared back into the fire; his brow furrowed.

"For what?" I asked, confused.

"For – liking you." I stared at him, waiting for him to say more, but he didn't. I was more than confused. Sometimes, when he spoke, it felt like he was speaking in rhymes and riddles that only he understood. I was trying to decipher what he meant so much, that it took me a moment to register that he had just admitted to liking me. I'd pretty much figured that much out, as I didn't really have him pegged as the type of guy that goes around kissing any girl he meets, but still, it was heart-warming to hear it from his lips.

"I like you too," I said quietly, tracing the lines of his knuckles with my fingertips. I was too shy to meet his eye.

"Mhmm," he muttered. "That's part of the problem."

"I don't understand," I admitted. What problem was he talking about? How could there be a problem? If we liked each other, that was all there needed to be – right? He closed his eyes and shook his head.

"It doesn't matter." It felt like it mattered. It felt like it mattered a lot. Even with his eyes closed, his expression was one of worry. I wished I could take it away from him, share the burden and solve whatever problem it was that seemed to make him so sad. I hated to see him this way. I reached out and stroked my fingers lightly down the side of his face. He caught my hand in his and held my palm to his cheek.

"Nate – what are we?" His eyes flew open. I couldn't decipher the look he gave me. Shock? Confusion? Maybe a little of both.

"What do you mean?" he asked carefully. I chewed my thumbnail absentmindedly, feeling shy again.

"Well – are we together, or..." The words got stuck in my throat as my breath became ragged. I was scared of his answer and as I ground my teeth together, I wished I'd never asked.

"Oh, that's what you mean." He visibly relaxed and I looked at him confused. What else could I possibly have meant? He blew his cheeks out, searching for an answer. "I still don't know if it's a good idea Grace. We shouldn't, it's..."

"Don't you dare. So help me god, if you say it's complicated one more time!" I snapped. I couldn't help it. If I heard that word come out of his mouth again, I might just explode. He winced.

"I'm sorry Grace, but it is. You don't know – I..." I pulled my hand out of his and circled my temples. My head was beginning to ache, and I didn't think it had anything to do with the cold or the wet but had everything to do with Nate and whatever his damn complication was! He was back and forth like a yo-yo, kissing me one minute and then telling me it was a bad idea the next! I felt like I was in an emotional washing machine, being tossed around violently and I didn't like it, not one bit.

"Look – the rain has stopped," he said quietly. Rising to my feet, I walked to the mouth of the cave, my arms crossed against my chest.

"Take me home please," I said, biting back the tears.

"I'm sorry Grace, I don't want to keep doing this to you," he said, coming to my side. He'd put out the fire and I was feeling icy cold again.

"Then don't," I whispered. He reached his hand out to stroke my face, but I stepped back from him. "I need to know where I stand with you Nate. I told you I'm not a toy to be played with. I opened up to you, told you things I've told no one. I told you everything!"

"I know, and I hate myself every time I see the hurt in your eyes." He looked so sad, it physically hurt, but I couldn't deal with the flip flopping around anymore. If he wasn't going to make a decision, then I would.

"Take me home please Nate." He held out his hand, but I refused to take it. I was barely holding it together. Every part of me wanted to cry and scream at him, but it wouldn't do me any good. He sighed and walked past me, leading the way back down the hill to the car.

We drove in silence all the way back home. I was furiously trying to keep myself from crying. He didn't think it was a good idea for us to be together, yet he offered me no explanation as to why or what the hell was so damn complicated in his life. It hurt me more than I would ever let him know.

When we pulled up outside the farmhouse, I didn't wait for him to open my door. I headed down the path, my clothes still damp and dreary – much like my mood. He grabbed my wrist and spun me around, but I didn't meet his eyes. I couldn't – my resolve would break.

"Grace, I'm sor…"

"Stop it Nate! Just stop apologising! I don't want to hear it." I bit my lip to stop it from trembling. "I don't want to see you again."

"What? Grace, no – don't do this." He looked crushed; panic streaked through his voice. I could have stood and sobbed.

"Goodbye Nate." My voice broke as I turned my back on him and headed inside. I held it together just long enough to get through the door, and then I collapsed against it, letting all the emotion go.

Thirty

It had been a seriously crappy night of tossing and turning, with plenty of crying jags in between. Maybe I'd acted hastily, and maybe I'd acted just a little bratty, but my brain couldn't comprehend what secret Nate was keeping from me and my emotions couldn't deal with his mood swings. I'd let him into my world and told him everything about me, yet he couldn't do the same – it was torture. There was something keeping him at arm's length, and I didn't know what it was, nor was I going to waste my time worrying over it.

I needed to talk to someone, I needed someone to vent to and the only person I had besides my mother, was Mia. I hated the thought of dampening her mood, I could feel the happiness in every text she had sent me since her and Tyler got together, but she was my friend; I needed a friend and she would understand.

So, I rushed around getting dressed, on a mission to go and see her at the library. I shoved my feet clumsily into my Doc Martens, preferring those over my Converse just in case I needed to kick somebody on the way. That was the type of crummy mood I was in.

Clouds were brewing overhead as I left the house. It was like the weather was emulating my whole demeanour, but the last thing I wanted was to get caught in a downpour again. I felt like my bones had only just warmed up from the last one I'd gotten caught in. The library was a good fifteen-minute walk away, so I pushed on, my head down against the wind.

There was no one around and the tiny, cobbled streets felt eerily quiet. The stone cottages stood side by side like sentinels against the coming storm. I could have taken the shortcut through the cemetery, but I didn't feel brave enough, not today, so I wound my way through the village as quickly as I could.

It was as I turned the corner on which stood the butchers shop, that I first heard it. The unmistakable sound of footsteps. My breathing quickened, as did my feet. I glanced over my shoulder but saw no one around. God, not this again. Why did I have to keep going through this? I'd had enough of living on edge.

It was dead, the weather keeping everyone inside where it was warm and dry. My skin began to prickle as the hairs on the back of my neck stood on end. I was being followed – I could feel it.

I turned again, into the main square. The memorial stood proud in the centre, faded poppy wreaths sitting at its base overlooked by the iron soldier. I wondered for a brief second whether it would be safer to duck into a shop, but as the footsteps closed in, all I could do was push on, my mind set on getting to Mia.

I headed out of the square to the path that ran alongside the river. I wasn't far from the library. I could already see it in the distance, its red bricks calling me to safety.

I was panting by the time I made it to the bridge, but I felt safer, I was so close. I slowed down, trying to return my breathing to normal as I stepped onto the stone arch. I reached the midway point and that's when I saw him, a figure blocking my path. He was dressed in army fatigues.

I couldn't see his face; all but his eyes were covered by a balaclava. Panic reared its ugly head and I found it difficult to breathe.

I turned to go back the way I'd come and froze. There was another, stood at the entrance to the bridge where I'd just been. I choked back a sob. What was happening? Were these the people who had killed Emily? What did they want from me? I looked around but I was trapped unless I wanted to jump into the rushing water below. It would be freezing and even if I were a strong swimmer, which I absolutely was not, the current was so strong, I wouldn't be able to battle it. I was getting frantic, looking for a way out, but I was petrified. It didn't look good; there weren't many other options for me.

The men looked burly enough to snap me in two in a heartbeat, so I didn't fancy my chances of trying to fight them off. If I ran to the very edge of the bridge, I could possibly jump down onto the bank, but it would mean having to run closer to one of them and I didn't want to go anywhere near them. They were stood stock still, neither making a move towards me, like they were waiting for me to move first.

I felt like screaming as I looked back and forth between them. My only option was to jump into the water. I would rather fight for my chance against the rushing current than let either of the men have me. My mind was full of Nate as I clambered up onto the rails, unsure of whether I would survive to ever see him again. I'd been stupid and selfish, I should have given him the benefit of the doubt, I should have given him time and space to explain to me what was so complicated. Now I would never know. I loved him, and at least if I were now going to drown, I could be happy in the knowledge that I had met him and known love. I just wished I could see his face one more time.

My move towards the rail was just the things my attackers were waiting for; they reacted.

The two men both started running towards me. I threw my leg over the cold metal, the bar digging into my stomach as I spun around. My feet slipped, and I screamed as I dropped, my hands grasping for something, anything! I grabbed the flat concrete of the bridge, my fingers stinging as it shredded my skin. Tears choked me as I stared up into the eyes of my followers. They were as black and cold as obsidian and as hard and unfeeling as it too.

I could see the smile behind the balaclava as a boot came down onto my fingers. They were crushing my bones! I cried aloud as the crunching sound churned my stomach. One of them leant over the rail, trying to make a grab for me but I did everything I could to swing away. There was no way I was letting these monsters be the ones to end me. I yelled in pain again, looking to the purple clouds above and praying to someone I'd never believed in.

I heard the whistling before my eyes found the source. There was something falling from the sky. No – not falling – flying. It landed with a crash, making the whole bridge shake and dislodging one of my hands. I screamed as I swung helplessly, unable to pull myself back up. I couldn't see the masked men anymore; the impact must have knocked them both away from me. I was fast losing my grip. The river beckoned to me from below; its cold, murky waters calling me to its depths. I couldn't hold on for much longer. I closed my eyes as my fingers slipped and braced for the cold – but it didn't come. In fact, it felt like I was being lifted up. I opened my eyes and couldn't believe what I was seeing.

"Nate?" I gasped, incredulously. His fingers closed tight around my wrist as he pulled me up and over the railing. I fell into his arms, hardly daring to believe he was here. I grabbed him, hugging him so tight, I could barely breath, scared that if I didn't, he might disappear, and I would be alone again. I looked around for the masked men. They were getting to their feet on either side of us, and they'd multiplied. There were now four of them. I'd felt how strong Nate was, but I doubted even he could take on four men.

"Back off," he growled through clenched teeth. He spun me, so my back was to his front, wrapping an arm protectively around my waist. I was shaking so much, it felt like my legs would give out at any second. It was terrifying; not just because I was being attacked, but because Nate was here too, and I feared something happening to him.

"Give us the girl, scum!" one of the men called. His voice was gravelly and hoarse, and it made my entire body cold, like ice had just been shoved beneath my skin.

"I said, BACK OFF!" Nate shook with rage against me. He took his hand off my waist, and held his arms outstretched to the men. I didn't know what to do. I stood looking from one side to the other. We were trapped, we were dead, there was no escape and there was nothing to do but fight.

The men looked to each other and then ran at us. I prepared my best, full bodied scream, but I didn't need it. Everything happened in the space of a heartbeat – Nate closed his eyes, a blast of energy radiated out of him and the men flew backwards into the trees. The sounds of bodies crumpling as they hit solid wood, filled the air. I cringed, my stomach rolling at the sickening noise they made. What the hell had just happened? What had I just witnessed?

I was starting to hyperventilate. I could feel Nate behind me, but I had no reasonable explanation as to what just happened or how, and I was starting to freak out. I stepped away from him. He was Nate – my Nate, the Nate that I knew and loved, the one who had saved me from a killer hangover and his brother, the one who had taken me on the best date ever and yet – he wasn't, he was different, he was something else. He looked scared and he was watching me warily. He stepped towards me but I backed away from him, hitting the railing that I'd moments ago, been swinging from.

"Grace, please," Nate said, his voice breaking. "We have to get out of here. Just trust me – please." He held his hand out to me, I was confused and scared, but he was right, we needed to leave before they came back. I took his hand and he pulled me in close. "Close your eyes Grace." His eyes pleaded with me, so I laid my head against his chest, and closed my eyes.

His arms wrapped tight around me and I gasped as I felt a sudden shift. My body felt like it was being pulled through a vacuum and my feet no longer had anything solid beneath them. I squeezed my eyes as tightly shut as I could, my fingers digging into the black shirt that clung to Nate's body. I felt his grip on me ease, but I didn't dare let go. I didn't know what was happening and I didn't want to. I felt sick; like the one time I'd been on a boat ride at the seaside.

"You can let go now," Nate whispered against my ear. My knees knocked together as I opened my eyes and forced myself away from him. A noise, not much more than a squeak, burst from me. I couldn't believe what I was seeing. We were stood at my front door. How the hell was we stood at my front door? Pesky lights began to dance before my eyes again, as my breathing quickened, and the panic built. It was all too much to take in.

"Nate – I need – sit." It was all I could manage.

"Whoa there," Nate said, catching me before I fell, lifting me into his arms like I was nothing more than a bag of sugar. He took the keys from my pocket and let himself into the house, sitting me down gently on the sofa. I bent over, forcing my head between my legs, trying to calm myself, trying to get back some level of control.

It was impossible – what had just happened was impossible. Nate looked terrified when I finally lifted my head. He was still the same Nate whose lips I'd kissed, whose eyes told me so much more than he ever did, and yet he wasn't – was he? He couldn't be.

"I know you're going to have questions, and I will try and answer them." I gave snort of derision. Damn right I had questions! Like how in the hell had I gone from being attacked on a bridge, to being stood outside my house? How the hell had he known exactly where to find me – again? Right at the point when I needed him the most, he just conveniently fell from the sky! No – not fell – flew. It didn't make any sense!

"Who are you Nate?" I kept thinking back, going over and over the moment that the men had flown backwards through the air. He hadn't laid a hand on them; he hadn't needed to. He looked desperately sad and hung his head.

"You don't want to know." The sorrow in his voice gave me the urge to wrap my arms around his neck, kiss him and tell him everything would be ok. I wanted to comfort him and tell him I didn't care, but I couldn't do that. I'd told him I never wanted to see him again, and though I had already decided that I'd been too rash, it didn't mean he could just rescue me and make me forget. I still wanted answers, I deserved answers.

"I wouldn't be asking if I didn't want to know. Nate – who are you?"

"The better question might be – what – am I?" My brow creased in confusion, but the cogs in my mind were already in overdrive, working hard to decipher how he could possibly achieve what had happened on the bridge. I was no comic book geek, but I knew my way around a fair few superhero stories, and as I looked at him, I wondered whether I'd found myself a real life one.

"Ok – what are you?" I asked uncertainly. He sat back in the chair and looked utterly destroyed. Even in my darkest hour after Emily had been murdered, I'd not looked as lost as he did now. My chest burned, the ache for him unbearable. As I watched him go through a million and one emotions, I realised I couldn't do it. I couldn't leave him sat suffering as he was. It was shattering my already fragile heart and although I wanted answers, I couldn't bring myself to cause someone I loved so much pain just to get them.

I stood unsteadily on my feet and went to him. His head was back, and his eyes were closed. I could see the trace of where a lone tear had slipped down his beautiful face and it made a lump form in my throat. I put a leg on either side of his, straddling his lap, and lowered my lips to the wetness on his cheek. Just as he had kissed away my tears, I now kissed away his. He opened his eyes and stared at me, confusion and disbelief swimming through the green.

I ran my fingers down the side of his face, letting my hand rest on his shoulder as I leant into him, my lips meeting his. I could taste the salt of the tear as I ran my tongue over his lip. He moaned softly, his hands pulling me closer to him. They slipped up my back, underneath my shirt and my skin exploded under his touch. Every tingle, every spark, shot pleasure through my stomach. He kissed me hungrily, his tongue dancing with mine. He fell from the chair to his knees, laying me on the floor. I wrapped my legs around his waist as his lips traced the line of my jaw, his teeth gently nibbling at my throat. I arched my back, needing to feel him, all of him, needing to take his pain away.

"Grace – I – I need to tell you…" he said breathlessly.

"I don't care," I whispered, pulling his lips back down to mine. It might be strange and stupid, but I found I really didn't care 'what' he was. Whatever it may be, it didn't change the fact that I loved and wanted Nate – nothing could change that. He pulled back and closed his eyes in defeat.

"But I do." He pulled me up until we were sat opposite each other. I let my breath go in a sigh, but one look at Nate's face told me how important it was to him. He shuffled back to sit against the chair, but there was no way I was letting him get away. I went with him, sitting between his legs. Whatever he was about to tell me, I wanted him to know that I was on his side, that I would stay close to him no matter what.

"Grace, I'm not – human." I swallowed hard and tried to keep my face devoid of any emotion. Not human? What did he mean by not human? My heart thumped against my ribs as panic began to creep under my skin. He looked human and when I was in his arms, his hands exploring every inch of me, he certainly felt human. I shook my head confused.

"I don't understand." He rubbed his eyes, struggling to put into words whatever it was that was floating around inside that complex mind of his. I silently willed him to go on. He was about to open up, I could feel it; perhaps I was about to learn what all the complications were about, why he couldn't just be with me like any normal person would.

"I'm immortal Grace – I'm not human." It felt like my heart had literally stopped. Was he being serious? How could he be immortal? How could he – live forever? My head was spinning with the mere possibilities! I thought back to the bridge, to the clearing in the woods, to the bar and before that, to my monster hangover. He'd always shown up exactly when I'd needed him to. Well, apart from the bar; we'd both been gobsmacked when we'd clocked each other there.

I remembered wishing for him on the bridge and how he'd magically appeared, how the masked men had flown through the air, how we'd gone from being over the river to being at my front door in the blink of an eye. None of it made any sense – and yet it could – if he weren't human.

"Are you – are you my guardian angel?" He didn't look much like a fairy godmother so it was my next best guess, the only other explanation that could fit the bill. He looked at me like I was crazy and to be quite honest, I was starting to think maybe I was a little bit crazy. Ever since I'd moved to Stonewell, things hadn't been quite right. But that wasn't strictly true; things hadn't been quite right since the night Emily was killed.

"Not quite Grace, I tend to work more for the other side." I narrowed my eyes. The other side? But that would mean –

"The other side? As in...?" He couldn't meet my eyes, which was answer enough in itself. No – he couldn't be! Nate wasn't bad; in fact he was good, truly good! He'd saved me, he looked out for me and protected me. I couldn't believe it – wouldn't believe it! I didn't care what Nate thought he was, I knew him better than that.

"I don't care," I said, defiance in my voice. Nate looked at me incredulous.

"What do you mean, you don't care?" he asked carefully. I squeezed his hand.

"I don't care Nate. I don't care who or what you are. I don't care what side you're on. I don't care what you think of yourself. I don't even care if you're the devil himself! I – don't – care. I like you anyways." His eyes widened in shock. I was breathless, and more than a little afraid. I stubbornly ignored the little voice in the back of my head that kept telling me I could be in danger with him. I refused to believe it. We'd been alone plenty of times – if he'd meant me any harm, he'd had more than one opportunity to do so, and he hadn't. Hell – he'd seen me at my most vulnerable, in his bed with a corking hangover, and been nothing but kind and caring.

"There's so much you don't yet know Grace, and I'm – I'm terrified." I couldn't fathom what he could possibly be afraid of. He'd just dispatched four men in one powerful outburst. He'd just told me he was immortal for crying out loud! What could he be scared of?

"Do you think they'll come back?" I asked, briefly glancing towards the window, remembering the figure I'd seen watching me from the cemetery. Perhaps Nate knew something I didn't, knew that there was more to the men than meets the eye and was fearful of what they might come back with.

"Most definitely Grace, but that's – that's not what I'm scared of."

"What is it then?"

"I don't want to lose you." It was barely more than a whisper. My heart felt like it was about ready to fly out of me. I knew the connection that I felt between us wasn't something that I'd conjured up. He felt it too – it went deeper than just being attracted to each other. It was probably childish and stupid of me to be elated at such an irrelevant detail, especially when he'd just confirmed that the masked men would most certainly show up again, but all that mattered was that Nate cared for me, as I did him. I placed my hands on either side of his face, so I could look into his eyes.

"You won't lose me Nate."

"You don't know the whole story."

"And I don't want to. Seriously Nate – I'm staying right here."

"But…" I shook my head and pressed a finger to his lips, silencing him. In time, perhaps I would want to know more, but I was already dealing with the fact that he wasn't human. Add to that the fact that my life was in imminent danger from masked assailants that were making it their mission to dispose of me for reasons unknown, and my mind was pretty much chock-a-block. As I was reeling through it all, something dawned on me.

"Is this the complication?" I asked, trying to keep the hopefulness to a minimum. If this was it, and he had finally told me, then it would mean we could be together – wouldn't it?

"Not – entirely." He said no more than that and I sighed. My inner five-year-old stamped her foot and crossed her arms, pissed off that there was still something out there that I didn't know about that could keep Nate and I apart. I sat the bratty part of me in a dark corner facing the wall and turned to him.

"I haven't had chance to say this yet but thank you for saving my life today." I was still processing what I'd learnt but I needed him to know how grateful I was. He smiled and my heart skipped a beat.

"You're welcome. They will come again Grace. This isn't the end. You have to know, that they will come for you again." His face twisted into a grimace and I could feel the anger that was building within him again.

"Then I hope you're always around to save me," I said, letting my hands slip down and rest upon his heart.

"It would be better if you didn't need saving at all." He looked sad, serious and brooding as he said it. As pieces of information floated around my head, trying to fit into the big picture that was Nate, something bothered me. The way he knew they would come again, the way he had spoken to them on the bridge. I took a deep breath before speaking.

"Nate – do you – do you know them? Do you know why I'm being hunted?" I could feel my lungs straining against the dread that weighed down my heart. Nate couldn't know – could he? Because that would mean he already knew about Emily and that would mean – I didn't want to think about what that would mean. I couldn't.

"It's a very good question and it's – it's difficult to answer. I, well, I…" He trailed off. I slumped against the sofa, a million and one things making my head feel like it was about to implode. I was overwhelmed and exhausted. Nate knew full well why they were coming for me. It wasn't that he didn't know, it was that he didn't want to tell me, he was holding back.

The room was growing dark and I knew it wouldn't be long until my mum returned, but that was no comfort. If the men were going to come for me again, I didn't want my mother around; I didn't want anything to happen to her. I yawned involuntarily. How the hell could I be so tired after everything that had happened? I should've been wired.

"You need to sleep," Nate said.

"There is no way on this earth that I'm sleeping when there's masked nutters out there on the loose, baying for my blood!" I stood up, thinking a coffee might help.

"Grace, I'm not going to let anyone hurt you, I promise. I'll stay." I froze and swallowed hard, spinning slowly to face him again.

"Stay? As in, stay the night?" I squeaked. Nate smiled. It was part teasing, part seductive and all irresistible. It was the side of him that I loved the most, the side that I'd first met, the morning after I woke with him beside me. It was the side that filled my whole body with tingles. Did I want to wake up beside him again? Absolutely. I wasn't too sure my mother would be happy with the arrangements though.

"Your mum won't know I'm here," he grinned, plucking the thought right out of my mind. I didn't even want to know how he did that. He took my hand and led me up the stairs to my room.

"Make yourself at home, I guess," I said, gesturing around. I was such a pathetic tangle of teenage hormones. The thought of having Nate stay over with me had completely wiped my mind of anything and everything to do with what had happened, sending me instead into a tizzy of giddy excitement. My face felt like it was on fire as Nate wandered around my room. I'd woken in his room, in his bed no less, but this felt totally different. He was now in my inner sanctum, in my private space – it shook me.

I left him nosing around to go and do the mundane things you do before bed; you know, wash your face, brush your teeth and raid your mother's pyjama drawer for something that wasn't covered in small pink bears with holes in all the wrong places. I pulled out a pair of silvery grey, silk bottoms and dug around for the matching top. There was absolutely no way I was sleeping with Nate in my room, it was going to be impossible. Five minutes ago, I'd felt tired but now, the thought of him staying the night had acted like a caffeine shot straight into my bloodstream.

He was sat in the window when I walked back into the room. Even his profile was sexy. The pyjamas were a little on the long side, but they were better than Carebears. I'd whipped my hair into what I hoped was a sexily messy bun to try and control the frizz fest. He turned, his eyes drinking me in. I felt like he was undressing me, just with his stare and I felt my skin flush all over.

"Are these of me?" He gestured to the pad in his hands.

I hadn't even noticed he was holding my sketches. I groaned, covering my eyes with my hands.

"That depends – if I say yes, will you be offended?" I never heard him move, but he was suddenly before me, pulling my hands away from my face.

"Why would I be offended? These are amazing." His voice was husky and deep, full of emotion. It stirred my insides. I felt embarrassed but I took the compliment.

"I don't usually sketch people – or headstones for that matter. I was having some pretty weird dreams is all." I was babbling, a serious case of verbal diarrhoea; I was aware of it, but I couldn't stop. Something flashed in Nate's eyes, but he didn't say anything, and I didn't question it.

"Come on, it's been a long day; into bed." I felt like I was being shepherded like a toddler, and like a toddler I wanted to stamp my feet and throw a tantrum. I didn't want to go to bed. I had Nate here, sleep was the last thing on my mind, but I could tell from one look, that arguing would be a lesson in futility, so I slipped beneath the cover silently. He laid beside me and I snuggled into his arms, my back to his front. He dropped soft kisses along my bare shoulder, fingering the thin strap of the pyjama top. I shivered and dug my fingers into the duvet. His lips traced their way to my ear.

"Goodnight Grace," he whispered. I laid thinking there was no way I was going to fall asleep, but the rhythmic movement of his chest along with the sound of his breathing was like a lullaby, and before I knew it, I was gone.

Thirty One

Where was I? It was cold and dark and there was a thick mist snaking its way around my bare feet. I tried to recall what I'd been doing before I had fallen asleep, glancing down and taking in the grey silk of my mother's pyjamas. I panicked, spinning around and looking for Nate, but he was nowhere to be seen. Had I been sleepwalking? No – I couldn't have. He would have woken and would never have let me leave the house. No, this had to be a dream – but everything felt so real. I reached out blindly and took a step, my hands finding cold, hard stone. Squinting through the fog, I tried to make something out, anything at all that might tell me where I was. Headstone – it was a headstone. So, I was in the cemetery. The darkness felt suffocating, like a blanket was covering the whole place.

"Grace?" I spun, the long silk of the trousers snagging on something I couldn't see. Goosebumps covered me from head to toe. I hadn't heard that voice since before the move and as it tinkled through the air, fear and dread filled me.

"Emily?" I whispered. She couldn't be here, she was – gone. I didn't want the nightmares again; I couldn't handle them, not now. But this felt different; it didn't feel like the nightmares, it didn't even feel like I was asleep, it felt like I was in total control. This was in my head, this was my imagination conjuring her up, and so she could be here – couldn't she?

"Grace, over here! We don't have much time and I need to speak to you." She sounded so far away and, in the darkness, through the dense fog, I had no idea how to find her. I jumped as something grazed past my ankle. Looking down, I frowned as I watched brown, crumpled leaves blow over my foot. Well – that was weird. I hadn't seen those for a while. What was going on? Something in the back of my subconscious registered, and I immediately knew where she would be; it still didn't help me though. It was incredibly difficult to decipher which way was up, never mind where the gnarled tree with the angel beneath it would be.

"Emily? I can't see!" I called helplessly.

"Follow my voice Grace – please, you need to hurry!" I closed my eyes, trying to trust my instincts and shuffled forward slowly. The gravel was cutting into my feet as I walked but I didn't care. I needed to find Emily. I stumbled, my eyes flying open just in time to stop me nosediving into a headstone. The fog was lessening, but shadows seemed to loom everywhere, rising above me and moving independently of the inanimate stones. It had to be a trick of the mist. I could just about make out the tree in the distance.

I started towards it, my only purpose to find her, to find Emily. My hair clung damply to my forehead as I pushed on. Finally, I saw her. She stood with her back to me, looking up at the magnificent marble angel that had haunted my dreams.

"Emily!" I called, running towards her. She turned to me and smiled, enveloping me in a hug.

"Grace, I don't have much time. There's something you need to know!" I clung to her, barely registering her words. I didn't want to let go. She smelt the same as ever, her citrus shampoo bringing tears to my eyes. She held me at arm's length. "You need to know – there are people coming for you Grace…"

"I know," I nodded. "I saw them today. Are they the ones that – that – took you?"

"That doesn't matter right now; you need to know that they will try to get to you again these men. You need to be careful who you trust, they aren't telling you everything you need to know, they aren't telling you about –" She paused, looking around her confused. "I have to go, I think – I have to go now."

"Wait! No Emily, please don't leave me again!" I tried to grab her hand but all I grasped was air. She was gone. I spun round in the dark, looking for her, listening intently. I heard – footsteps; heavy and fast, no way they were Emily's. Fear told me I needed to run, but it was too late. Forceful hands pushed me from behind, sending me flying to my knees. I cried as the gravel shredded my palms.

I tried to get up, but a boot between my shoulder blades, pushed me back to the ground. I was spun quickly onto my back and came face to face with one of my masked aggressors. I couldn't get past how black his eyes were, black and endless as the night sky. I tried to kick at him, tried to fight but he straddled my hips, pinning me to the floor. He was holding a silver knife and even behind the balaclava, I could see he was smiling.

Reaching up, I tried to remove his mask. If I was going to die in this weird, not quite asleep world, then I wanted to see my killer. I clawed at his face as aggressively as I could, but it was no use, he was stronger than me and swatted away my arm like it was nothing more than a *nuisance fly. I grabbed at his shirt, ripping the top button open. My eyes bulged as I took in the welted skin on his chest. It was a brand – burned into the skin, but what was it? It looked like – gates? It was the last thing I saw. He plunged the knife down, and I screamed.*

Thirty Two

I screamed and sat bolt upright in bed, my face stinging from the tears I must have shed in my sleep. The pyjamas clung to my drenched body and the duvet felt like it was suffocating me. I tried to kick it off, but it wouldn't budge.

"Shhh. It's ok, you were dreaming Grace." That voice – his voice. It was like balm on a burn, soothing me through to my very core. I buried my face in his shoulder and wrapped my arms around him. It felt reassuring and safe.

"No – it wasn't just a dream Nate. It felt too real," I whispered, digging my fingers into his shirt. My pulse steadily returned to normal and I sighed, laying back into the pillows and meeting his eye.

"Do you want to talk about it?" he asked, concerned, his fingers brushing a strand of hair behind my ear.

"Emily was there Nate. She was there and she felt so – real. It all felt real. It's like I can still smell her on me. She was trying to tell me something but then – then one of the men showed up. He had a knife and he – he was burned – I saw his chest and it had a brand on it. What do you think all that means?" I shook my head, knowing how crazy I sounded, although after everything I'd learnt in the past forty-eight hours, maybe it wasn't so crazy after all. Nate was quiet, guarded; like he knew something but whatever it was, he wasn't sharing.

It was light outside and I sighed, thankful because I

didn't want to go back to sleep. My head started pounding as I let the past two days sink in. Nate was still deep in thought as I turned to him. He looked so perfect lying next to me, how could he not be human? How could he be on the other side to Guardian Angels? That would make him a – I couldn't bring myself to even think it.

I would've thought it was some sick joke, that I was being Punked, if Nate didn't look so crushed by the whole thing. He was obviously telling the truth, but I was finding it hard to grasp the facts. I'd watched my fair share of horror movies and read the books to match, but that was all fiction. Except – what if it wasn't?

I thought back to the hours I'd spent in English Literature, learning about the French Philosopher, Albert Cadmus, for our final exam project. He'd said, 'Fiction is the lie, through which we tell the truth.' So, the truth was that anything was possible. Anything that anyone had ever written about, used to scare people, to get peoples adrenaline pumping from between the pages of their epic novels, could all have come from nuggets of truth. It could all exist out there. It was a terrifying thought. Almost as terrifying as the fact that there were men out there, that had me marked for some reason. I shuddered as a thought swam through my head, a question that I had asked but remained unanswered.

"Nate – those men – are they the ones responsible for Emily's death? Is this all linked somehow?" My voice broke as the stab of guilt pierced my chest, shooting right through my heart. My lovely Emily – taken. It should never have been her; it should have been me. It was always meant to be me and my earlier fears that they would find me and finish the job were now concrete.

"Grace, this isn't your fault. You didn't know, you still don't..." He trailed off. It was nice that he was trying to reassure me, but I knew that this was on me. For whatever reason, those men were after me, and if I had been a better friend then she would still be here, she would still be alive. I should have insisted she stay home when she told us about being followed – she was being followed.

"They were following me," I whispered, realisation dawning on me.

"What?" Nate said, looking at me cautiously.

"Emily told us she was being followed but she wasn't, was she? They were never following her; they were following me." I stiffened. We'd spent all our time together, practically joint at the hip. How could I have been so blind? So stupid?

"Grace..." Nate looked pained.

"What am I supposed to do? We moved to the other side of the country and they've found me again!" I was gripped by the panic, choking back down the bile that tried to force its way up my throat.

"I will protect you Grace. I promised you that and I don't intend to break any promise I make to you," he said seriously. I nuzzled into his neck, my heart still hammering, the panic still holding me within its reach. What if he couldn't always protect me? What if they once again came after the people I loved? He couldn't protect them all; my mother, Mia, Tyler – it was impossible.

"You can't protect everyone – no one protected Emily," I said quietly. Nate sighed, sitting me up.

"I am truly sorry about that Grace, really I am." He thought for a moment before speaking again. "Knowledge is power, and I think maybe it's time you held a little of that power." He watched me nervously and I held my breath. Was he going to explain a little more about himself, was I going to be fully immersed into his world? Was I going to learn why these men wanted to hunt me down? And was I going to learn how Nate knew anything about that? As all the questions ran through my head, I couldn't help but wonder if I would be able to handle all that information. It was already pretty surreal to think the man I loved wasn't the same as me – wasn't human.

"We need to go and see Mia," Nate said. What? I frowned at him, incredibly confused. What did Mia have to do with all of this? What would she know? After everything that had happened, I didn't want to put her at risk; she was already in danger just for knowing me. The thought sickened me to my stomach.

"No Nate! I already lost one friend to these crazy buffoons; I won't lose another!" He looked to me, the intensity in his eyes making me almost fearful.

"Grace, you need to trust me. I know it's a big ask right now, but if you want to know things, if you want – explanations – then we need to talk to Mia. You need to talk to her, you need to confide in her about – about me, about what I told you and we spoke about yesterday." It was like he was trying to tell me more than he was saying, like there was a hidden meaning behind his words. How could Mia know anything? She told me herself that she didn't even know Nate that well. Neither did I for that matter, but I trusted him implicitly, so what more could I do? I nodded bleakly.

"I need to shower first," I mumbled. I was even more confused and had even more questions, but I bottled them up. There was no point asking Nate; he was so cagey. It felt like he knew everything, he knew why the men were after me, he knew who the men were and yet he didn't want to share any of that info with me.

"Want company?" My jaw dropped at the huskiness in his tone and I cursed myself for once again letting the thought of him wipe all worries and doubt from my mind. I could see he was teasing, and it definitely took my mind off everything – mainly because my mind was now filled with images of Nate naked and wet.

"I, um, just – I'll be five minutes," I stammered, rushing to the bathroom. I was all over the place, struggling to contend with raging hormones, paralysing fear at the thought of being attacked and the confusion of not knowing what the hell was going on.

I took as little time as possible in the shower. Nate skated around my questions and avoided answering them properly which left me completely in the dark, but he had told me I needed to speak to Mia and perhaps she wouldn't be as tight lipped. He obviously knew something I didn't – a lot of things actually and perhaps she knew them too. Mia was my friend, she wouldn't be as intent on keeping me out of the loop, I was sure of it. The only thing bothering me; if Mia did know something, why hadn't she told me already?

Circles – my mind was running in massive circles like a poor hamster stuck on its stupid wheel. More and more questions came and went, flashing in and out as more and more things came to mind. It was frustrating, tiring and confusing and it was a state that I was becoming less and less fond of.

Nate was stood, once again looking out of my window when I came out of the shower, wrapped in nothing more than a flimsy towel. In my haste to get beneath the water, I hadn't taken any clothes with me. Being naked but for a towel was enough to send my stomach into a roll, but somehow, not having clothes around him seemed to be the least of my worries.

Nate turned and I froze. I didn't move just in case I exposed – anything. The muscle in his jaw was working on overdrive and I watched as he balled his hands into fists. His chest moved rapidly as his breathing quickened. I flushed at the effect I was having on him.

"I forgot my clothes," I said sheepishly.

"I can see that."

"Could you turn around for a second? Please?" He took a step forward and I swallowed – hard. Now really wasn't the time for any of that kind of stuff. He struggled for a moment, debating whether to listen to me or not, but he did as I asked and I breathed a sigh of relief. He closed his eyes and spun back to the window.

I fanned my face as I headed to my drawer, pulling out underwear and slipping it on beneath the towel. I chucked on a pair of jeans that were discarded on the floor and pulled out a t-shirt. It was possibly the quickest I had ever gotten dressed.

"Ok, I'm done." His hands were still balled into fists but at least his face seemed more relaxed as he turned back around. He walked towards me and pulled me into a passionate kiss, crushing his lips to mine, his hands knotting themselves into the back of my shirt. All his pent-up emotions came across in that one kiss. I was breathless when he finally pulled away and stepped back to look at me.

"Sorry," he gasped.

"Don't be." I ran my fingers over my lips and smiled. He groaned softly and shook his head.

"I'll take you to the library." It was a good idea. If we spent any more time alone in my bedroom, I dread to think what would happen. Even through all the madness, it was having an effect on us both. I thought about how we had ended up at my house and my stomach dropped. Was I travelling by – Nate? If I closed my eyes, I could still feel how tightly he had gripped me and how we'd just appeared at my door. Teleportation? Was that a real thing? Magic maybe? I wouldn't put anything past him.

"How?" I asked warily. Although the feeling hadn't been entirely awful, it had still been disconcerting and had left me shaken and breathless with legs akin to jelly. He gave me a dark, teasing smile.

"By car." He pointed out of the window to where his Jag sat. How had that gotten there? Could he teleport things as well as people? "I went and got it this morning while you were still sleeping." So – not teleportation then. God, I was an idiot.

"Nate, how did we get here yesterday?" I wasn't going to ask, but the memory of the sensation wouldn't leave me. All the mystery was messing with my mind and it felt like it was slowly killing me.

"I'll show you sometime," he said, the teasing smile still on his lips but a shadow of doubt crept into his eyes. Again, not a straight answer, but I was fast becoming used to it, as frustrating as it was.

My mind was so far away on the drive to the library. The dream that I'd had still niggled at the forefront of my mind; how Emily had felt so real, how I could still sort of smell her on me. Then there was the fact that I was pretty sure I was about to find out that both Mia and Nate had been keeping BIG secrets from me. I was terrified of what I was about to learn. I'd handled Nate's revelation well considering, but it was like a house of cards – one false move and the lot was going to come down around me.

I was still so deep in thought that I didn't even notice when we pulled up outside. The red brick building that I'd only yesterday been heading towards. My eyes darted around, looking for the bogey men who might leap out and try to get at me again. There were more people around, and none of them appeared to be wearing balaclavas, but it still didn't stop the waves of panic induced nausea.

"Don't worry Grace, I'm right here." Nate took my hand in his and it was only then that I noticed how much I was shaking. He saw and looked pained. I nodded, still unable to get out of the car.

"Nate, I'm, I, I don't know if – I don't – I'm terrified." It was little more than a whisper towards the end as I choked the words out. He leant across and kissed me softly. I sighed against his lips. He would keep me safe; if I kept telling myself that, then I could do this.

"Let me talk to her first," he said, before jumping out, running round to my side, taking my hand and helping me from the car. I pulled up my hood, trying to be as inconspicuous as possible. The way I was fidgeting and glancing around though, it probably only served to make me stand out more. We walked through the giant oak doors, through the looped detectors and into the heart of the library.

I scanned the rows, pulling Nate's hand as I weaved up and down the aisles. There was no way I was letting him go. He was my rock, my safety net; the only thing keeping me together at this moment. It could all change depending on what Mia had to say, but for now, he was my anchor.

Where was she? She was never usually this hard to find. There hadn't been a single visit to the library where I hadn't seen her smiling face, bobbing about with an armful of books. Something was nagging at the back of my mind, telling me that this felt off.

"Maybe it's her day off?" I said, but the way my skin prickled told me that wasn't the case. I couldn't explain it, I just knew something wasn't right; this was confirmed when Nate shook his head worriedly.

"She should be here," he murmured. He grabbed hold of a passing boy and I recognised him straight away. He worked alongside Mia at the library, he was the one that had argued with a customer over late fees. He looked scared as he stood before Nate, and he had every right to. Nate's face reminded me of when he had shown up at the clearing and Dan had had his hands on me. He was fierce and intimidating.

"Where's Mia?" he growled at the boy.

"I – I – I don't know. She didn't show this morning, her parents called me in to cover." I inhaled sharply. That wasn't like Mia at all. Something was wrong, something was very wrong. Nate let go of the boy and turned to me. My eyes stung as images of Mia being attacked, flooded my mind.

"Call her," he said softly. He was trying to keep it together, for my sake no doubt, but he couldn't hide his fear from me. He was worried too, and that was never good. I felt woozy and sick – this wasn't right. I pulled my phone from my pocket and dialled.

"This is Mia. I'm obviously super busy right now so

leave a message and I will call you back – probably."

"Answerphone," I said helplessly. "What's going on Nate? I want to know – right now!"

"Not here. Let's go." He grabbed my hand and pulled me outside. I felt like a ragdoll being dragged along behind him. My legs were shaking, and my breath was short. He practically shoved me into the car and jumped behind the wheel, not bothering to put on his seatbelt before pulling out.

"Where are we going?" I asked, my voice sounding feeble. I was fast learning that I wasn't very good in a crisis and I hated it. I felt weak and powerless. Every time I blinked, I had visions of Mia being held down by the men in the masks. I felt sick.

"To see Dan," he replied firmly. I looked at him agog. What? Was he for real?

"What the hell Nate?" I cried. My voice sounded too loud in the confined space of the car, but I couldn't help it. Mia was missing, quite probably because of me, and we were driving towards someone else who wanted to hurt me? How did it make one iota of sense? "Why the hell are we going to see Dan?"

"Because he can help." I was reeling. I didn't want help from him! I would have been happy to make it through the rest of my life without ever seeing him again. I was pretty sure he was just one more person on the list of people who meant to do me harm, and there was no getting past that fact. Nate might be able to push it all aside, but I didn't know if I could. I thought of Mia and sighed. I had to – I had to if I wanted to know where Mia was, if I wanted a chance at finding her safe.

"Nate, what are you not telling me?" I asked. With Mia

missing, and her phone off, my patience was wearing thin and all I wanted were some answers.

"Plenty of things!" he shouted. I jumped, stung by his sudden change in tone. He'd never shouted at me before, never even lost his temper. Even with Dan, even on the bridge when he had been at his angriest, he'd been fairly calm. I glared out of the window, crossing my arms across my chest. His change reminded me too much of Dan, of our failed date, of the way he had changed. I was scared.

"Don't do that Grace." His voice wavered, once again soft and tinged with regret.

"Do what?" I snapped.

"Don't cross your arms, don't shut me out." I turned and stared at him, gob smacked.

"Shut you out? Are you kidding me? You don't want me to shut you out, but it's perfectly fine for you to shut me out all the damn time, is that it?" I sounded hysterical, and if I'd been in Nate's shoes, I would have stopped the car and kicked me to the curb. I slid a look sideways. He didn't look angry, he just looked – defeated.

"Grace, I know it sounds paltry right now, but I am sorry. If I promise to tell you everything after we find Mia, will you just trust me right now?" I chewed the inside of my cheek, thinking over his words. Other than never telling me anything I wanted to know, he hadn't actually given me reason to distrust him; he had in fact saved me a couple of times – even saved my life. What choice did I have, really?

"Everything?" I clarified. I watched the corner of his mouth twitch into the hint of a smile. He reached across for my hand, interlacing his fingers with mine.

"Everything."

Thirty Three

I felt sick as I walked through the door of Dan and Nate's house. There were fresh flowers in the vases, and the place smelt the same as the last time I'd been here, just like the beginnings of spring. The first time I'd walked through those doors, I'd been apprehensive, worried about whether I would fit in and make friends, whether I would be liked. Now as I walked in, I was apprehensive for entirely different reasons.

I didn't want to see Dan again, I was petrified. He'd developed some weird vendetta against me, but if he could help us find Mia, then I didn't have much choice but to see him again.

Nate squeezed my fingers encouragingly, but as he walked into the lounge, I cowered behind him like the wimp I knew I was. He'd made a promise to protect me and I knew from the way he had saved me in the clearing that it even extended to his own brother – I could only be thankful for that. Dan was sprawled out in front of the TV. He smiled lazily when he saw us, his eyes taking me in and instantly taking on an edge.

"Well, isn't this a nice surprise? I told you I would be seeing you again Grace. Granted, I didn't think you would just walk on through MY door." I shivered, every hair on my body on end. He looked at me the way a lion does its prey, as it stalks it through the long, savannah grass.

"Dan, cut the bullshit and drop your agenda for a minute.

Mia is missing," Nate growled at his brother, his teeth clenched. Dan's face changed in a nanosecond, and he looked to Nate like I was no longer there. For an instant I felt relieved, but then his reaction sunk in, and I felt worse. If both of them were so worried about the fact Mia was missing, then it was deadly serious.

"What do you mean she's missing? Isn't she at the library?" he said, jumping up from the sofa, his hands on his hips.

"Oh, good one Dan! Why didn't we think of that Nate? Of course, she must be at the library!" I rolled my eyes. "Idiot," I mumbled. Nate barely hid the smile that teased at the corners of his mouth, but Dan gave me a look that instantly dispelled any bravado I'd had.

"What about with Tyler?" Dan asked. Nate shrugged and I watched as Dan pulled out his phone and dialed. Holding my breath, I crossed my fingers and prayed they were together somewhere, perhaps playing hooky to spend some quality time together, rather than the alternative of her being hurt by ruthless killers somewhere where I would never find her. He listened for a second and cursed, his eyes turning worriedly to us. My heart sank, all hope lost.

"Grace, can you give us a second?" Nate asked, turning to me. I arched my brow at him. Was he serious? Mia was missing, possibly even Tyler; probably taken by masked men who were after me, he'd brought me to his brother who, for reasons unknown, hated my guts and wanted to see me suffer and he was asking me to leave so they could have a private little powwow? I rolled my eyes and stomped from the room. This was stupid! It was idiotic! Why was he still so hell bent on keeping secrets from me? How the hell could Dan help us, and why would he even want to?

The door closed behind me and I glared at it, before remembering that the lounge also led to the kitchen. I tiptoed through the hall as quietly as I could, elated to find they hadn't shut the door. I pressed my back to the wall, ensuring I stayed out of sight and listened to their voices. They were low, but I could just about make them out.

"Does she know?"

"Not everything?"

"So, you haven't told her?"

"No – but I will."

"Nate, Nate, Nate – what a naughty boy you've been! Does she know what we are?"

"Not – exactly." Dan laughed, that hideously creepy laugh that had echoed around me during our last encounter. His voice cut through me like a knife when he next spoke, my skin crawling.

"Do you think she will still like you so much, when she knows the truth?"

"I don't – I don't know." Nate faltered and my chest throbbed for him. I wanted to barge in there and shout that nothing would change my feelings for him, it didn't matter what he told me, I would always love him, but I couldn't. I had to stay quiet.

"But that's not what's important right now Dan."

"No, you're right. Do you think they have Mia?"

"And probably Tyler too by the looks of things. It must be them."

"But why would they take a Keeper? What are they up to?"

"It might not be because of that; they could just be using

her to get to Grace."

"But how do they even know her and Grace are friends?"

"They've been watching her Dan. They attacked her yesterday, on the bridge near the library. In broad daylight no less. I – I only just got there in time." Nate sounded cut up.

"Oh shit, is she ok? Seriously? They've gone too far now. Though this confirms a few suspicions of my own." Dan's voice had completely changed. It was almost back to how it had been in the beginning, when we had first met. He was quiet, concerned even. Why was he suddenly so concerned over me?

"What do you mean, what suspicions?"

"The day I took her to the Craft Fayre, she said she'd seen someone in the trees. I knew someone was there, I saw them myself, but never dreamed it would be them. I should have taken it more seriously." I frowned, completely confused. What the hell were they talking about right now? What was a Keeper? And who were 'they'? My heart was racing faster than a stallion trying to win its first race.

I didn't have a clue what was going on, but one thing I did know was that someone had my friends, someone who wanted me. An idea popped into my head. It was probably a stupid idea and not a very well thought out idea, but I didn't care, I didn't give it a second thought. I tiptoed from the kitchen and headed for the front door. If they wanted me, they could have me. There was no way I was letting anyone else die in my place, the way Emily had. This ended – now.

I ran down the driveway as fast as I could. It wouldn't be long before Nate and Dan figured out I was no longer in the house, which only gave me a short amount of time to get away and try and find Mia and Tyler. Where could they be? I could head to the cemetery and see if the men found me there? The muscles in my legs began to burn as I dipped into the trees. It was a ten-minute drive back to the village, which meant at least a half an hour walk, if not more, and that was presuming I could even find my way back without getting completely lost.

I stumbled, falling flat into a puddle, cursing as I realised my coat was unzipped. Ice cold, dirty water seeped into my t-shirt and I was caked in mud. I instantly began shivering. What a joke. What had I been thinking? I was nothing more than a helpless mess who didn't know what she was doing. I was desperate to help my friends, but I was next to useless. My immaturity was showing. As I sat in the freezing mud, I choked back tears, feeling utterly deflated.

The stupidity of my plan hit me in the face, and I felt crushed. I couldn't possibly find my way to Mia alone, I'd never paid enough attention to the route we took to Dan and Nate's house, but the thought of going back to them, with my tail between my legs, made me want to retch.

I sat in the puddle, shaking my head at myself and thinking of Nate, of all the confusing things he had said. I just wanted someone to tell me what was happening, tell me what was going on and what sort of mess I was wrapped up in. What was it that he and Dan had been talking about? What was he so worried about me discovering? He had found it hard to tell me he wasn't human, but I had accepted it without question, so what made him think he needed to shelter me now?

"Grace?"

"How the hell do you do that?" I groaned, swiping angrily at my tears. I didn't even want to look at him, especially as his voice was so warm and was filled with such tenderness. I was an idiot, nothing more than a silly little girl, and now Nate knew it too. It was all too much to bear. I rested my head on my arms and sobbed, the tears uncontrollable as they rushed down my face.

"Oh Grace." He lifted me into his arms, and I couldn't even put up a fight. I felt completely sapped of energy. What was I going to do? I couldn't live through losing Mia. Losing Emily had been more than enough for an entire lifetime; I couldn't lose another person I cared about. He carried me back to the house, and it was pitiful how far I had gotten. I could have laughed hysterically at myself, but I couldn't even muster enough energy for that.

"Are you crazy?" Dan shouted when we walked back through the door. "There are people out there trying to kill you, they probably have Mia and Tyler, and you decide to go running off? Are you insane? You don't know what's at risk!" Anger radiated from him, but I didn't care. I laid my head on Nate's shoulder.

"Dan, leave it," he said in a low voice. It was a warning.

"No – I will not leave it! The last thing we need is for her to be taken too!" I'd heard just about enough, his voice grinding on my last nerve. I lifted my head and looked at Dan, a swell of anger filling my chest.

"What the hell do you care if they take me? They'd probably be doing you a favour wouldn't they?" I spat at him. He faltered, his face changing. His eyes shone and I saw the old Dan, the Dan that I'd liked.

"Of course I care Grace," he said quietly, reaching out,

but then he seemed to think better of it. "You don't know what you're talking about." For the first time ever, I saw a vulnerability in him, one similar to what I sometimes saw in Nate's eyes and I wavered, taken aback by it.

Nate pushed past him and carried me up the stairs, ridding me of my chance to question it. They were both hiding something from me, something that I intended to find out – in time.

The house looked entirely different in the light of day. I noticed for the first time that all the framed pieces of art that adorned the walls, were paintings of all different shapes and sizes, yet they all seemed to have one thing in common – they all depicted heaven or hell. I chose not to look too closely into what significance that might have.

He pushed the door to his room wide open, closing it with his foot and setting me back on my feet. I looked down at my soaked shirt, feeling pathetic. He pushed my coat back from my shoulders, letting it fall to the floor. I froze as his hands found the hem of my shirt. His fingers grazed my bare skin and I gasped, inhaling sharply. A fiery heat spread through me as his hands ran up over my ribs and he lifted it right over my head. I swallowed. He reached into the drawer where I'd first taken one of his shirts, and pulled one free, pulling it down and covering me once more. He exhaled heavily and pulled me into his arms.

"That was quite possibly one of the hardest things I've ever had to do," he whispered. I bit the inside of my cheek, feeling guilty for how distracted I'd gotten by his hands, how easily I'd forgotten that Mia was missing. "You should try and get some rest."

"No way Nate, we need to find Mia and Tyler. They

could be…" I didn't want to think about what might be happening to them. I really meant it, I wanted to find them, but there was hardly any fight left in my voice.

"They aren't going to hurt them Grace, it isn't them they want. Dan is going out to look for them now." He brushed the hair from my face. "We will find them." I nodded. I was feeling exhausted, and in the state I was in, I was no good to Mia or Tyler anyway.

I laid on Nate's bed, the intoxicating scent taking me back to the first time I'd seen him, the way he'd been sat next to me so nonchalantly looking through a travel book. It felt like eons ago and as I looked at him now, I felt my heart swell. I couldn't have been more thankful for meeting him. He moved towards the door.

"Wait!" I called, stopping him in his tracks. "Will you stay with me? For a while? I don't want to be alone." He looked towards the door, obviously torn between going out and hunting with Dan, or staying with me, but eventually he nodded, coming back to lie beside me on top of the covers. His hard, muscled stomach peeked out from underneath his shirt and I shuffled closer, running my fingers lightly over his skin. He was holding his breath.

"Will you still tell me everything when we find Mia?" I asked quietly. There was obviously a lot of things I needed to know, if I made it through the day. If the opportunity to give myself up for Mia and Tyler arose, then I would do it in a heartbeat. I didn't want to think about how much that would hurt Nate. It would be the right thing to do, to keep everyone safe. I looked up to him through my lashes and saw a shadow of worry flit through his eyes.

"I promised I would." He didn't sound happy about it.

He was quiet and sad. I hated to see him this way.

"It won't change how I feel about you, you know," I said gently. I pressed my palm flat against his stomach and he inhaled sharply.

"You don't know that," he breathed. "You know next to nothing." He wouldn't meet my eye again, but I shook my head.

"It doesn't matter Nate. You can't change what's in here." I ran my hand up under his shirt, resting it over his heart. He tilted my chin up, his eyes full of desire. I parted my lips and sighed softly. It was all the invitation he needed. His lips tasted sweet as they touched mine, the kiss soft and gentle at first. His hand slipped beneath the shirt he had just pulled over my head, resting on my ribs. Heat spread through me like wildfire as I arched my back. His kiss became more urgent, his teeth catching my bottom lip teasingly. I crooked my leg over his hip and pulled him closer. He moaned, the sound primal and sexy.

"Hope I'm not interrupting anything." Dan's voice was like having a bucket of iced water thrown over me. He was back to his old self again, all concern from before, gone. Nate closed his eyes in frustration and rested his head against mine.

"What do you want Dan?" he said, subdued.

"We need to talk."

"Did you find them?" I asked, pulling away from Nate and sitting up. I didn't know how he possibly could have in such a short time, but I was ever hopeful.

"Does it look like I found them?" I scowled at him and he smirked right back at me. "No Grace, I didn't find them, but I think I know a way to."

Thirty Four

"So, let me get this straight," said Nate, rubbing the bridge of his nose. He sounded exasperated. "You want Grace to call Mia's phone, leave a message, and then wait for a reply?"

"Exactly!" I covered my mouth with my hand, but I couldn't help it; a snort of laughter burst from me. Nate cocked a brow at me, and Dan's eyes glinted with amusement too. He was far too excited by his stupid idea and the whole thing just seemed – laughable.

"Sorry," I muttered.

"No need to apologise Grace, I know you think my idea is awesome." I shook my head and my lip curled involuntarily at his slimy tone. I didn't even care that he saw. I was sat on the sofa, and as the debate continued into whether it was a good idea, I watched them closely. They were stood together and for the first time, I noticed just how different they were.

Nate had gorgeous green eyes, hair as black as night that curled around his ears and had a certain wildness to it. He was broad shouldered and hid well-toned muscles beneath his black attire. One look at him and you knew he was strong, but not in a scary way. He was warm and drew you in with his easy demeanour.

Dan on the other hand had eyes of blue topaz; light in colour yet they held a darkness to them that often scared me. His hair was mousy brown and slick, and he was tall and willowy, slight. All the warm, welcoming aura he'd given off when I first met him was near enough gone – save for a few, individual moments – and now he made me want to run very fast and very far in the opposite direction.

It was as I looked between them that I was struck by the connotations of what Nate had told me about himself. If he wasn't human, wasn't mortal, then that would mean –

"Oh my god! You aren't human, either are you?" I asked in surprise. I met Dan's eyes and he smiled.

"Soooo," he said slowly, dragging the word out. "Is that all he told you about us? That we aren't human? That's precious."

"You didn't answer my question." I gave him a stony glare, but it only seemed to serve as encouragement. I got the impression that Dan was sly and calculating, and his sarcastic nature got my back up, but he also scared the crap out of me. It was an unbelievable difference to how he had made me feel when we first met.

"No, I'm not human Grace, I'm a…"

"Enough!" Nate shouted. He glowered at Dan, a warning in his eyes. "Leave it be."

Dan smiled an evil smile and shrugged. Nate's knuckles were white and even though I hated seeing him so angry and I hated seeing the pain in his eyes that he got whenever he thought I might discover something about him, I couldn't help but wish Dan had finished his sentence. Whatever it was that they were, it was something that Dan revelled in and Nate thought would drive me away.

"So, about my plan," Dan said finally. I rolled my eyes.

"I'll call her, but it's not going to work." I pulled my phone out and was once again greeted by Mia's voicemail.

"This is Grace. I know you have my friends. Call back if you want to make arrangements." I hung up feeling cold and stupid. What made Dan think they would be listening to her voicemail? It was an idiotic idea.

"Let's get comfy, we might be waiting a while," Dan said, sliding onto the sofa next to me. I looked him dead in the eye, bolstered by the fact that Nate was standing a few feet away and I knew he could move fast if he needed to.

"Get. Away. From. Me." My teeth were clenched together as I addressed him, spitting each word out. It was more to stop them chattering with the fear I didn't want him to see, than any real anger. I tried to keep my voice from wavering. It was difficult, because the more I looked at him, the more I could see the old Dan, the one who had been nice and kind to me; plus, I knew he was still in there because he'd been concerned this morning when I'd overheard his and Nate's conversation, and then again when Nate had brought me back inside from my little escape attempt. One evil grin though, was all it took to go back to him scaring the bejeesus out of me. He was sat so close – too close.

"Now, now Grace. Let's have some manners. This is my home you're in after all."

"It isn't just yours. You think you're so slick, don't you?" I said, shaking my head and trying to stay calm. "I'm not afraid of you Dan." He laughed, leaning in close so his face was only inches from me. His blue eyes sparkled and held mine intensely.

"Yes, you are. I can smell it on you, and when all this is over, you and I have some unfinished business." I glanced over towards Nate, but Dan's hushed voice brought my eyes back to his. "He won't always be around to protect you, you know." He reached out towards me. I could feel his hand coming but I was powerless to stop it. I couldn't move; every part of me was screaming to stand up, to get away from him but I was held in place, unable to break free.

"Knock it off Dan," Nate growled. Nate – I blinked, feeling dazed. I looked from one to the other. What had just happened? Nate was fuming and Dan was smirking.

"I'm just having a little fun. Nothing wrong with some harmless…" My phone rang, silencing Dan midsentence. Seeing the caller ID, I looked to Nate, my jaw dropping.

"It's Mia," I said faintly. I could hardly believe the stupid plan had worked.

"Well, probably not, but they will hopefully lead us to her and Tyler," Dan said. "Put it on speaker." I accepted the call, doing as he'd asked. My hands shook uncontrollably.

"Hello?" I said, trying to sound confident, like I wasn't completely terrified that one wrong move might put my friends in even more danger.

"We have them, your so-called friends. Come alone and do not fight, and we will let them go unharmed." The voice, it sent chills down my spine. I recognised it as one of the men who had attacked me on the bridge; his gravelly tone was hard to forget.

"How do I know you're telling the truth? How do I know you haven't already hurt them?" I looked between Nate and Dan desperately, and they both nodded, Nate giving me a thumbs up. So, I'd done something right then, it was good to know. There was a muffled sound, a grunt and then a whimper. A lump formed in my throat.

"Grace?"

"Mia!" I cried. "Are you ok?"

"Peachy," she croaked, her voice sounding hoarse. How long had these monsters had them?

"Is Tyler with you?"

"Yea, but he's out cold. Listen Grace, don't you dare..."

"There, now you know she is alive." I ground my teeth together, shaking with anger. How dare this man take my friends? How dare he threaten them!

"If you hurt a single hair on their heads, I swear I will..."

"Your friends won't be harmed, as long as you come – alone. If you do not come, we will kill them both and then we will come for you anyway. We'll text the location." I blinked, listening mutely to the dial tone before my phone cut it off.

"You were getting a little feisty there Grace – I liked it." I glared at Dan.

"Why don't you just shut your fat mouth!" I snapped, all the anger from the call coursing through me. Nate laughed loudly and I threw him a glare too, just for good measure. He coughed and looked at the floor, but I could still see the ghost of a smile on his lips. They'd just threatened Mia's life, threatened Tyler's! This was no time for laughter.

"You did really well there Grace," Nate said softly. "Your quick thinking showed us that Mia is ok, and Tyler too. Now we just need the location." My phone beeped.

"All Saints Church?" I read out; my brow furrowed. Both Dan and Nate groaned.

"How – unoriginal," Dan sneered.

"They've got to be under the church, there's a huge basement," Nate muttered, wrapped up in his own thoughts.

"Wait a minute," I blurted. "Is this the church in the cemetery by my house?"

"Yes," Nate confirmed. "We should have guessed really, if they've been watching you from there and you felt like you were being followed, but I thought they might have been a little more creative." My mind started racing, first over the fact that I couldn't recall ever telling Nate that I thought I was being followed, and secondly, because they were so close to my home. How long had they been there? Had it really taken them such a short time to find where we'd moved to?

It certainly explained my unease whenever I walked through the cemetery; the feeling of being watched, the dark figures and sinister noises. It all made so much sense now. Something plagued me though; they'd been so close this whole time, why hadn't they taken me out on one of the many occasions I'd been alone?

"We need a plan, there will be a few of them."

"There were four on the bridge."

"Ok, so at least four."

I zoned out, no longer listening. I knew what I needed to do. The instructions had been implicit, and I wasn't going to ignore them and put Mia and Tyler at risk. Come alone, they'd said; so that was what I would do.

"Just nipping to the toilet," I mumbled to no one in particular. Nate looked at me, but I couldn't meet his eye. He knew me too well, would be able to read me. He would know what I was about to do, and he would try and stop me. He turned back to Dan and they continued formulating their plans that no doubt, I wouldn't be a part of. I wasn't going to get caught out this time. I retrieved my coat, peeled back my phone case and thanked my lucky stars that I'd still got my emergency twenty-pound note hidden there. Loading up a taxi app, I ordered one, leaving a note for them to stop at the bottom of the drive before the black gate. I might not be able to run back to the village, but I could get a lift.

I slipped as quietly as I could out of the front door once more, this time determined to get to Mia and Tyler alone. I needed to save them, even though I knew that it would mean a trade of my life, for theirs. I still had no idea why these men wanted me, but I sure as hell knew no one else would die in place.

I ran down the drive, keeping my mind distracted, not thinking of either of the boys, concentrating solely on Mia and Tyler. The taxi was waiting for me when I got to the bottom of the winding driveway.

"Where to, love?" the man asked, as I clambered into the back seat.

"All Saints Church please." He nodded, pulling away from the curb. I couldn't even look back as we set off towards the village.

I ran through a million scenarios in my mind on the way, but not in any single one of them did I make it out alive. Dan had said there would be a few of them, at least four if my previous attack was anything to go by. A tear slid down my cheek as I thought of my mother. She'd already lost so much by moving us, and she'd moved to keep me safe. Well, it hadn't worked. Whatever the reason was that I was being hunted, something that I was still struggling with because as far as I was concerned, I wasn't anybody special, it was big enough that as soon as they'd realised their mistake with Emily, they'd promptly found me.

I swiped at my cheeks, trying to clear my mind of the ones I would leave behind. It seemed unfair that I'd just met Nate and now I wouldn't ever get the chance to tell him how much I liked him, how much I loved him. Mia and Tyler too, I would never get to tell them how much their friendship meant to me, even in the short time I'd known them.

We pulled up outside the church and I pulled out the twenty, handing it over to the driver.

"Wait love, this is too much," he called as I jumped out.

"Keep it," I said. I wasn't going to need it anymore. The sky was turning a deep, inky blue, the night threatening to fall. The church loomed before me, large and imposing against the backdrop of headstones.

I didn't waste any time, pushing my way through the heavy doors. The smell of burning incense, stung the inside of my nostrils. Candles flickered all around, lighting up the stained-glass windows and it was deathly silent. I couldn't see anyone; the pews were empty.

My footsteps echoed loudly around the large gables, robbing me of any element of surprise. Not that an element of surprise was going to help me against the men that I knew were holding my friends. I didn't think there was anything in the world that would help me against them, but I wasn't looking for help; I just wanted to get my friends out alive and well.

Nate had mentioned a basement, but having never been inside the church itself, I didn't have a clue where to start looking for it. I chewed the inside of my cheek nervously, my heart beating so fast I was surprised it didn't give out on me. Slowly, I made my way towards the altar. I could see a small door to the right of it, that I assumed would lead to back rooms and possibly the entrance to the basement.

I was parallel to the altar when the door slammed behind me. I yelped; the sound magnified in the too quiet church. Turning sharply, I came face to face with one of the men in the masks.

"Did you come alone?" he asked, his voice chilling me to the bone.

"Yes." I tried to sound strong, but it was no use, I was nothing more than a petrified seventeen-year-old girl.

"Good," he snarled, before everything went black.

Thirty Five

"Grace – Grace, you need to wake up right now!" Someone was whispering urgently in my ear. I didn't want to wake up; I'd been having a lovely dream. I was at a picnic and Nate was there. He'd brought all the posh food again and then Dan showed up, but he was smiling and warm, then Mia had shown up. She had sat down and held Dan's hand, which was weird, but everyone was so happy and joyful. I didn't want to wake up – and yet, I knew I had to.

I forced my eyes open quickly and cried with delight as I looked into the hazel eyes that I'd been so worried I would never see again.

"Mia!" I sat up quickly, regretting it the instant I moved. I reached behind my head and winced as my fingers ran over a lump. It was very tender and sore, and my hair felt matted and damp. As I pulled my hand away, I gulped at the sight of drying blood.

"Grace, are you mad? You shouldn't have come. They're going to kill you!" I shook my head, trying not to whimper at the pain it elicited.

"I know."

"You know? What do you mean, you know?" she asked surprised.

"I know Mia. I came to save you and Tyler. Where is he?"

"I'm here," he croaked from behind me. I'd never been

more thankful to see him. It was clear he had tried to put up a fight, his split lip bringing forth a tsunami of guilt. "What's going on?"

"They said they would let you both go if I came alone – so, why are you still here?" I looked around, trying to gather my bearings. It was dimly lit, and everything was caked in a thick layer of dust. The walls were brick and the roof low. There was a cold draft blowing around me and the floor was packed dirt. There were no windows, just one door. The last thing I remembered, was being stood in the church, facing one of the masked men. I couldn't tell whether that's where we still were; there was nothing distinguishing about the room at all.

"Well – they didn't. I hardly think these are the kind of men that keep their word Grace. Seriously, you shouldn't have come, what were you thinking? This is so much bigger than us." I looked at her confused. She had a purple bruise across her cheek and her skin was pale. Her eyes looked tired.

"How did they – when did they get to you?" My mind was fuzzy, and my head was hurting badly, but there was something bothering me. Why wasn't I dead yet? I'd handed myself to them, practically served myself up on a silver platter – what were they waiting for? They hadn't waited with Emily; they took her out in a dirty alleyway. Something didn't feel right.

"We were coming out of the library. It was dark, I didn't even see them coming. I think they drugged us," Mia said, shaking her head.

"They definitely drugged us. I feel hung-over, like I had a few pints of Dan's punch," Tyler said, rubbing his head. Dan – god, he and Nate would be furious, and they would probably hate me for what I'd done. I wasn't sure how long I'd been out, but they must have discovered I'd gone by now. My eyes filled with tears as I looked at them both, feeling completely hopeless.

"Did they – did they – do anything – to you I mean?" My mind was running over stories in the news of terrorist cells, taking people and brain washing them, of human trafficking rings that kidnapped people and sold them like property, of cults that had taken people for human sacrifices. Chills ran through me – that had to be it. That had to be why I was being hunted. I'd been selected by some crazy cult leader as a sacrifice. I couldn't think of another reason that a band of merry freaking men would be chasing me down and taking my friends.

"No Grace. I'm not going to lie and say they were nice, offered us a cup of tea and a chitchat, because they didn't, but they haven't actually hurt either of us." I looked from Tyler's split lip to the bruise on her cheek and arched an eyebrow. "Well, apart from that," she mumbled.

"Oh Mia, I'm so sorry," I said, pulling her into my arms.

"How did you know I was missing anyway?"

"We came to look for you in the library. Those men attacked me and I thought I was going to die but then Nate saved me and we were talking and he told me some things and then he told me I needed to talk to you but you weren't there and so I called you and your phone was off so…" I didn't take a breath, most words running into one until Mia interrupted me, her eyes narrowed.

"Wait – Nate sent you to see me?" She watched me with a serious expression on her face.

"Yes, he told me – well – he told me something and then said I should talk to you." Nate had told me to speak to

Mia, but he hadn't mentioned Tyler, so I was reluctant to say any more in front of him. If Nate had some sort of secret identity, then I wasn't going to be the one that blabber-mouthed it around. Mia tilted her head, thinking something over.

"How much did he tell you?" she asked. I blew my cheeks out in a sigh.

"Not a lot to be honest. Not that it matters now anyway. I should have just let them have me on the bridge, I didn't know they would come for you. I don't even know why they're coming for me." She interrupted me again.

"Grace, there's something I need to tell you, something that you need to know. I haven't been entirely honest with you." I blinked at her. What did she mean? How had she not been entirely honest with me? I knew there was something they were all hiding from me obviously, that was why Nate had been taking me to see her in the first place, but the look on her face told me it was something big and my stomach churned at the thoughts of what it could be. I looked to Tyler, he was suddenly sat up too, listening intently.

"Go on," I encouraged, though my heart was racing. Was I ready for this? Was I ready to know whatever it was that they all knew? Could I handle it?

"When I told you I didn't really know Nate – it was a bit of a lie." I narrowed my eyes at her. She'd known Nate all along. But she'd been so convincing! The whole 'Nate is an enigma' thing had sounded so genuine. My mind went into overdrive.

"Wait – are you the complication?" I asked, my voice breaking. Mia looked confused.

"I don't know what you mean."

"Are you and Nate together Mia? Is that why he keeps running away from me, pulling back and telling me it's complicated?" She laughed loudly, making me jump.

"No! Not at all, we aren't together. You know I'm with Tyler. But I do know Nate, have done all my life and – and I know what the complication is." I furrowed my brow and looked at Tyler. He looked as confused as I felt. We were both so out of the loop, but surely, I'd misheard. How could she know about the complication, yet Nate couldn't tell me?

"So – what is it?" I asked. Mia scratched her ear, glancing between myself and Tyler, suddenly looking nervous.

"I'll tell you Grace, but you might not like it."

"I want to know," I said firmly.

"Ok, well, you're not quite who you think you are – you're actually very special." I snorted, shaking my head. What on earth was she talking about? She continued. "Do you know anything about your fa-" The door swung open, cutting her off.

"On your feet – all of you." I looked into the cold, black eyes of the three masked men and all thoughts of what Mia had been about to tell me were forced from my mind.

"Let them go!" I said, stepping in front of my friends. "I kept my word, now you keep yours."

"We will. Your end is nigh girl, then they will go free." I didn't want to think about my end, it threatened to send me into a hysterical panic attack, and I didn't want to show these beasts any more weakness than was necessary. One of them grabbed me roughly by the arm and I let loose a whimper as his fingers dug into my skin, the other two grabbing Mia and Tyler and dragging them along behind.

I blinked, my head pounding as he led us down a dark corridor. There were no windows here either, and I realised Nate must have been right, we were underground. It was very claustrophobic, and I felt every breath as I dragged them past my lips, letting them go shakily. At the end of the corridor were small, narrow stone stairs leading upwards.

The stairs opened up into the church and I sighed, my lungs no longer feeling like the walls were closing in to crush them. We were behind the altar. There was a carpet pushed to one side and a heavy wooden door laid open from the floor. I looked around. There were six masked men. Any hope I had of escaping dissipated and I felt beaten. We stopped before what looked like a sacrificial table. There was a red cloth laid out on it, with what looked like painted runes on rocks. I looked at it in horror. I was right – I couldn't believe I was right, but I was! I was going to be sacrificed, I just didn't have a clue why! Being right was no comfort though, if anything it amped my fear up to a barely controllable level.

"Is this right?" The man who was holding me turned to Mia. She looked behind her, then looked back to him with a look of pure confusion on her face. I glanced at Tyler, but he just shrugged. I was glad I wasn't the only one that knew absolutely nothing.

"Are you talking to me?" she asked in surprise.   I couldn't help but smile, even though my heart was racing, the panic threatening to overwhelm me.

"Yes you – is this right?" He gestured to the table. Mia looked at me, pure bafflement on her face.

"How should I know?" Hysteria must have been setting in, because I found this hilarious and I could feel a giggle bubbling up from my stomach. I tried to squash it back down; it would be completely inappropriate to laugh out loud around a bunch of murderers.

"You are one of them, a Keeper are you not? It is in your bloodline – you should know, you should know everything." Something niggled in the back of my mind, and then it hit me. I knew where I had heard that before. When Dan and Nate had been talking, they had questioned why the men would take a Keeper. I looked to Mia bewildered. She gave me an apologetic shrug and looked worriedly at Tyler. She turned to the man and bit her bottom lip.

"Well, this is awkward, you see – they don't know what you're talking about. I haven't quite got around to filling them in," Mia said, smiling sweetly.

"Silence! I have no concern for whether they know about you and what you are. Now tell me – is this right?" She stared at the man and glanced over the table. A look washed over her pretty features; I recognised that look – she was scheming.

"No – this isn't right. There should be..." She looked around the church. "The fleece of a new-born lamb, and – and – a golden orb that has been blessed. And you're missing the pillow." The men were stood stock still, listening intently to every word she said. Mia's eyes were full of amusement. I bit my lip hard, trying not to laugh. She was stalling – it was a dangerous line to walk and I worried for her. I wasn't sure what she was stalling for, it wasn't like we were going to get out anytime soon, but I appreciated it all the same.

"The pillow?" The man was obviously confused, which only heightened my hysteria.

"Yes," she said seriously. "You do not have the crocheted pillow of holiness." It was a step too far, and the man finally realised what she was doing.

"You think this is a joke? You think this is something to laugh about?"

"Well," Mia shrugged. "I thought I was pretty funny."

"You are lying. You are taunting us. How dare you. That was not a good idea," he growled. He dropped my arm and before I could react, he stepped towards Mia, slapping her across the face with the back of his hand. She flew through the air with the force of the hit, laying in a crumpled heap on the floor."

"No!" Tyler and I screamed simultaneously. I tried to run to her, but the man caught me around the waist and lifted me into the air. I kicked, punched and scratched at him, screaming as loudly as I could. How dare he! How could he do this? They'd promised to let my friends go; they'd promised they wouldn't get hurt!

His hand came down on my mouth; his rough fingers making me gag. My vision blurred as tears filled my eyes, but I wasn't going to give up, not without a fight. I bit into his hand as hard as I could and he shouted in anger, releasing my mouth but still holding me tight to him.

"Grab the Keeper," he shouted roughly. Two of the men grabbed Mia, dragging her forward by her arms. Her head slumped forward like a doll; her eyes still closed. I sobbed, cold dread filling me. What were they doing? She looked so helpless and small in their big, brutish hands. I couldn't even tell if she was breathing.

"Time to teach you a lesson girl," he whispered into my ear.

The fear squeezed my lungs, making it almost impossible

to breath. I shook my head. This wasn't the plan; this wasn't the deal – Mia and Tyler were supposed to be safe; they were supposed to have let them go! This couldn't be happening. I was scared and I was angry and most of all, I was heartbroken. I hadn't wanted this; I'd only meant to save my friends.

If only I'd stayed with Nate and Dan, perhaps all this would be different. Perhaps they would have been able to save us all; if only I'd relied on them, had trusted that they would come up with a plan. Instead, I'd acted irrationally and gotten us into even more trouble. Nate had a knack of showing up, just when I needed him and I wished with all my heart that he would find us, that he would swoop in and save us like a hero – my hero.

My heart shattered as I thought of Nate. I was never going to see him again, never going to look into those beautiful eyes, never going to run my fingers through those wild, black curls ever again, never feel the heat spread through me at his slightest touch. I was glad we'd met, however briefly, because he'd shown me what it was like to love someone, truly with all my heart and soul, love someone.

"Kill her," he ordered.

"NO!" I screamed. My eyes burned with tears and I fought as hard as I could; I couldn't let them do this! I would not lose another friend to these despicable excuses for human beings. Tyler struggled against his captor too, trying to get to Mia. The two men who were holding her up looked at one another briefly, before turning back to the monster by my side. They looked uncomfortable.

"We cannot kill a Keeper; you know the rules. We will not break the rules." I had no idea what they were talking about, what rules it was that they had to follow, but I was grateful that Mia was one of these so-called Keepers – whatever it was, it meant she would be safe, that they couldn't hurt her. I let my breath go in relief. The man dug his fingers deeper into my skin and grunted in annoyance.

"Fine then – kill the other."

"NO!" I yelled again. "Don't you dare touch him! You promised, YOU PROMISED! Let him GO!" I felt sick. Tyler wasn't a Keeper, he was just my friend, just my sweet friend as Emily had been, and I knew without a shadow of a doubt they were going to hurt him.

"Wait, what? No man, what the hell!" Tyler kicked as they dragged him forward. I felt a hand come down on my mouth once more and I could do nothing but watch as Tyler struggled, my shouting and screaming ceased. I was shaking my head, trying to free myself. No, I couldn't let them; they couldn't hurt him, not Tyler! They couldn't do this; they'd said they would let him go! I needed to save him; they couldn't do this to me again. I kicked and fought as much as I could, but it was useless. I was no match for the man in the mask.

I stared in horror as one of the men pulled a silver blade from inside his jacket. It was a blade that I'd seen before – in my dreams. I felt dizzy and faint, and I couldn't breathe as the man's arms gripped me like a vice. I knew what was coming, I'd seen it and I'd seen this knife. My eyes widened, panic bubbling to the surface. Everything seemed to happen in slow motion.

I saw the look of horror on Tyler's face; I could see the fear in his eyes as tears slipped down his cheeks. He knew what was coming too, and we were both powerless to stop it. I screamed against the man's hand as I watched the knife come down through the air slowly, retching at the sound it made as it passed through Tyler's ribcage, straight into his heart. His eyes widened, then they went dark, the gorgeous light, his happy life snuffed out like a mere candle flame.

I bit down hard, as hard as I could until I tasted blood and I screamed, my eyes streaming with tears. It was a sound like no other I'd ever produced, something deep and shocking. My heart was shattered, and my lungs were trapped beneath the weight of the guilt that flooded through me. It was so difficult to breathe. I'd watched them take the life of my friend, and it was all too much, it was too much to take. They needed to pay, I needed to make them pay! How dare they go back on their word! How dare they take the life of someone so special.

I shook with violent anger I'd never experience before. I felt white hot fury igniting my insides, beginning at my core and burning through every fibre of my being, a powerful hatred that seemed to build within me to a devastating crescendo, until I could take no more.

"ARGHHHHHH!" I screamed, closing my eyes as a pain ripped through me, a force exploding from every part of my body. I fell to my knees, heaving as the pain crippled me. My nose was bleeding, and my eyes were streaming as I opened them, panting, struggling to get my breath. I gasped, panic driving through me once more. I shrieked and whipped my head around, unable to believe what I was seeing. The church was on fire!

Mia was laid a few feet away from me, Tyler's body was a few feet from her and there was no sign of any of the men. I dragged myself over to Tyler, pain radiating through every bone, nausea sweeping through me as I took in his blood-soaked shirt. I pressed on the wound, calling his name between sobs, but it was too late, he was gone.

This was wrong, it was all wrong! I gagged and coughed, smoke filling my lungs. What had happened? The flames were instantly out of control. Had I done this? But how on earth could I? I didn't have time to think about that. I needed to try and get Mia out while I still could, while I was still conscious. I looked down at Tyler.

"I'm so sorry," I cried, my heart breaking all over again as I took his hand in mine. "I'm so sorry I couldn't save you Tyler. Please forgive me." I closed his eyes gently, laying a kiss upon his forehead before going to Mia.

"Wake up! Mia, you have to wake up!" I shook her furiously, unable to control the cries that poured out of me, ripping through my chest. It was no use; she was still out cold. I choked, my chest burning as I breathed in the toxic air around me. Flinging Mia's arm over my shoulder, I tried to lift her, but I couldn't. My body was wracked with pain, my strength all but gone. I was just too weak.

"I'm so sorry Mia. I'm so, so sorry Mia. It's all my fault, this is all my fault." I cried, my tears stinging my skin as I laid beside her, pulling her into my arms and waiting for the fire to take us.

Thirty Six

As I opened my eyes I blinked, lifting my hand to shield them. It was so – bright. Where was I? What had I been doing? My head throbbed and my lungs felt like they were full of soot. I smelt smoke – the fire! The church! Oh god – Tyler. I sobbed. We didn't make it; we couldn't have made it out; no one came to save us. Me, Mia and Tyler, all taken out by those sick, twisted beings. But where were they now? I rubbed my eyes, trying to accustom myself to the light.

"Hello Grace." I spun quickly.

"Emily!" I cried, running to her. "Have you come to take me with you?" She tilted her head, looking confused.

"Take you with me – where?"

"To wherever you go now – to – heaven?" She gave me a sad smile and shook her head.

"No Grace honey, not even in the slightest. You're dreaming." Dreaming? Really? So, that had to mean I was still alive somewhere, right?

"Where are we then? Why is it so bright?" She shrugged her shoulders, smiling.

"This is your dream Grace, well," she pursed her lips thinking, like she was almost about to say something else but then she just grinned. "Anyway, it's not me. You're in the driving seat here." I looked around, blinking to try and clear the light, to focus. I groaned as shapes started to form. Headstones – the cemetery.

"I've had just about enough of this place."

"Yes, I imagine you have. Anyone would be a tad fed up by now if they were in your situation. Hey, there's someone who wants to see you. I brought them, I thought it might help." What did she mean? This was a dream – how could she have brought someone? I turned back to her baffled. She was sat upon the plinth of the headstone that I now knew so well, looking up at the giant marble angel.

"Grace?" That voice. I instantly crumpled to the ground. It sent shockwaves of pain through me. I looked up, unable to control the sobs that began in my chest and burst out as I looked into the chocolate brown eyes of Tyler. It was so incredibly raw. I felt like I'd been sliced open from head to toe and someone was rubbing salt into the wound.

"I must be in heaven if you're here," I choked. "I'm so sorry Tyler. I am so, so sorry. I tried, I wanted to get free, I tried to save you! I wanted to give my life for yours and they – they – they said they would let you go! It should have been me." Tyler rushed forward, dropping to his knees and pulling me into his arms.

"Hey, shush now. It's ok. I'm ok Grace. Emily has explained a few things, she'll look out for me. She seems – nice. I don't want you to blame yourself at all, this wasn't you. Promise me, promise me you won't blame yourself."

"Yes, it was," I cried, soaking the shoulder of his shirt. "If you'd never met me, we wouldn't be having this conversation, you'd still be alive and fine and-"

"If I'd never met you, I would still have been mooning around over Mia, not having the balls to ask her out. Our time may have been cut short Grace, but it was incredible.

I will cherish it and I wouldn't change it for the world. So, don't you dare blame yourself, you hear? And – and I need you to do me a favour."

"Anything," I blubbed. How could I deny him a single thing, in this weird dream world, or any other? He'd died in my place, just like Emily. Two friends I'd now had snatched from me, lost to reasons and explanations that I knew nothing about. The pain in my chest was becoming unbearable.

"Mia is going to have a hard time coming to terms with this, and I need you to help her. I need you to look out for her. Dan too." I looked at him with a furrowed brow, confusion etched onto my face. He smiled. "He might act the macho alpha male, but he isn't, and this is going to hurt him too. Mia has been friends with him so long, he's known her much longer than I have, so I need them to repair their relationship. Can you do that?"

"I – I'll try," I whispered.

"And Grace, you need to know, you are so much stronger than you know, than you believe. You need to lend them your strength. They're going to need you." I nodded, tears blurring my vision. I didn't feel strong, in fact, I felt completely helpless and weak. I was really struggling with the fact that I'd now lost two friends and for what? Tyler smiled, kissed my forehead and then stood. He gave me a small nod before walking off into the light. I wanted to run after him, wanted to keep him with me, take him back to Mia. I didn't want to lose him all over again. Emily's citrusy scent blew to me on the slight breeze and my chest constricted further.

"Why are you here?" I asked, wiping at my eyes. It was a lesson in futility because the tears kept on flowing.

"I was hoping you would ask." She jumped down from the plinth and came and knelt in front of me, taking my hands in hers. "I shouldn't be here. If anyone found out – if they knew – well, let's just say I would be in trouble, but I had to come and warn you. They will come for you again. They will keep coming for you until they either succeed or you reach eighteen. For now, you have some time, a little respite to recuperate. They're regrouping. You took them by surprise Grace, they didn't account for any – complications." She smiled at me; the same way Mia did whenever she said something cryptic.

"Emily, I don't understand, please, you have to help me. How do you know all this? How can you even be here talking to me like this, telling me things?" She squeezed my hands, a single tear running down her cheek.

"Grace, listen to me carefully now. I shouldn't be here; I don't have a lot of time, but I had to tell you."

"Tell me what?"

"Things aren't always as they seem – don't go jumping to the wrong conclusions." I shook my head. All the talking in riddles made my brain hurt. I didn't have a clue what she was saying, I was completely befuddled.

"The wrong conclusions about what?" She dropped my hands and stood, turning her back and wandering in the same direction that Tyler had. Before she completely disappeared into the light, she threw a knowing look over her shoulder and said, "About you."

Thirty Seven

"Grace – Grace, please wake up, please. Don't leave me." The pain in his voice was evident as it broke, but I didn't want to open my eyes. I didn't want to lose the smell of Emily or the warmth of Tyler. All that waited for me if I opened my eyes was a world of pain and regret, of guilt and anger. Here, in my dream world, I had conversations with my dead friends like everything was ok – here, in this half-conscious state, I could almost imagine that none of it had happened. My chest hurt immeasurably – like someone had ripped it open, torn out my heart and stamped on it.

I'd closed myself off for so long that I realised I'd never properly grieved for Emily and now – well, now I had to grieve for two of my friends, two of my friends that had been brutally murdered in my place. If I stayed asleep, perhaps I wouldn't have to deal with the reality of that.

"Grace, please wake up, I can't lose you – I need you." That voice; how could I possibly ignore that voice. It was so soft; it made me warm and happy and yet, it was so full of sadness. There was only one person that could take that sadness away – me. I needed to wake up.

"Nate?" I croaked. My voice was hoarse, my throat swollen like I'd swallowed a million razor blades.

"Oh, thank you, thank goodness." I felt his lips come down on my forehead. I opened my eyes slowly. They felt itchy and heavy, like they were full of soot. Where was I? I smelt like smoke, but I was laid on something soft and familiar. I rubbed the blurriness away, blinking as I realised, I was in my room.

"How did I get in here?" I coughed and it stung. My lungs had taken a serious battering.

"I brought you here." I nodded slowly, not wanting to look into his face. What had I done? I'd been so stupid. I sat up, looking down at my hands in my lap. Big mistake. A sob caught in my throat as I held my hands in front of me, hardly able to stop them from shaking. They were covered in Tyler's dried blood. Tremors wracked my body, pain shooting through every part of me, both physical and emotional. "Oh my god, oh god, what did I do? What did I do?"

"Grace, you didn't…"

"Don't lie to me!" I screamed at Nate, finally meeting his eye. He looked devastated. All I ever did was cause people pain. I rocked back and forth, unable to control the screams that escaped me. Black lights kept dancing into my field of vision, threatening to take me back to the dark abyss of unconsciousness.

Nate scooped me up, carrying me through to the bathroom. He turned the taps on, taking my hands and forcing them beneath the running water. I couldn't watch. I closed my eyes and cried as he lathered up my hands, washing away all signs of Tyler from my fingers.

"I'm so sorry you had to go through that Grace, but it was not your fault," he whispered against my ear as he dried my hands.

"Where's Mia? Did you, did you get to her too?" I asked, my voice quiet and hardly recognisable as my own.

"Yes, Dan got Mia out of there. She's in your room." I

looked up at him for a brief moment, before pushing past him. Once again, I'd been so wrapped up in myself, I hadn't even noticed that she was mere feet away from me. I was a horrible person. I was scared Mia would hate me, but she couldn't hate me any more than I hated myself, so I had to see her.

She was sat on my window seat, weeping silently, her knees pulled up to her chest. She turned to me and my heart broke all over again. The flow of hot salty tears worsened as it slipped through the ash on my face. I'd been so stupid and reckless; I'd acted immaturely, and it had cost the life of someone we both cared about. She stood and walked to me; I wasn't sure if she was going to slap me or hug me, but then she pulled me into her arms and pulled me down onto the bed. We sat and cried together. The pain rippled through me as flashes of the night slipped into my mind. Tyler – how could they do that to him? I felt sick as I relived the moment over and over in my head.

"I'm so sorry Mia," I sobbed. This was all my fault. It could all have been avoided if I had stayed away from everyone. I'd chosen to make friends again, but it had cost someone their life. I should have known better, should have known to stay away from everyone and save them the heartache. Tyler would still be here if it weren't for me. She shook her head, her chest heaving from uncontrollable sobs.

"This wasn't your fault. You didn't kill him – they did," she spat. I looked to Nate as he came and sat beside the bed. His eyes were glassy, and his face was wet. He'd been crying too and though I hated seeing him this way, I knew it would only get worse – because I wanted some answers.

"Who are they?" I asked. It was time I knew the truth, time I got to the bottom of who these monsters were that had killed my friends and why. That was what I needed to know most of all – why?

"They're Guardians," Nate said quietly. I could have cried anew. He was answering me, and not in his usual censored way either. He was finally trusting me, trusting that whatever he told me, I could handle it. I took a deep breath, processing his words, letting them sink in and waiting for my mind to formulate a response.

"But I thought Guardian Angels were good?" I asked. Nate shook his head.

"They aren't Guardian Angels Grace. They're Guardians, they're something entirely different," he said, sounding disgusted. Mia turned back to the window but continued to hold my hand. She was crushed and it was slowly killing me, ripping me apart. I just wanted to take her pain away, but I couldn't do that. I turned back to Nate, trying to focus on what he had said and what answers I wanted, the reasons behind all of this. I knew it was going to take a while to sink in and it would take some understanding, but I needed to try.

"I don't get it," I said, shaking my head. He took a deep breath and took my free hand in his.

"All angels value life Grace, especially Guardian Angels. You could even say that's what keeps them alive, what keeps their existence going. It's the very reason they're here at all." I furrowed my brow, still struggling to understand. It felt like I was stuck in a maths class with a complicated equation.

"But I thought – isn't that what they do? They come for

you at death, right?" It was a hard and surreal conversation to be having, not only because of the confusion but because every time Nate spoke, Mia squeezed my hand and with every squeeze, I could feel her pain. It was excruciating.

"They don't take a life – they never would. It would be immoral for them to do so. They collect souls and they escort them to the afterlife. Guardians however are entirely different. They're a society of mortals that have existed for millennia. They were created to do the dirty work that Heaven won't sully its hands with." He sounded angry and resentful. "They have a free pass for what comes after which means they're capable of despicable things."

I couldn't bend my mind around it all. That certainly wasn't something they taught you at Sunday School. It was hard to digest. Heaven was real, not only real but they had a band of mercenary humans to do their bidding? Why the hell would they even need that?

I thought of Tyler, of lovely Tyler who wouldn't harm a fly, of the way one of the masked men had ordered his execution and it had been carried out without so much as a second thought, without a hint of remorse. I felt sick.

"Ok, but what does all this have to do with me?" I asked meekly. All this talk of angels and heaven, it was difficult to swallow, but even more so because I had no clue what it all had to do with me. Why were they being sent after me?

"Because you're the one Grace," Mia said softly. She squeezed my hand again and I could see the tears still rolling freely down her face.

"The one what?" I was suddenly terrified of knowing. I

could see the smoke-filled sky outside my window and my body still ached from the pain that had coursed through me before my anger had erupted and the church had gone up in flames. Had I done that? Had that really been me? Nate was watching me closely; his face was a picture of concern and fear.

"It's difficult to explain," Mia murmured. "To understand all of it, you have to go back to the beginning."

"The beginning of what?" My hysteria was steadily on the rise, creeping into my voice. I wasn't sure how much more I could take. It was all too much. I ached from head to foot, my head felt like it was splitting in two, my heart was shattered, and I was slowly finding out that I wasn't who I thought I was, my life wasn't what it seemed, and I hadn't had a clue about any of it.

"Creation," Nate mumbled. He didn't meet my eye, instead looking at my hand in his. Creation? What did he mean Creation? As in the creation of the earth? The whole seven days spiel? It was seriously threatening to overwhelm me. My brain couldn't function anymore, it was on the verge of a breakdown. I needed time to process it all, I needed time to come to terms with what I'd witnessed, what I'd just done. I'd watched as the life of my friend was snatched away right before me and I was fairly sure I'd levelled a church.

I laid down on the bed, once again feeling weak and helpless. Tyler had said I was strong, but he was wrong, he didn't know all of this – did he? He said Emily had filled him in, but then how would she know? I squeezed my eyes shut tight, wanting to forget it all. It hurt to think about it. The events of the day had left me traumatised and all I wanted to do was shut the world out. Mia laid down too, wrapped her arms around me and hugged me tight. I felt her whole body shake as she cried silently into my pillows. Nate was pale and he looked drained, but he gave me a small smile.

"I'm not going anywhere Grace. Get some rest." I refused to let go of his hand as I let the day wash over me, and I cried myself to sleep.

Thirty Eight

Please let it have been a dream, please let it all have been a nasty nightmare. Over and over again I said it to myself, but it was no use. The pain that still radiated through me and the smell of smoke that clung to every inch of my body told me that it had all been very real.

I opened my eyes, trying to rub away the blurriness. My room was still dark, which meant I hadn't been asleep for more than a couple of hours. I rolled over and found that I was in Nate's arms. He stirred as I moved, opening his eyes to look at me. They were bloodshot and tired, exactly how I imagined mine looked.

"Where's Mia?" I whispered, squinting around the room. She'd been crying into my pillow when we'd fallen asleep, now she was nowhere to be seen. I felt a small stab of panic.

"She went home. She wanted to shower and clean up before she headed over to see Tyler's parents." He looked sombre and the ache in my chest returned as all the grief and pain weighed me down once more.

"She must hate me – I would hate me," I whispered. I really would in her position. If Nate died at the hands of someone else because they wanted to get to Mia, I wouldn't know how to cope, how to get past that.

"She doesn't hate you at all," he said, brushing my hair from my forehead. "Grace, there is a lot you need to know to be able to understand everything, things that Mia knows, that make her understand better…" I stopped him before he could go any further. I didn't want to listen, wasn't yet ready to know. I felt too fragile, like a china cup teetering on the edge – one false move and I would irreparably break. I was struggling to keep it together, struggling to deal with the loss of Tyler, which had opened me up to the loss of Emily and the whole thing made me feel like I was wading through a thick swamp of pain and regret that was pulling me deeper and deeper in.

"Nate, I think I need – I need some time – to myself." The shock and pain that shot through his stormy eyes almost made me falter.

"Grace, please, I can explain, I…" he said, his voice breaking. I shook my head and laid my hand on his chest.

"It's not that Nate, it's not about that. It's not you, or who or what you are. I just need some time to come to terms with this, with everything that's happened. Just – just give me some time and then we can talk, and you can – you can fill me in on the rest." I pulled my hand away and looked down at them, where they laid upon the cover because I knew if I looked into his eyes any longer, then my resolve would vanish and I would give in to him and – I just couldn't do that, not right now.

"Are you sure this is what you want?" His voice was choked and was barely more than a whisper.

"Nate, this isn't forever, it isn't goodbye. This isn't the end of us, of you and me. Please don't think that. Just – give me time." I chanced a look at him; his eyes swam with tears, but he nodded, giving me a small, sad smile.

"Ok, give me a call – when you're ready." He stood, leaning down and placing a soft kiss upon my forehead before leaving. He didn't look back.

I rolled over, the bed suddenly feeling too big and too cold. I began to shiver uncontrollably, and then the tears came. Big fat tears that seemed never ending. I was glad Nate had left because it wasn't a pretty sight. It wasn't like in the movies where a woman cries delicately into a tissue and single tears roll elegantly down her face. No, this was full on wailing, my nose running as much as my eyes, my cheeks red and swollen and my eyes puffy.

I needed to shower. I needed to get the stink of fire and death off me. The house felt so cold and empty, but I was glad, I was glad my mother wasn't around. I felt absolutely sick to my stomach at the thought of having to ask her about who I was because, well – she must know. I couldn't for one second believe that she was oblivious to the whole thing and that thought terrified me, because if she knew and she'd been keeping it from me, it meant she could have saved them, she could have stopped my friends from getting hurt.

I walked into the bathroom and turned the heat up on the shower until it was nearly unbearable. It was what I needed; I needed to feel something other than the crushing pain and overwhelming guilt. Climbing under the spray, I let myself go, opening myself up to it all; Emily, Tyler, to a world that I didn't feel that I belonged in anymore and I welcomed the tears as they once again rained down my face, mingling with the hot water.

I stood there under the spray until my skin was red raw. I just wanted to feel something, anything other than heartache, but it was no good. It was going to take a lot more than a hot shower to wash away all the guilt and the hurt and the – the confusion.

I no longer wanted to think about what Mia and Nate had

told me about the Guardians. Nor did I want to start thinking about who I was, why I was 'the one' or how I managed to set an entire church on fire. It was too much, too raw and I could feel myself slowly descending into a sinkhole of depression that I wasn't sure I would ever climb out of.

I needed to do the same as I'd done when we'd moved. I needed to bottle it all up, compartmentalise it for now, until my mind was healed, until it was ready to really take it all in. I shut the water off, shaking my mind clear. Wrapping myself in a towel, I barely made it back to the bed before collapsing into it. Curling into a foetal position, I closed my eyes and prayed I could sleep until the pain lessened – IF it lessened.

Thirty Nine

I studied my reflection in the mirror. My skin was pale but no longer sallow, the purple bruises that had darkened my eyes were nearly completely gone and my hair no longer looked like I spent my days down in a coal mine. The cut on the back of my head had healed rather quickly and the bruises that had covered me from head to toe were all gone. On the outside, I was healed, but the inside was a different story. It had been a rough ten days.

Nate had kept his word. He'd given me time and space – just like I'd asked him to. I'd been tempted on several occasions to call him, but something always held me back, something that told me I wasn't quite ready – to see him or to receive any more of an explanation.

Mia had been texting regularly, each time asking whether I was ok and every time she did, I was wracked with guilt. What did it matter if I was ok? Emily wasn't ok, Tyler wasn't ok, and neither was she. It didn't matter what they said, no matter how many times they told me that it wasn't my fault, I knew better. I'd spent ten days trying to overcome the sea of guilt, trying to escape the undertow that threatened to pull me beneath the waves and drown me, ten days of seeing no one. No one – except my mother.

News of Tyler's death had spread through the village, whispered about in dark corners and deserted streets. The papers had reported it as a tragic accident. The way they told it, some faulty wiring and a candle were to blame;

causing a fire that had spread rapidly and violently as the whole church had basically been a tinderbox. Tyler had been the unfortunate victim of a freak accident. No one else was mentioned, no other names being reported. The police weren't investigating as the death was not claimed to be suspicious.

As soon as she had heard, my mother had asked me whether I was ok. She'd met Tyler once before; she knew we were friends. I'd responded that we'd been close, and it was a bit of a shock. I'd never lied to my mother, not really, but it was the only thing I could do. She was worried enough about the fact that I'd now lost two friends, if she found that I'd lost Tyler to the same monsters that attacked Emily, then we would move somewhere new and she would lock me up. That wasn't something I could let happen.

I'd tried on a few occasions to pluck up the courage to ask her about how much she knew, because deep down, a big part of me knew that she had to know something. She acted like she was completely in the dark, but there was no feasible way she could be. How could she not know that there were people after her daughter? How could she not know that it all had something to do with heaven and creation? How could she not know who I was? But I'd chickened out every time. I couldn't bring myself to tell her that I'd been there, that I'd come face to face with Emily and Tyler's killers, I couldn't tell her what really transpired in the church because I was utterly terrified of what I would find out.

I took one last deep breath before making my way downstairs. My mother was sat in the kitchen, she had a cup of hot coffee waiting for me, but I didn't touch it. It smelt appealing, but I hadn't been able to stomach much more than water and the occasional slice of toast since the fire. I knew she was worried, but I couldn't bring myself to care too much.

"Are you sure you don't want me to come with you?" she asked, but I shook my head.

"No. I want to go alone thank you." My voice sounded alien to my own ears. It was monotone and lacking any sort of feeling. She eyed me warily, but I ignored her. I grabbed my cardigan from one of the stools and offered her a small smile. "I don't know what time I'll be back." She didn't argue, she just watched me leave, concern etched into every line of her face.

As I slipped out the front door, I sighed. The sun was out, and it was warm on my face. There was no wind and there wasn't a single cloud in the sky. It was a beautiful day, yet I pulled my cardigan tight around me. There was a deep-seated cold that had settled into my bones the morning after the fire, and I hadn't yet been able to shake it.

There were lots of cars around as I pushed my way through the creaky old gate. People were milling between the stones, making their way slowly towards a portable cabin. That's what the church had been reduced to – a portable cabin. There'd been talk it would take three months to rebuild, restore and fix the damage the fire had caused to the church and until then, Sunday Mass, Sunday School, christenings, weddings and even funerals were being held in the cabin.

I kept my arms crossed tight over my chest and my eyes trained on the floor before me. There were faces I recognised from my jaunts in the library, but I didn't actually know anyone. I was fine with that. The less people I knew, the less people I had to lose.

I entered the cabin and was immediately hit by the smell of flowers. To say it was little more than a glorified tin box, they'd done a very good job of making the inside pretty, with wooden pews and an altar, just like in the proper church. I shuddered involuntarily as I glanced towards the altar.

It didn't take long for the whole place to be full. All the seats were taken, and people were stood shoulder to shoulder along all the sides. I stuck myself in a corner, glanced around and saw Dan. My chest hurt as a fracture line appeared across my fragile heart. He was leant against the wall, tears falling from his clear blue eyes and part of me wanted to go him, to draw him into a tight hug and tell him he wasn't alone, but I couldn't do that. Part of me was glad he was lost in his grief. If he didn't hate me before, he most certainly would now. His best friend was gone – because of me. I knew he would be angry, would be furious that I'd left and gone to the church without them. If I hadn't been so stupid, perhaps we wouldn't be stood in a cabin, mourning the loss of Tyler. I stepped back, hoping to blend into the walls. It didn't feel right for me to be anywhere near his funeral, but I wasn't going to miss it, no matter how much guilt I felt.

Music started and I watched as the coffin was carried in by six men in suits. A man and a woman with cocoa skin the same shade as Tyler's, walked into the cabin behind them. Between them was a mousy haired girl. They were all clutching each other's hands for dear life, like they might not make it if they didn't. Mia. My eyes began to prickle with tears as I watched her walk down the aisle, clinging to the parents of her first boyfriend that she had so tragically lost – because of me.

Everyone was devastated by the loss of Tyler, but the ceremony was stunning, a true representation of the happy go lucky character he had been. He couldn't have had a better send off. Tears slid silently down my face the whole time. I saw Mia glance around a few times, and I knew, I could feel it in my heart, she was looking for me. It made me feel sick to think of how bad a friend I had been, how selfish. I'd not kept my promise to Tyler, but I had every intention of rectifying that, once I knew everything I wanted to know.

His parents invited everyone over to their house afterwards in a celebration of his life, but I couldn't face it. I couldn't go and make small talk with all the people who had loved him so dearly, knowing that I'd been the cause of his death, knowing I was the reason he was no longer with us, that he would still be here if not for the unfortunate event of meeting me. Plus, there was something else I needed to do.

So, instead of following the crowd, I wandered through the cemetery until I found the angel headstone. I didn't know how, but I knew Nate would know I was looking for him and I knew he would know where to find me. After ten days, I finally felt ready. It was time to face the music.

I sat on the plinth, just as Emily had in my weird, almost too real to be imagined, dream. I lifted my face to the sun, closing my eyes against the bright light and enjoying the warmth. I'd been dreading Tyler's funeral since Mia had text me the details. This was the second funeral of a good friend I'd attended in the space of a year. It was heart wrenching, but now that it was over, I could feel a sort of calm descending over me. After ten days, after setting Tyler to rest, I finally felt I could handle whatever truths were about to come my way.

"Grace?" I opened my eyes and sighed. I'd missed that voice, and I'd missed that face and until he was stood before me, I hadn't realised just how much. Nate looked at me with his beautiful green eyes and I smiled sadly. He looked how I felt – grief-stricken, tired and hollow. His normally clean-shaven face had a shadow of stubble and he had a general unkempt air about him. He didn't move and I knew he was trying to gauge me, trying to gauge how I was doing. I jumped down from the plinth and walked right into his arms.

"I missed you," I whispered against his chest. A lump formed in my throat, but my eyes were finally dry. I didn't feel like I had any tears left to cry. He squeezed me tight, like he was fearful I might run off.

"I missed you too, hell I missed you so damn much Grace." His voice cracked as he spoke. "Mia wouldn't let me see you, she said I needed to give you your time and space. It damn near killed me." I breathed him in, his familiar spicy scent like aspirin, healing some of the pain I still felt.

"Thank you for understanding," I said softly, looking up into his gorgeous face.

Witnessing Tyler's life being taken, seeing it ripped away before my eyes, had shattered my heart and being around Mia and Nate, especially after the things they had told me, had just served as a reminder that if not for me, he would still be alive. Now though, as his arms enveloped me, I felt like the pieces were coming back together and he was the glue.

"I have questions," I said, burying my face into his chest again, absorbing his warmth and drinking in his strength.

"And I will answer them all," he replied softly. "Shall we go to yours?" I thought about it for a moment but shook my head. My mother was at home and I didn't want her listening at the door. Similarly, I didn't want to go to Nate's house on the off-chance Dan had done the same as me and skipped the memorial, instead going straight home. Staying in the cemetery wasn't a good idea and the library was out. The questions I had weren't for the public's ears.

"I have an idea," Nate murmured softly. He took my hand and led me to his car.

Forty

Nate kept his fingers interlaced with mine as he drove out of the village and I didn't protest. I felt the need to cling to him just as much as he did to me. The buildings fell away to woods, and the woods fell away to fields, the fields opening to hills and moors filled with sheep. It was then that I realised where we were going. Before long we parked at the bottom of the hill we had picnicked on and a sense of peace washed over me. I turned and smiled at him, his eyes glinting as he smiled back.

The sun beat down as we made our way up the hill. Nate still had my hand in his and I wondered whether he was as scared as me of letting go. I'd thought about him every single day and it had been physically painful to stay away from him, but I'd still been trying to process everything, trying to deal with the fact that heaven was sending men to kill me, and I was 'the one' whatever the hell that meant. It had taken some time, but I'd finally gotten to the point where I could accept the things I'd so far been told, and I was ready to learn more of the truth about myself.

He helped me hop up onto a small rock and then we entered the cave. Nate swung his backpack, that he'd insisted on grabbing from the boot, from his shoulder and dropped it to the rock. He pulled out the picnic blankets and a pile of sticks of various sizes. I watched as he deftly built what looked like a tiny tepee.

"If I do something, do you promise you won't get

freaked out and run away?" He looked anxious. I wasn't sure there was anything left in the world that could possibly freak me out, but I nodded. Sitting down beside him on the blanket, I placed my hand on his knee encouragingly. One thing I had come to terms with in the ten days since the fire, was that I knew truly little about the world around me and things that had seemed the stuff of fantasy and fairy-tale, were actually very real. I wasn't sure much could shock me anymore; I'd mentally prepared myself for everything I had yet to learn.

He gave me another sidelong glance before turning to the sticks. I watched curiously as he held his hands before them, rubbing his thumb and forefingers together until suddenly, a sound like a match being struck echoed around the cave and the sticks were on fire. I froze, wide eyed, my heart beginning to race. I blinked, barely able to believe my own eyes. Nate had just created fire – something I was pretty sure I had done in the church but on a much bigger and much scarier scale. Could that mean?

"I'm like you," I gasped. I looked into his eyes, the reflection of the flames dancing amongst the green.

"Sort of," he conceded, a small smile playing on his lips. I pulled him until we were sat opposite each other cross legged, our knees touching. I held his hands and chewed the inside of my cheek, a million questions racing through my mind. This was crazy! I gulped before speaking, needing reassurance from him.

"I need you to promise you will answer all my questions Nate, no more holding back, ok?" He nodded, his eyes never leaving mine. "And in turn, I promise I won't run, I won't freak out and I won't leave you."

"Sounds like a fair deal. I promise." He smiled, before looking at me a little sadly. "I shouldn't have left you in the dark for so long Grace. I should have realised when I started having feelings for you – I should have told you then." I smiled, my belly firing up the way it always did around Nate. It was good to know the guilt and the pain hadn't stripped me of everything.

"That doesn't matter, as long as you're honest and tell me now." I watched his face for any signs he might be withholding, but he was an open book.

"Go ahead," he said softly. I nibbled my lip, thinking through all the things I wanted to know, trying to decide what was important and what was just morbid curiosity.

"What am I? Am I immortal like you?" My voice squeaked towards the end and I cursed myself. It was a purely selfish question and one that shouldn't have bothered me, but it did. If Nate was going to be around forever, then I wanted to be around with him. Well, as long as we could get past the fact that heaven had some sort of vendetta against me and wanted me dead of course.

"Yes – you are immortal, and as to what you are…" He trailed off, his face contorting as he thought about how to answer.

"You promised," I reminded him, squeezing his hands. He couldn't hold out on me now. This was it; I was so close to finally learning the truth, the whole truth as well, not just the little bits that seemed relevant at any given time.

"I know, it's just – it's a bit of a difficult question. I could tell you what you are, but then you might to the wrong conclusions about yourself." He looked pained and I realised he was saying the same thing Emily had said to me. My heart thumped loudly. What conclusions would I jump to? What was I? Could it be something so awful that I wouldn't even want to know about it?

"I burnt the church down, didn't I?" I asked quietly. It was a futile question because I already knew the answer, but somehow, I needed Nate to confirm it.

"I – I think so, yes, but you cannot blame yourself. You didn't know, you didn't mean to do it." I nodded. He was right, I knew that. I hadn't intentionally started the blaze because I hadn't been aware I was even capable of such a thing, I hadn't known what I was doing at all, but it was still scary and something of a shock. In the past ten days, there had been moments where I'd woken up and I could feel the pain in my bones, feel it coursing through me as it had in the church just before it'd exploded into flames. It was a terrifying sensation and I'd thrown myself into a cold shower, scared that I would suddenly combust in bed and set the house on fire.

"How did I do that?" I looked down at my hands in Nate's. I'd just watched him light a fire, but he had been in control and it had been intentional. I didn't even know I could do it and I'd somehow burnt down a whole building.

"To be honest Grace, you shouldn't have been able to – not yet anyway. I can only guess that it was because you were in some real distress. I think only a complete emotional overload could have caused it." He watched me closely, like at any moment I might snap and go crazy or run away, but I'd promised I wouldn't, and I thought, considering all that I was learning, I was holding it together pretty well.

"They were going to kill Mia but then two of them – two of them said it was against the rules so they, they – Tyler –

they made me watch Nate and they…" I choked, unable to finish as my breathing became strained, flashes of that night coming back to me.

"Shit Grace," Nate whispered, pulling me to him and holding me tightly in his arms. My heart pounded as I relived those moments. I could still remember the taste of coppery blood in my mouth so clearly, as I'd bit down as hard as I could into the man's skin. I could feel the burn of the bile as it had risen up my throat when I'd watched the knife slice through the air. When I closed my eyes, I could still feel the heat of the fire on my skin afterwards, I could remember how warm Tyler's hands had been as I took them in mine, remembered how his blood had covered my skin as I apologised to him for something that seemed so out of my control.

"They stabbed him right here," I whispered, pressing my hand flat against his heart to show him. He pressed his lips to the top of my head, and I closed my eyes.

"We can stop if you want to Grace, we don't have to do this." I shook my head. I'd said I wanted to know everything, and I'd meant it. I had no intention of turning away from it all now, not as I was so close. I took a deep breath, composing myself, shaking away all the images of the events of the church. I looked into his green eyes and brushed a light kiss against his lips. I knew my next question would be difficult for him to answer, but I wanted him to know that it wouldn't change anything.

"What are you Nate?" He stiffened, as I'd expected he would. He pushed me away gently, so I was once again sat opposite him. I didn't know whether it was for his benefit or for mine. I gave him a reassuring smile and squeezed his hand.

"I suppose the technical term would be – demon." He shook his head, his features twisting in anger. I shook my head too. Since telling me he worked for the other side, the term had floated in and out of my thoughts, but I refused to believe it. Demons were bad, but there was nothing bad about Nate. He was profoundly good.

"So, what does that make me?" I was trying to hold it together for his sake, but I began to shake. It was just my hands at first, but then my whole body started shivering. I looked to him pleadingly. This wasn't the time to sugar coat it, I just wanted the truth.

"You, well, you are the first female born of Lucifer." My jaw fell open, the shock evident on my face. I tried to get the words to sink in, but my mind kept telling me I'd misheard him, that there was no way he'd just told me I was born of Lucifer.

"Say again?" My fingertips were barely holding onto reality and I was scared of what he'd just said, scared that if I discovered any more about my true self, I would slip and fall into the abyss of folklore and fairy tale and I wouldn't be able to claw my way back out. I grasped tightly to the one thing I knew to be true – I had Nate. Although I wasn't exactly clear on the finer points of his status as a demon, I didn't for one second believe him to be a bad guy. He'd saved me from that fire and that wasn't even the first time he had ever saved me.

"Grace, it's really not what you think." His tone was serious, and he looked at me with what I could only describe as adoration in his eyes. How could I be? What did it even mean? The devil? I shook my head, clearing my throat.

"So, you're telling me that, that I'm related to Satan, that

I'm – he's?" I was astonished. How could I be? How could I not know about something so huge? I almost wished I knew more about the bible, perhaps it would help to clear the confusing fog that had settled in my brain.

"Yes." His eyes were full of amusement and there was that glint, that teasing glint that I loved so much and hadn't seen for what felt like an age. I didn't know whether to laugh or cry.

"Does this mean I'm bad?"

"Bad is a relative term Grace." I pulled my hands from his, rubbing at my temples. When I'd set out to Tyler's funeral, I'd been dead set on getting answers, but now that I was getting them, I wasn't sure it had been such a good idea. The grass always looks greener on the other side, but now I'd crossed that bridge, I wondered whether I might have been better staying where I was – in the dark. I narrowed my eyes as his words tumbled around my brain; if Nate was a demon, and I was some descendant of Lucifer –

"Is that why you're here? You're here because of who I am?" My voice cracked. I didn't want to believe it, I wanted to believe he was here because we had a connection, because he felt things for me, but it was hard to deny the facts. He lifted his chin so that my eyes met his, and he looked fierce.

"I won't lie to you Grace, not ever. I've known you a lot longer than you've known me and at first – yes, it was why I was here. To protect you." I pulled my knees up, crossing my arms over my chest, feeling incredibly exposed.

"I don't understand," I whispered. He never took his eyes from mine, the intensity in them shone in the dark cave. What was he saying? How could he have known me a lot longer than I'd known him? How could he know me at all?

"I've been there since you were born. Always there – always watching,"

"Always protecting," I uttered, repeating his words as my brain caught up. "That's it isn't it? That's – that's the complication?" He smiled and looked relieved, like I'd finally found the last piece of a massively difficult jigsaw puzzle.

"Yes. I was sent to protect you to make sure you came of age, and I managed to do that from a distance for a long time. However, you sort of threw a spanner in the works when you ended up in my bed at Dan's party. Even I wasn't expecting that. You looked so peaceful – so beautiful. I wasn't expecting the reaction it would have on me, the reaction that YOU would have on me." The way he was looking at me sent the butterflies in my stomach into a frenzy and my mouth suddenly felt very dry.

"Are you in trouble?" I asked, taking his hands once more, wanting to feel close to him again. The electrical impulses that always travelled just below the surface of my skin at his mere touch, still astounded me. I hoped they never went away.

"I don't very much care anymore Grace. All I care about is you, keeping you safe, and not for anyone else's reasons either, but for my own." His cheeks flushed with colour and my heart quickened. I climbed into his lap, wrapping my arms around his neck and pressing my lips to his. The kiss was sweet and full of unspoken emotion. I pulled away, resting my forehead against his with a smile.

"I knew I couldn't be the only one feeling it, I knew

there was something here."

"I'm sorry for pushing you away Grace, I just – I was scared." I sat back a little, his arms still around my waist but just far enough I could look into his eyes. Nate – scared? What on earth could he have been scared of? He was so strong and powerful. He didn't elaborate further, and I didn't want to push him. I changed the subject, asking the next question that had been on my mind.

"Nate, if I'm immortal, why are the Guardians even coming after me? Why bother trying to kill me?" It seemed like a waste of everyone's time to keep trying to get rid of someone who was immortal.

"Immortal isn't invincible Grace. You can be killed, so don't ever assume that you're safe. It takes something special, something very particular but it is possible." I chewed the inside of my cheek, trying to keep my face impassive. If I could be killed, that meant Nate could be killed too, and that thought made me feel sick to my stomach. I was fairly sure I knew what could do it too.

"A silver dagger," I mumbled, as the images from my dream and Tyler's attack swam before my eyes. He looked shocked.

"How do you know that?"

"I saw it, the night I dreamt of Emily. The man whose chest was branded, he pulled it from within his jacket. Then I saw it for real, they – they – that's what they used on Tyler." He looked disgusted.

"They're vile creatures Grace, unbelievable in their ruthlessness. They've lost almost all their humanity, traded in for a twisted job and a golden ticket. They make me sick," he spat.

"Why do they want to kill me in the first place?" This

was the big question, the one that would finally fill me in as to why two of my friends had lost their lives. Nate inhaled sharply though his teeth, and he took a moment to answer.

"There was a prophecy, not long after The Fall, a prophecy that foretold of your arrival. They've been sent to kill you to stop that prophecy from being fulfilled." Of everything I had learned, this was the hardest to swallow. I felt like I was trapped in some sort of cult classic. Could this really be happening to me? Yet as I rested my forehead to Nate's once more, I knew it all to be true. I knew that I could trust every word he was saying. This was what he had been so scared of telling me.

"This is so surreal," I whispered, shaking my head. A prophecy? I was fulfilling a prophecy. How could that be? How could I not know that I'd been born because someone had predicted I would be? I didn't even read horoscopes because I thought they were a load of old tosh.

"Wait," I said suddenly. "Did you say The Fall? As in when the angels fell to earth?"

"Yes," he said sadly.

"You were an angel once?" I asked, stating the obvious. He nodded and sighed.

"It's not as cut and dry as you may think. It wasn't a case of good versus evil – it still isn't really. I told you before, bad is a relative term. Sometimes, those who are portrayed as the bad guys have never had the chance to explain themselves, to tell their side of the story, to share what really happened." Was he trying to tell me, that the devil wasn't really a bad guy and that he'd just never had the chance to share? It was hard to believe. What wasn't hard to believe, was that Nate used to be an angel and no matter what else I discovered; it was how I would always think of him.

I let my breath go as I realised I'd been holding it and looked into the flames, watching as they danced around. Nate's arms tightened around my waist and I ran my fingers absentmindedly through the curls at the nape of his neck. It was going to take a lot more than one conversation to get my head around it all, but at least I had him, and he would explain everything to me that I wanted and needed to know.

"I know it's a lot to take in. I'm sorry I didn't tell you sooner," he said. He looked across to the flames too and again, I could see the shadows of sadness hiding in the green that made my heart constrict. I held his face in my hands, turning him gently so I could look directly into his eyes.

"I understand why you didn't Nate. You were worried about what I would think of you, but I'm still here aren't I?" I raised my brow in question, a small smile tugging at my lips.

"Yes, which is just – unbelievable." I laughed for the first time in over ten days.

"You just told me I'm a descendant of the devil and that some prophecy foresaw me coming and heaven is sending men to stop me fulfilling said prophecy, yet the unbelievable thing is that I'm still here?" He smiled and ran a finger down my cheek.

"I don't deserve you," he whispered. "I thought you would be running for the hills by now."

"You deserve me and so much more Nate, and I promise, I'm not running anywhere." I brushed my lips against his in a featherlight kiss, my heart warming as I felt him smile.

We sat in silence for a while, my brain trying to absorb everything and put it into some sort of order within my head. I was a relative of the devil born to fulfil some prophecy and a group of nasty humans doing heavens bidding were trying to kill me to stop me fulfilling it. Add to that the fact that I had some sort of supernatural power that I hadn't known anything about nor was in control of, plus I was totally in love with a demon who had been watching over me since birth. My life was about to take one hell of an epic turn.

"Grace, you need to know they will come again," Nate said softly. I thought back to what Emily had said.

"Until they succeed, or I turn eighteen."

"How do you know that?" he asked, unable to hide his shock.

"Emily told me – but she said I have some respite because they hadn't accounted for any complications and apparently setting a church on fire is a pretty big complication. They're regrouping." He didn't look surprised, though he did look a little confused and there was something else – something that I couldn't quite put my finger on that flickered through his eyes. I didn't try and decipher it too much, I already had enough to think about. The fact that he wasn't shocked by a dream apparition telling me things would have surprised me, if not for the fact that I was now living in a world where angels, demons and prophecies existed. Ghostly visitations whilst asleep were a drop in the ocean of craziness that I'd opened myself up to.

"She visited you?" he mumbled, almost to himself. "How did they not know? She must have some balls." I assumed by 'they' he meant those upstairs. I grinned at the thought of Emily having 'balls' because it was exactly what she had. She'd never really cared much for authority on any level. I thought about how she had brought Tyler to see me too, how I'd made him a promise to take care of Mia – and Dan. I felt guilty that I hadn't even yet tried to keep that promise, but I would – soon.

"Where does Mia come into all this?"

"She comes from a family of Keeper's – Keepers of knowledge. She'll be one eventually, but she hasn't been initiated fully yet. The Keepers are impartial, they don't work for either side, they just – know everything. They document it all." I thought about it for a moment, unable to shake a funny feeling that was filling my stomach.

"When we were in the church, the Guardians had what looked like a sacrificial table set up and they kept asking Mia if it was right. They said she should know because it's in her blood." Nate raised an eyebrow.

"A sacrificial table? Someone is feeding them unreliable information. That's ridiculous." He shook his head.

"Then why did he think Mia would know? What did they mean when they said it's in her blood?"

"Mia's family have – an ability. They're the only family of Keepers to have it. They have the ability to See." I narrowed my eyes, confused. "It was one of Mia's ancestors that had the vision that predicted you would one day come. It was Mia's family that gave that prophecy."

My mind was blown. There was absolutely no way on this earth that we had just happened to move to Stonewell. It couldn't all be some big coincidence that I would end up in the village of the family of Keepers who saw me coming, in the same village as two demons, one of which was sent to watch over me, but then – that confirmed it. It confirmed all the suspicions I'd been trying to trample. My mother knew more than she was letting on. Maybe it was time to ask her, to find out how much she really knew.

"I need to go home. I need to speak to my mother." Nate grimaced.

"Are you sure?" he asked cautiously. I knew he was still trying to protect me, but he couldn't wrap me in cotton wool forever.

"I'm not sure of anything anymore. My world has pretty much been turned on its head, but I refuse to believe she knows nothing about any of this." I didn't want to believe my own mum would keep such a massive secret from me, but how could I deny the facts? Her instinct would be to protect me obviously, but knowledge was power and if I'd known all along, then perhaps my friends would still be alive.

Nate extinguished the fire and took my hand, helping me carefully from the cave. We were silent all the way back to the farmhouse, which suited me fine because after everything I'd just heard, I was happy to sit and mull it all over.

The whole thing still threatened to overwhelm me, to push me over that edge that I was so delicately balancing on, but I was learning that I was in fact stronger than I'd ever believed and I was dealing with it – just like Tyler had said. It was going to take a period of adjustment, but I could learn to live with who and what I was.

Forty One

"Do you want me to come with you?" Nate asked as we pulled up outside. He seemed anxious and I couldn't tell whether it was because I was asking him to leave again or because I was about to go and question my mother. He'd been quiet ever since I'd said I wanted to go home and speak with her.

I shook my head. This was something I needed to do alone. It might have been nice to have Nate around for moral support, but he would be there for me afterwards. I wasn't sure what was going on, how much my mother knew, but I was as determined to get those answers as I had been to discover the truth about myself.

"I'll be fine. I'll call you when I'm done, and then will you take me to see Mia?" Nate smiled and nodded. A shadow of doubt passed through my mind as I worried about the other half of my promise – to repair the relationship between Dan and Mia and to look out for him too, but I pushed it away. One step at a time. He pulled me towards him across the car and brushed my lips lightly with his.

"Please don't make it another ten days though Grace, I don't think I could handle it." I laughed and jumped out, waving as I watched him pull away and disappear down the road. My heart was racing at the thought of seeing my mother and letting her into the world of madness that I'd found myself in; a world of fantasy that was suddenly very real. Of course, that was assuming she didn't already know about it, which was unlikely. That then posed the questions, if she had known all along, why hadn't she told me anything? Even just a little hint that not everything was as it seemed, that perhaps my life wasn't as perfectly normal as I'd always believed would have been nice. There was only one sure fire way to find out, and that was to ask her.

"Mum! Mother!" I yelled as I walked through the door. The house was cold as I walked through the rooms looking for her, which made my heart sink. "Mother!"

I walked into the kitchen and groaned as I saw the note stuck to the fridge confirming what I'd already realised. She'd been called out on an emergency job and would be back in the morning. Fantastic. I rolled my eyes, cursing.

Questioning my mother would have to wait. I was annoyed that I'd let Nate drive off without first thinking to check whether she was even home. I sighed, thinking I might as well change out of the black dress and tights that I'd worn to the funeral before calling Nate back and heading to see Mia. I just hoped she was back from Tyler's parent's house.

I made my way upstairs to my room. I was going to have to apologise to Mia for being such a rubbish friend. Yes, I'd had a lot going on, but so did she and thanks to Nate, I now knew she was part of my world too. I could trust her and lean on her. Maybe I should have been doing that the whole time.

I pushed open the door to my room and screamed, my heart jumping into my throat. My breathing quickened, coming thick and fast as panic gripped me in its iron claws. Terror spread through me like ice.

"What – what are you doing here?" I choked out, my voice breaking. I watched frozen, unable to move as he walked towards me. He looked dishevelled and upset, like he'd been crying for days and I felt that fracture line in my heart throb once more. If I weren't so petrified of him, I would have felt sorry for him. He'd lost his best friend after all, but the anger, hurt and danger that shone from his topaz eyes dispelled any such feelings.

"Hello Grace – about that unfinished business."

Acknowledgements.

I would just like to take this opportunity to say a big THANK YOU to a few people.

First of all, thank you to my amazing husband who has supported me through the entire process. He has helped me hash out problems, spin out storylines and create plot twists. Plus, he never looks at me funny when I laugh or cry whilst writing.

Secondly, to my children – G, F, I & C – for all the times they've had to run wild without much complaining so that I could immerse myself in this little world that I created. Mummy will make it up to you one day, I promise.

And finally, a big thank you to all you lovely people who have spent your hard-earned cash buying my book and taking the time to read it. Without you, this wouldn't have been possible!

Printed in Great Britain
by Amazon